SEALED CORRESPONDENCE
A Novel by
Richard Rudomanski

D1519457

This book is a work of fiction. The characters, incidents, and dialogues are products of the author's imagination and are not to be construed as real. Any resemblance to actual events or persons, living or dead, is entirely coincidental.

Libby & Tom

Enjoy Sealed Correspondence

CHAPTER 1

May 2010, Horsmonden, England:

Rogue antique dealer, John Miller, had been clearing out the farm house for most of the day. He had bought the entire contents of the estate and worked his way room to room loading up his Ford pickup, taking it to his shop in town, and then returning to repack his truck. By late afternoon he had worked his way to the attic. It contained four generations of family possessions piled up to the hand hewn rafters; most of it was junk.

Horsmonden was sprawling farm country handed down from father to son, common folk, with common tastes, who were happy with common things, and Miller waded through the worn out furniture and the broken empty trunks. As he made it to the south gable wall, and he moved an old table and chairs, Miller discovered and unopened pine crate. He freed three sides and examined the color of the wood. He could tell it was old, very old, its patina golden and rich. Miller maneuvered the furnishings away from the box so he could slide it toward the stairs. He tried, but it was too heavy for one man to push. Still, he was able to move it away from the outside wall maybe an inch, maybe two. He slipped his hands in between the wall and the crate and pulled it toward his body. It moved, and he observed writing on the hidden fourth side, big black painted letters, but it was still obscured by its proximity to the wall. Tired, he leaned against an old beat up dresser staring at the pine box and thought.

After a few moments, he wrestled with the crate again. This time he was able to swing it around enough to get his body between the wall and the writing on the back. He pulled the flashlight from his back pocket, switched it on, and illuminated the letters line by line as he read the black painted words on the box.

Boston Harbor
Aboard Lucretia
1786
Property of Colonel William Smith

Four days later over the Italian peninsula on the Amalfi Coast, a helicopter approached Senior Brosconni's seaside villa.

Heading south, the blue and white Bell 429 hugged the Italian coastline as its rotors chopped through the air at eighteen hundred feet. As the transport approached Atrani, the pilot banked left and headed inland, straddled the S373 toward Pontone, and slowed to a hover just above the steep cliffs of Ravello. On board, in the passenger cabin, was Christina Sheppard. Recognized as the world's leading antiquarian detective, her 2nd Ave. showroom, in Manhattan, received daily requests for her expertise from around the globe, but in the last six years she had traveled only four times to examine a piece. Sheppard was scared to death of air travel. Her phobia had kept her grounded now for the past three years. But the extraordinary phone call she had received in New York, from an employee of Senior Brosconni, had left Christina Sheppard with no choice.

"Ms. Sheppard," the voice had said in a thick Italian Napolitano accent.

"Yes, this is Christina Sheppard" she responded as she sat in her winged back chair behind her eighteenth century Sheraton desk.

"My name is Antonio Capano, Ms. Sheppard; I am employed by Senior Brosconni."

Oh please, not another high profiled Italian egomaniac, she thought, as her eyes examined the inventory slip of the Chippendale secretary which had arrived earlier that morning.

"Senior Brosconni is a very promin-"

"Yes, yes," she said impatiently, "I've heard of the shipping tycoon, get to the point."

"Please, Ms. Sheppard, I understand your aversion to air travel, but this piece is important; it was discovered only three days ago."

3

Sheppard rolled her eyes.

"I'm listening," she said.

"It's a Carlton House Desk that was found in a crate in an attic. The crate was dated 1786. The piece is in pristine condition: the gilt-tooled, pale green writing surface looked as it did the day the master cabinetmaker glued the leather into its recessed niche."

Sheppard leaned back in her chair and let her head fall against the leather.

"You're losing me, Mr. Capano, what's so special about this desk?"

"Signora, Senior Brosconni believes it's a Hepplewhite."

Sheppard's body snapped forward and her elbows landed on her desk. Antonio Capano had just uttered the name which collectors from around the world had searched to find for the last hundred years. An authenticated piece of the master cabinetmaker, George Hepplewhite, was deemed by dealers as the holy grail of antiques. Not a single piece of the famed craftsman was known to exist, and after studying the photographs emailed to her office, Christina Sheppard was forced to face her worst fear—air travel.

And now, as the 429 descended to the concrete helicopter pad on the cliffs of the Tyrrhenian Sea, the thirty six year old attractive blonde in the black silk blazer and shoulder length hair felt close to panic. Her milk white hands clutched the leather of the seat as the helicopter's landing gear touched down. And as the rotors slowed to silence, she had thoughts of the return trip home, and she shuttered.

But for now, she rationalized to calm her nerves, her ten hour nightmare was over.

Outside the cabin, about fifteen meters away, a man stood in the shadows of the columned portico with his hands clasp behind his back. He was five foot six, had short salt and pepper hair, a dark clean shaven beard, and was wearing a black Armani suit. As he watched Sheppard disembark his Bell 429, with the help of one of his staff dressed in a white sports coat and black bow tie, he lifted the heels of his Ferragamo loafers off the ground and balanced on the souls of his shoes. He waited with impatience, and Sheppard, still trying to regain her composure, strolled in a languid gate as she captured the breathtaking views of the towns and the coast. And as she approached the shipping tycoon, she straightened her blazer, and she reached out with her hand.

"Senior Brosconni?" She asked.

He made no effort to reciprocate.

"Ms. Sheppard," he said in a thick Italian accent, "follow me," and he turned and strutted off in front of her and paraded down the terracotta, tiled walk toward his opulent seaside manor—Villa Marcella.

Constructed in 1572 by Gianni Bordatelli, of mercantile nobility, Villa Marcella sat high above the Amalfi cliffs overlooking the Tyrrhenian Sea. Built strategically on a ledge, only accessible from a steep inclined road from the east, the Bordatelli family lived secure from the invasions common in medieval Europe. Brosconni found its impenetrable location appealing. The need for high security, surveillance cameras, and infrared motion detectors were trumped by the steeped cliffs, sole entrance, and rough terrain. Brosconni's ride to power had been riddled with hostile takeovers, ruthless employment practices, and countless broken lives. His enemies were as vast as his fortune. Tactically placed above the Amalfi Coast, Brosconni believed, like himself, Villa Marcella's existence belied defeat. And as Brosconni marched toward its limestone facade, his gate was confident and quick.

Sheppard had fallen back. The columned portico accentuated the magnificent vista; it was laced with Bougainvillea and as Sheppard took in the richness of the deep burgundy flowers, she felt her tense body begin to relax. On a whirlwind for the past three days, it felt good to finally come down, and she took a deep breath and exhaled.

Prior to her departure from JFK, Sheppard had received one of the most coveted honors of the antique industry from the Antique Dealers Association of America. The ADA had held its "Annual Award of Merit" dinner at the Jacob Javits convention center in New York and had chosen Christina Sheppard as their 2010 recipient. In giving the award, the chairman had described Sheppard as a distinguished leader in the antique industry, whose unique methodology and investigative genius had given new meaning to the professional designation of Antiquarian Detective.

Thanking the chairman, the governing board of the ADA, and the congregation of her peers, she offered some insight into her distinctive approach.

"Craft," she said, "is like personality: it demonstrates a particular reasoning and style. If you wish to uncover the most intimate details of a craftsman's art, those combinations of moves which unlock the brilliance of the art, one must learn their methods in the simplest of form. Get inside the mind of the cabinet maker," she concluded to the twelve hundred or so dealers from around the world, "and you will decipher how to get inside his work."

Sheppard had discovered at an early age her exceptional ability to interpret the cabinetmakers skills and their cunning ability to create security for their wealthy clientele. Her parent's exclusive showroom, in Manhattan, exposed her to Sheraton, Chippendale, and Linnell's famous designs. It became her classroom, and shortly after her sixth birthday exploring the joinery of a travel, lap desk circa 1800, she discovered her first secret compartment with a paper wrapped lock of hair inside. Thirty years later, experienced dealers confounded by the talents of the brilliant old masters called on Sheppard's unique gift. Brosconni knew it, and he was willing to pay the exorbitant fee she insisted upon when asked to examine the piece. And now, like always, he demanded results.

"Pick it up, Ms. Sheppard," he said, as he stepped through the west side entrance held open by Antonio Capano. He moved into the kitchen and raced through into the main hall. As he approached the marbled columned, arched opening to the living room, Brosconni stopped and nodded his head. Sheppard moved to his side and stared into the vaulted ceilinged room. In front of the large medieval fireplace, placed upon a rare Persian Tabriz, stood the eighteenth century masterpiece, and Sheppard, now stepping toward the desk, felt her heart pound from inside her chest.

She arrived at the piece and froze. Her blue eyes scanned the D-shaped mahogany superstructure, circled the pierced gallery, and slid down the six drawers accented by the Hester Bateman, silver handles. As she inched around to the rear and studied the seams of the solid mahogany back, she summoned her eidetic recall in search of a similar piece in such condition. Sheppard's reputation in the world of antiques was as legendary as her photographic memory, and she had in her vault of images every significant Carlton House Desk that existed throughout the world. And after studying the magnificent piece for only a moment, she had no doubt.

"Remarkable," she said.

"Yes, it is!"

CHAPTER 2

Sheppard completed her initial examination, as Brosconni watched her visual inspection of each component of the hand crafted desk: the design of the inlays, the shape of the legs, the complexity of the rising tiers, the pierced brass gallery with anthemion motif, all evidence of superior workmanship—every detail a unique signature crafted by a long deceased master. As she approached the front, Sheppard put on the cotton gloves she retrieved from her silk blazer pocket, and she prepared to dissect the interior components which would expose the complexity of the artisan's craft. She removed the first draw and inspected the patina of the satinwood draw stock and the detail of the dove tail joints, and as she did, a man's voice startled her, and she turned toward the columned opening to the hall.

"Senior Brosconni," Capano said standing between the columns.

"What," Brosconni said aggravated by the intrusion.

"Senior Brosconni, I'm sorry to disturb you," he said in a soft spoken Italian accent, "may I have a word with you please?"

Antonio Capano had been Brosconni's head of staff for the past fifteen years. He lived in the small apartment above the detached garage with his wife and young son. He was the final stop in the chain of command and ran Villa Marcella with the discipline of a drill sergeant. Ten years before, Brosconni had fired Capano when one of the caretakers attending the gardens addressed Brosconni directly. Antonio begged for his job back, was re-instated, and had run the estate with an iron fist ever since.

"You know better than to interrupt me," Brosconni said, "what is it?"

"Senior, please, I need to speak to you for just one moment."

Brosconni turned his head toward Sheppard and raised his hand indicating for her to wait. He walked past Capano, and as he did, he flipped his hand abruptly, commanding his butler into the hall. He stared back through the open archway to Sheppard who was now standing at the balcony looking out to the Tyrrhenian Sea.

"What is it?" He said.

"Senior, I'm sorry to disturb you but…."

"Get on with it."

"Senior, my mother, she is very sick."

"So?'

"Senior, I need to see her tonight, I need to travel to Atrani to see her; she is very ill senior."

"No!"

"But Senior,"

"No!"

Brosconni marched back to the desk impatiently eyeing Sheppard who was leaning on one of the marble columns at the veranda opening.

"Ms. Sheppard," he said, as he snapped his fingers and pointed to the desk.

Sheppard turned at the crude command and shot a cold stare to Brosconni. *What a jerk*!

As she arrived back at the desk, Sheppard uncovered the first hidden compartment after removing three drawers and the bottom floor of the opening. The secret slot was empty. Sheppard now moved to the under belly of the desk and proceeded with the "Braille" method of examination running her fingers from right to left across the lower bottom, moving a step closer to the front with each pass. On her fourth sweep, Sheppard detected a slight depression in the smooth surface with her pointing finger. It was part of the cabinet maker's intentional design: the needed hold to operate a spring or a slot. She pushed. The soft sound of wood hitting against wood resonated into Brosconni's ears. He moved closer to Sheppard stopping just behind her left shoulder. Sheppard turned to Brosconni and pointed to the Chippendale chair in the corner.

"Bring that over here," she said.

Brosconni picked up the wood framed, armless Chippendale and positioned it just behind the back panel of the desk. Sheppard brought the wrought iron floor lamp over and placed it next to the chair and switched it on. Then she circled around the chair and sat down. Knowing a master like Hepplewhite would create more than one move to unlock his sophisticated compartments, Sheppard focused on the boxwood inlay which ran across the bottom of the desk. The sound of the first release had alerted her to the probability of a second latch which she had uncovered years before in a Sheraton piece. So she ran her finger along the banding until she reached the corner and then pressed gently inward. Another muted sound from behind the mahogany veneer pierced the silence and the back panel released. She reached forward toward the panel, and with the tips of her fingers she pushed gently using her right hand. The mahogany panel slid on two wooden tracks, making a rubbing sound of wood on wood. Brosconni squeezed tight to Sheppard's left, and as the panel reached its limit, the opening revealed four shelves stacked two high.

On the bottom left tier was a piece of paper folded in half, on the upper right were two pieces of correspondence, folded, tied with string and sealed shut with unbroken red wax stamps. Sheppard reached to the bottom left shelf and carefully slid out the paper. She walked around to the front of the desk, laid the paper on the pale green writing surface and reached down to her leather satchel on the floor. She pulled out two sheets of Mylar, carefully unfolded the paper, and placed it between the two plastic sheets: the Mylar would protect the paper from the oils and touch of her hand and protect the print from the ultraviolet light of the sun. As she sealed the sides and top, Sheppard couldn't help but notice the print, and her heart began to thump again inside her chest.

At the top, stamped in black ink, the name pierced the deep blue of her eyes.

George Hepplewhite
Red Cross Street
London, England

Brosconni edged Sheppard away from the center of the desk and was now standing directly in front of the protected sheet.

He had searched for decades for a genuine Hepplewhite, and now, as he stood staring at the paper on the top of the desk, the bill of sale proved it beyond any doubt, and Brosconni felt an egocentric rush envelope his body.

"I've done it," he said, "I own the only known Hepplewhite to exist in the world."

"Senior Brosconni," Sheppard said, "the value of this desk is far more than you comprehend— examine the document further."

"Yes, yes, I see; it was commissioned by your American president, George Washington."

Sheppard was perplexed. She had been told by Capano that stenciled on the crate it had said property of Colonel William Smith. She looked to Brosconni.

"If we can authenticate this document, Senior, this desk becomes not only a one of a kind Hepplewhite, but a part of the birth of a new and independent nation. Historians in America will salivate to examine this desk and document the contents inside."

"Examine my ass, Ms. Sheppard. The world will learn of the piece, and that I own the desk, but no one will ever get to examine it or the documents inside—never. This desk belongs to me, Ms. Sheppard, and when we're through here, you are to speak to no one except to verify the desk exists. Anything more and I will consider it a breach of confidentiality, do you understand me? Let the fucking pen heads salivate, Ms. Sheppard, until they drown in their own saliva."

Sheppard stared at Brosconni in disgust, and felt herself edging backward away from the crass tycoon. She had no desire to continue. She felt ill from his statements and couldn't imagine unlocking two hundred and twenty four years of secrets to entertain his perverse and self obsessed ego. She side-stepped around to the rear of the desk.

"I am tired, and I need to rest." She said.

Brosconni's face went hard and cold.

"I did not fly you from New York to Rome to put off the examination until morning—proceed!"

"What is your given name?"She asked.

"What?"

"I said, what is your given name, it certainly is not Senior, mine is Christina and yours?"

"Enrico, Enrico Filipo Brosconni, now, Ms. Sheppard—proceed!"

"Enrico, you don't mind if I call you by your given name, Enrico, do you?—good. I fear you have a misconception of our relationship. You sent for me because I am the best at what I do. I unlock the complex stories of rare antiques as a service to individuals like yourself, and if you catch the distinction I made, the operable word here is service, not servant. No one, and that includes you, Enrico, tells me how or when to do my work. I am closing up the back compartment, those remaining documents will remain undisturbed until they can be handled properly and, if I am ready, we will resume the examination in the morning. Now, have your butler show me to my room!"

Frozen in a narcissistic trance in the soft cushioned chair sipping decanted Chianti, Brosconni devoured the image of the centuries old desk. In his left hand was the Mylar covered bill of sale illuminated by the soft light of the wrought iron lamp. His eyes swept from the document to the desk and then out past the veranda to the lights of the towns below. He swirled the glass, eyed the hand written commission, and gloated in his greatest victory to date—a genuine Hepplewhite.

He pulled a small fob from the left pocket of his Armani blazer and pressed the little button on the face. A moment later, Antonio Capano appeared. He stood at the opening to the hall.

"Yes Sir?"

Brosconni looked at his watch, ten past ten.

"Are the grounds secured?"

"Yes sir."

"Who's in the security room tonight?"

"Carlo Brigatto, sir."

"I want you in the house tonight."

"Yes sir."

"You're to check on Brigatto every hour on the hour, is that understood?"

"Yes sir."

Brosconni went silent in thought. He took a slug of his wine as he looked out toward the sea.

"What about Sheppard?"

"She's in her room, asleep."

"I want the motion detector in her hallway shutoff, use the cameras. If she leaves her room, I want to know immediately—understood?"

"Yes sir."

Brosconni looked down to the document. He swirled what was left of the wine in his glass and then in one pass consumed it.

"Will that be all sir?"

Brosconni didn't answer. He stood up, walked over to the desk, and rubbed his fingers on the pale green writing surface, then turned and moved in the direction of the hall with the document from Hepplewhite's shop still in his hand.

"Sir?"

Brosconni continued down the hall. Antonio watched his back, as he picked up the empty wine glass from atop the chair table. Brosconni turned toward the second floor stairs, and Capano listened to the sound of Brosconni's leather souls as they slid on the marble treads. He stood at the columned opening until Brosconni disappeared and then flicked the light switch off, stared at the darkened silhouette of the Hepplewhite, shook his head, and turned and walked away.

.

CHAPTER 3

As the sun crept through the marble balustrades on the balcony, Sheppard slowly opened her eyes. Without moving her head, she gazed at the night table next to the bed, 6:15. She'd been asleep over ten hours—the first rest in twenty four. Christina hadn't slept on Brosconni's Gulfstream over the Atlantic, in fact, every time she started to feel woozy, she jerked her head up, and with her heart pounding like a base drum, she went to the bathroom and washed her face. Six years earlier, she had lost her husband and her parents on the same private jet. They were returning from the sale of a Sheraton on the west coast. Descending to ten thousand feet on their approach to Teterboro airport, in New Jersey, the pilot sent a may-day call. There was smoke in the cockpit, the jet was losing altitude, and the last words the air traffic controller heard was, "we're going down!"

They found the wreckage in the New Jersey Meadowlands strewn over half a mile of swamp. The bodies of her husband and parents were torn apart and badly burned. Six years had passed, and the images still flashed like a slide show in her mind's eye every morning when she awoke: pieces of the burnt fuselage bent and twisted, an engine upside down smoldering in the swamp, a set of landing gear with its shattered wheels sticking out of the marsh, burned pieces of her husband's clothes floating in the water, the remains of her loved ones covered with blankets; it's how she started her day. And as her recall flashed images from the inside of her brain, she rubbed her eyes with both her hands and tried to erase her memory.

She rolled onto her back, stretched her arms, slid to the side of the bed, and attempted to shake off her morning nightmare. As her feet hit the floor, the echo of a man's voice bellowed down the long upstairs hall and blew through her door and into her room. *What was that*? She turned her head and listened. The sound escalated and approached the second floor hallway. It was Enrico Brosconni; she recognized the voice now. His words were in English and Italian, alternating with each sentence as he screamed.

"Tutti, nel salotto—ora!"

"Everyone in the living room—now!"

His voice grew louder and stronger and echoed throughout the Villa. It was clear he was approaching her room. The anger in his voice froze her body as he pounded on her door.

"Sheppard, downstairs—now!"

Sheppard backed against the wall as the violent pounding continued, and she felt the vibrations on her face and chest. *This man's insane*, she thought as she slid along the wall toward the bathroom opening.

As the screaming trailed away, Christina moved into the bathroom. She put on the terrycloth bathrobe, which hung from the hook next to the marble vanity. She picked up her brush and straightened the snarls entangled on the back of her head and put on the pair of slippers from beneath where the robe had hung. And as she sat on the water closet, the screaming intensified, again.

When she arrived at the entrance to the living room, Brosconni stood where the Hepplewhite had been and pointed his finger first at Capano, then to another man in a guard's uniform, and screamed in Italian as he pointed to the Persian Tabriz. He whirled around toward Sheppard.

"What do you know of this, Sheppard, where the fuck is my desk?"

Christina almost fell backward by his anger and his lewd talk.

Brosconni whipped back around and pointed to the man in the uniform. He was red in the face, and in his fury, he became confused which language he was speaking.

"What did you see last night—answer me!" He screamed to the security guard.

"Nulla, ho visto nulla, della telecamera ha visto nulla, Senior."

"Bullshit, every hall in Villa Marcella is covered by cameras. No one could enter or leave this room, what the hell did you see?"

"Nulla, ho visto nulla Senior, nulla."

"Capano, get me General Capalli of the Carabinieri on the phone—now!

No, not in here you idiot, call from outside this room. No one touch a God damn thing."

Brosconni froze as if to gather his thoughts. He rubbed his forehead and then his head jerked up.

"Sheppard don't move." He turned to Grippato, the security guard. "You, get in the hall—now!"

Brosconni stomped in front of his security guard into the vaulted hall.

"I see anyone in this room, I'll drop you myself. Grippato get Nonti, tell him if he's not here in ten minutes, he's finished. I want everyone assembled in the front foyer. No one leaves the grounds, and you, you idiot, stay out of the security room."

"Yes sir."

"Senior, General Capalli is on the line."

"Give me the phone." He said as he yanked it from Capano's grip.

General Alberto Capalli was the head of Italy's crack Carabinieri Art Squad: a national investigative branch of the military; a special police squad used to stop major art theft and trafficking to foreign countries. In 98,' they recovered ten stolen paintings, including the story of the Virgin, by Benozzo Gozzoli (1420-1479). Six separate countries where involved in the investigation. The painting was returned, unharmed, after the masterpieces were discovered in a Spanish diplomat's house.

Brosconni and Capalli met in 95, when Alberto Capalli was a Lt. Colonel working out of the regional branch of the Carabinieri called the Campania unit. Responsible for Naples, the busiest port in Italy, Brosconni had a vested interest in forming a working relationship with the military police. Colonel Capalli fit the bill. Now, with Capalli a General in charge of the Carabinieri Art Squad, and Brosconni's 18th century Hepplewhite missing, Enrico went straight to the top. And, as expected, the General responded. Brosconni explained the events of the past seventy two hours with particular emphasis on the last twenty four.

"Enrico, I'm sure you have secured the room, yes?"

"Of course," he said in a sarcastic voice.

"I am sending the Polizia di Stato immediately to secure and search the Villa. Don't let anyone touch anything near the living room. I am handling this personally. I'll have forensics there as quickly as possible. Enrico, remove the DVD's from the security room and don't let them out of your sight, and, give me the name of that American woman again—we'll run an international background check on her right away."

CHAPTER 4

The circular island, at the end of Villa Marcella's driveway, was a sea of blue Alfa Romeo 159's. The gray and blue uniformed officers, with their bright white holsters and 9mm Berettas', scurried in and out of the Villa to the chorus of police radios which crackled in the warm morning air. Standing to the left of the portico entrance was the entire staff of Villa Marcella, herded together by two armed officers who stood guard. Inside, under the supervision of Enrico Brosconni, an entire search of the 1572 Villa was being conducted room by room. Every square foot of the interior was torn apart with the exception of the cordoned off living room. Enrico Brosconni was convinced his prized Hepplewhite was hidden somewhere within his opulent seaside manor, and he was determined to push the commander hard, until it was found.

"Impossible," Brosconni said with a cold stare to the commissario capo (the commissioner chief) standing at the entrance to the living room, "nothing could be removed from this room without detection." Brosconni pointed with his finger as his hand swung in the air. He stood in front of the commissioner with his black blazer, white button down oxford, and the lids of his eyes opened so wide, Russo was stunned by the attack. "The only way to escape Villa Marcella is the grounds in the front," he said as he jabbed his finger toward the front entrance door, "and they're saturated with hi-tech infrared detectors and night vision cameras. The cliffs in the rear are three hundred feet high. No human could scale that incline with a desk tied to their side. It's in here somewhere," he said, "find my God damn desk!"

General Capalli had issued orders to the commissioner chief upon the dispatch of his squad. He had been told to secure and search the Villa with the exception of the living room. Forensics, he said, are to wait until I arrive to conduct their investigation. And as he completed his orders he made one last command.

"I want the American woman isolated until I can speak to her personally," he instructed, "post a guard outside her door."

Now, as the search continued, Sheppard sat on the balcony off her bedroom with an officer stationed in a chair in the hall. She watched the tiny cars down below traverse the narrow road cut into the cliffs of the Amalfi Coast. The cob webs of jet lag hung over her brain, but even in a fog Christina's ability to recall every detail of every minute, starting with the call from Capano at her New York show room to the final conversation last night, not surprising, remained intact.

Sheppard's infallible memory had stunned most of her colleagues as she answered questions and recited verbatim vivid images of every antique she'd ever examined. The accuracy and volume of detail she described was astonishing: the number of secret compartments, the trigger she located and manipulated to unveil the master's craft, the contents she discovered inside. It was as if the piece stood directly in front of her as she spoke, and each image, each sound, each object, was a photograph in her memory which waited to be excavated into her conscious observation whenever she flicked the switch. And now, as Sheppard rifled through the images of Brosconni's treatment of his staff, it sickened her to think anyone could be so callous or cruel.

Prior to the Polizia di Stato arriving at the villa, Brosconni had assembled his entire staff in the front hall. He paced back and forth with his hands clenched behind his back and let the tension amongst the assembled group thicken. When he stopped, he turned toward the mixture of uniformed staff and glared at them as if they'd been condemned. He waited a moment more, and then he barked out an order.

"Capano," he said, "step out here."

The silent moans could not be heard but yet they were as loud as the church bells on Sunday. Even though Capano was their hard fisted boss, his fellow workers cringed as he edged forward and stopped in the middle of the hall.

"You ignorant son of a bitch," Brosconni shouted out, "I gave you instructions to watch Marcella for one God damn night and my desk is taken from right under your nose."

Brosconni stepped forward and stopped in front of Capano eye ball to eye ball as he spoke.

"You're about as intelligent as your brain dead, twelve year old kid. Get out of my face."

Capano shuffled back to the group and no one dared touch him as he stood there alone.

Christina looked over the rail as a shiver ran down her spine. She had never met Antonio's son, but she had been told by the helicopter pilot on the flight from Rome, his son had severe brain damage at birth. He functioned chronologically at one quarter his age. Still, in the face of Brosconni's brutal attacks, Antonio didn't flinch. He couldn't afford to, because if he did, he'd be fired on the spot.

Christina's head snapped around at the sound of a chopper approaching the villa from the north side. She studied the sky as she shook her head in disbelief. The whole affair was like a bad dream that had come back to haunt her. A few years after her husband's death, Sheppard had worked on a piece purchased by a Rockefeller heir in rural New York. It was a 1770 Chippendale secretary desk. She spent one day in their mansion inspecting and evaluating the piece. That night, while the Rockefeller's were out to dinner, the house was robbed at gunpoint. Two pieces were taken: a twenty thousand dollar Ming vase, and the hundred and fifty thousand dollar

Chippendale. Questioned on three separate occasions by the Tarrytown detective heading the case, the discomfort Sheppard felt, by the questions Detective Krass asked, made her skin crawl. And now, what were the odds it would happen again?

CHAPTER 5

General Alberto Capalli marched from the helicopter pad straight to Villa Marcella's front entrance with his two aides by his side. The forensic team (two green vans parked directly in front of the Villa) had arrived forty five minutes before. Six men and two women in military uniforms stood by the trucks talking as Capalli passed. They saluted The General and stood at attention until he disappeared through the door. Alberto Capalli demanded nothing less.

Capalli was second generation military; his father had been a colonel in the Aeronautica Militare (Air force) Special Forces. A member of the 17 Stormo Incursori, Colonel Capalli was trained for co-opt raids on areonautical compounds. He indoctrinated the young Alberto to the rank and order of military protocol and expected the same from his son as he did from his troops. By twelve, Alberto was enrolled in a military academy, rose rapidly in class, and as a senior ascended to student commander in charge of all the student troops. Now, General Alberto Capalli, as head of the Carabinieri Art Squad, conducted civilian investigations with the same precision and exactness as the skilled commando who first taught him his trade.

Alerted by the incoming chopper, Brosconni and Commissioner Russo met General Capalli in the foyer as he walked through the door. The General wasted no time.

"Enrico, Commissioner," he said and nodded to each, "what have you found?"

"Nullo, nothing, we have searched every inch of the Villa General, the Hepplewhite is not here." Russo said.

The General's eyes rolled to Brosconni.

"Do you have the DVD's Enrico?"

Brosconni reached into his blazer and retrieved two DVD's clipped into individual jewel cases. He handed them to Capalli. Brosconni's cold, lifeless stare went unnoticed as Capalli turned toward his aide.

"Take these to the truck," Capalli ordered, as he handed them to his aide. "I want these digitized to check for sequential interruptions in the time line. Order a complete work up on last night's security guard. Have him taken to a separate room and questioned."

"Yes General." The aide said.

"Instruct forensics to bring their equipment into the foyer and wait for my orders."

Brosconni, having held in his anger long enough, was about to erupt.

"I wa…………………….."

The General held his hand up and stopped Brosconni mid-word. He was still focused on his aide.

"Inform me the minute you have analyzed the surveillance, understood?"

"Yes General."

"Go!"

Capalli turned to Brosconni.

"Who is in charge of the Villa, Enrico?"

Brosconni, still enraged, ground his teeth as his hands were clenched into tight pulsating fists.

"Enrico," Capalli said again.

Brosconni raised his head.

"Who's in charge of the villa?"

"Antonio Capano."

"Where is he?"

"Outside with the others."

The General snapped his fingers signaling to his other aide, Capt. Penso, who was standing at the front door speaking to one of the guards. Penso jumped at the command.

"Yes General?"

"Call headquarters, run a national and international check on Antonio Capano. Take Capano to Senior Brosconni's office; I want everything he knows about last night."

"Right away General."

"Where is this American you spoke of?"

"She's in her bedroom," Brosconni said, "with a guard outside the door."

"Good, show me to the room where the Hepplewhite was taken."

They arrived at the tape strung across the columned entrance to the living room, and The General held up his hand signaling for Brosconni to stop.

"Don't touch anything." He said.

They slid under the tape, and Brosconni led Capalli over to the Oriental rug where the desk had last been seen. In the foyer just off the hall, the squad of six forensic investigators had placed their equipment on the marble floor. The sound of feet shuffling and tool boxes hitting the stone echoed into the living room, and Capalli turned his head toward the noise. Then without moving his body, he raised his eyes up the paneled walls to the height of the fifteen foot frescoed ceiling. Slowly his head turned, inspecting the floor, the rug, the furniture, every detail of the room making mental notes of the crime scene. His gaze stopped at the panel of doors.

"What's out there?" Capalli asked.

"The balcony overlooking the cliffs, no one could enter from that side of the Villa, impossible." Brosconni said.

Capalli shook his head and scanned the perimeter of the room. He continued his search as he spoke.

"Are there surveillance cameras in here?"

"Just in the hall."

Capalli nodded. The General looked down to the Tabriz as a voice sounded on his two way radio.

"General?"

He pulled it from its holster.

"Go ahead."

"General, there are no time discrepancies on the recording, the time line is fully intact."

"Very good, run through...... just a minute. Enrico what time did you vacate the room last night?"

"Around ten."

Capalli clicked the radio, "run through the surveillance starting at 9:30 last night until 6:30 this morning."

"Yes sir."

He looked up to Brosconni.

"I would like to speak with the American." He said as he holstered his radio.

Brosconni said nothing and moved toward the marble opening to the hall.

They exited the room, and Capalli stepped over to where the forensics team stood. He snapped his fingers and then waved his hand. The forensics squad scrambled. He turned and followed Brosconni down the hall in the direction of the marble staircase to the second floor. As they passed the office where Antonio Capano was being questioned, Brosconni shot an irate stare at the closed oak door.

They continued up the marble staircase as Brosconni talked to himself inside his head. He was calculating how many people he'd fire and at the moment it was quite a few. When they reached the second floor hall and arrived at Sheppard's bedroom door, the guard jumped to his feet and saluted General Capalli.

"At ease sergeant!" Capalli said.

The General knocked on the door twice. He reached for the door handle and raised his right hand as he eased open the door.

"Enrico, I will question the American, alone!"

Brosconni watched as the thick oak panels closed in front of him, and he felt the anger flush up his body, rising into the veins in his neck. He stood in the hall, staring at the wood paneled door, about to explode.

CHAPTER 6

Christina Sheppard was as tough as she was gifted by her eidetic memory. Left alone to run the showroom on 2nd Ave., in Manhattan, after the death of her husband and her parents, she was thrust unprepared into the multi-leveled skills of operating a large and successful international business. Depressed by her loss and pressured by the huge demands, Sheppard turned to an English dealer who happened into her showroom one summer day in search of a particular piece. His name was Jermaine Arket. Arket was a savvy Antique dealer from London and was taken by Sheppard's knowledge and stunning good looks. He counseled her over the next three years, personally and professionally helping her strengthen her emotional psyche and develop the foundation of a solid CEO.

As her skill as an administrator blossomed, her tact at neutralizing overinflated egos flourished. She was not intimidated by the outspoken, demanding personalities of her wealthy clientele as witnessed by her confrontation with Brosconni. And now, as she stood on the balcony and watched her bedroom door ease open, Sheppard's patience had run thin. She detested the idea of being a prisoner in Villa Marcella and loathed the sight of a military uniform coming through her bedroom door. She turned and looked toward the coast.

"Ms. Sheppard," the commander said as he approached the doors to the balcony, "my name is General Capalli. I am the commander of the Carabinieri Art Squad, and I need to ask you some questions—sit!"

Sheppard sat at the round café table on the balcony, and the General pulled out the chair on the opposite side. He removed his hat and placed it on the table and rubbed his military cut, salt and pepper hair with his hand. He wasn't a large man, and although he sat low at the table, his dark brown eyes exuded strength and control. And as he reached to the inside of his military issue general's jacket and pulled out a small hand held digital recorder, Capalli attempted to intimidate Sheppard with his piercing, unyielding stare. But Sheppard, undaunted, glared back.

Still locked in a visual tug of war, Capalli placed the device on the marble table top, pushed the button, and began his interrogation.

"Tell me about last night, Ms. Sheppard." His voice had an inquisitive push in its tone.

With a matter of fact look on her face she responded. "There is nothing to tell."

Capalli broke off and stood up. He positioned himself behind Sheppard and leaned on the marble balustraded rail. "Come Ms. Sheppard," he said and raised his head toward the cloudless sky, "a priceless desk has disappeared only hours after your arrival, and Senior Brosconni informs me you insisted upon stopping your investigation soon after it began. He labeled the abrupt termination.....I believe the word he used was....."suspicious." The General turned and faced Sheppard's back. "I find your defensive stance curious, Ms. Sheppard, what am I to think?"

"Quite frankly, General, I don't care what you think."

Capalli edged around the table and stood behind his chair. He put his hands on the top of the rattan back, and his face went steel cold.

"You can answer my questions now, Ms. Sheppard, or later at headquarters in Rome."

Sheppard stood up defiantly and leaned on the marble rail. Capalli continued.

"What do you suspect happened to the desk, Ms. Sheppard?"

"I have no idea, General, that's not my job."

"What exactly is your job, Ms. Sheppard?"

Sheppard cracked a sarcastic grin.

"You already know the answer to that," she said in a sarcastic tone, "let's not waste each other's time. Check the surveillance tapes, you'll see I went into my room and didn't come out until morning. Brosconni has every inch of the Villa monitored, and I'm sure you've already examined the tapes."

Capalli was informed on the way to her room the DVD confirmed what she said. His aide had radioed him as he walked down the hall.

He pulled out his chair and sat down.

"Tell me about Tarrytown," he asked in a coy even tone.

Sheppard turned her head toward the sea.

The General could tell Sheppard was irritated by the question. He pushed harder.

"I'd like to hear your side of it."

Her eyes snapped back and examined his face.

"Am I a suspect, General?"

"A priceless piece of furniture is missing, Ms. Sheppard, that's a fact. An incident like this doesn't happen very often, and yet for you, it seemed to have occurred twice. Those two objects taken in New York were never recovered, and I am told no one was ever charged. Now a one of a kind Hepplewhite is missing, vanishes into thin air, and you were one of the last to see the piece. Is that a coincidence Ms. Sheppard?"

Capalli studied the reaction to his question. He raised his eye brows as he stared at Sheppard. She looked beyond him toward the sloping landscape dotted with trees. Sheppard had expected this. And, she wasn't surprised by his approach. She had dealt with the macho arrogance of Italian men before. She pulled her gaze back to Capalli still waiting with his brows aloof.

"Well, Ms. Sheppard?"

"I think we're quite through here General. I neither like your questions nor your insinuations. If you've done your homework, and I assume you have, you know all about me, my reputation, and the respected business which I run. I have nothing to offer this investigation. I examined the desk, grew tired, and went to bed. Unless you're going to charge me, General, I would like you to leave."

Capalli reached for the recorder with his eyes trained on Sheppard. He shut it off, placed it in his coat pocket, and positioned his hat on his head. He turned toward the Tyrrhenian Sea and spoke with his back toward Sheppard.

"It's a beautiful view, Ms. Sheppard, I trust you'll stay and enjoy it for a few days."

"Are you telling me I can't leave?"

"Not just yet, Ms. Sheppard, I may have more questions for you."

Capalli turned and began to walk toward the bedroom doors.

"Good day Ms. Sheppard."

Christina watched Capalli walk through the bedroom, open the door, and disappear. As the sound of the heavy oak closed against the jamb, a rush of adrenaline pulsated inside her chest. She jumped up and shuffled over to the rail and looked down to the towns on the coast. *What happened to the desk*? She thought. *How did it leave that room*?

She recalled the interior of the living room. One by one each image froze into the still likeness of the confined space—like the snap shot from a digital camera—and she examined the details of each frame: the green marble lamp sitting on the table underneath the ornate mirror hanging on the wall, the medieval stone fireplace with its over sized opening and charred black fire box, the open panel at the back of the desk with its two tiers of open shelves. She studied the two documents sitting on the rectangular shelf, the wax seals still intact.

She turned and rested her buttocks against the marble rail and looked back toward the soft light illuminating the bedroom walls. Christina was now as fascinated by the crime, as she had been by the desk. She pictured that morning, standing at the marbled column entrance, as the images flowed into her head: *the doors to the balcony—undisturbed, the furniture, the paneled walls, the frescoed ceiling, nothing. Brosconni had said no one could enter or leave without detection—cameras.*

Sheppard brought up the image of the rug, the oriental on which the desk had sat.

It was undisturbed. She raised her hand to her face and laid her finger across her soft pink lips. Her mind's eye searched each image for a clue as to how the Hepplewhite could have left the room. And then, as if the answer had been telepathically transmitted from the far reaches of her mind, she knew.

CHAPTER 7

By morning every newspaper, news channel, and international network had the disappearance of the Hepplewhite as their lead story. In Italy, the papers touted the well known shipping tycoon followed by the significance of the historical piece. Internationally, the Hepplewhite received top billing.

"An antique desk believed to be commissioned by George Washington, the first President of the United States, has been stolen from a Villa on the Amalfi Coast in Italy. It was purchased by a wealthy Italian business man named Enrico Brosconni. Taken from his Villa Marcella, the desk is considered the only known piece of the eighteenth century master, George Hepplewhite. Because of its connection to the future American President, and its significance as a one of a kind Hepplewhite, some experts have estimated the Hepplewhite could bring as much as ten to fifteen million dollars at auction.

A member of a special branch of the Italian military, the Carabinieri, said on conditions of autonomy that the investigation has failed to produce any leads or determine how the piece was taken from the impenetrable sea side villa. World renowned antiquarian detective, Christina Sheppard, was rumored to have been flown in to evaluate the desk but was unavailable for comment. We will bring you more on this fast breaking story as it develops. This is Wolf Blitzer for CNN international news."

Sheppard stood behind Brosconni who sat on the couch in the viewing room watching CNN on the large screen TV.

"You asked to see me?" She said.

"I am on my way to Rome to meet with my lawyers, Ms. Sheppard, I want you to send the pictures of the desk to my mobile phone; Capano will give you the information you need. No one in their right mind will try to sell my Hepplewhite, not after my lawyers hold their press conference this afternoon—no one!"

"I want the use of your driver today."

"You what?"

"I have some research I wish to conduct."

Brosconni was in no mood to grant amenities to anyone, least of all Sheppard. He still believed either by her defiance or direct involvement she was responsible for the theft, and she would pay for that. Brosconni didn't believe in justice; he believed in retribution, and gender meant nothing to the tycoon's rage—neither did age. Ten years into his growing empire, one of his dock workers had been crushed by a metal container dropped from a faulty boom. The family was never compensated for the worker's death, and Brosconni docked the man the rest of the day's pay. The wife hired a lawyer, but he was no match for Brosconni's high priced legal goons, and she lost the case. She was left without a husband, broke, and a six year old son.

Out of desperation she tried a different tact. She pleaded with his office staff, day after day, to have five minutes of Brosconni's time. After countless attempts to speak with the tycoon, she waited one afternoon outside the shipyard office with her six year old son. As Brosconni headed to his car, she rushed Brosconni and begged to have a word with the heartless tycoon. Angered at the inconvenience of her lawsuit and having to pay his lawyers for their services on the case, he grabbed her by her sweater and threw her to the ground.

The six year old son ran toward Brosconni in defense of his crying mother. Brosconni caught the screaming boy by his nose, twisted it like a door knob until it broke, and threw him down next to his sobbing mother. Even though the boy's nose was bleeding and broke, he scrambled to his feet, crying, and lunged at Brosconni's back. Brosconni turned, kicked the boy so hard in his chest, he fell back on his head, unconscious. His tolerance had been pushed to the limit and for his angst the two of them paid. And now, as he sat and listened to Sheppard, he was incensed by her request, and it provoked within him a need to deal with Sheppard in much the same way.

"No!"

"I can help."

"What do you know?"

"Nothing, yet, but if you wish to reunite with your priceless piece you will need my help."

In less than twenty four hours, Sheppard had grown to detest Brosconni. The passion that burned inside Christina was not about possession, it thrived on the thrill and reverence of stepping back into the past. She often told a story of her grandfather, who established the antique business she presently owned. In the early 1900's President Monroe's great granddaughter damaged the deceased president's Louis XVI's desk. It was taken to Christina's grandfather's shop for repair.

Her grandfather, the late Thomas Lablanc, discovered over two hundred letters in secret compartments which lay undisturbed for over seventy-five years. The documents included previously unknown correspondence from Presidents Jefferson and Adams to Monroe.

"That priceless trove of lost history," Sheppard had stated in her proud recitation to the director of the Metropolitan Museum in New York, "belonged to all the people—my grandfather had said—not the few."

Brosconni believed the opposite. The last thing in the world Sheppard wished to do was to help out a man who lived on the outskirts of humanity. But last night Sheppard devised a plan, and she would use Brosconni's twisted obsession as a hook and his missing desk as the bait.

"How?" he asked.

Brosconni stared at Sheppard, in part inquisitive, in part incensed.

"What do you want?" He asked.

"I want your driver, I want complete access to Villa Marcella, and, I want your lawyers to draw up a contract which states the following: if by the time you return I disclose to you the first clue toward recovering the Hepplewhite, and we eventually recover the desk, for six months each year the desk will be loaned to museums around the world for public viewing. Also, any papers, documents, or correspondence found inside the desk will be permanently housed at the Smithsonian Museum in Washington, D.C."

"You're delusional, Ms. Sheppard. General Capalli has recovered stolen art and artifacts from around the world since his appointment as commander of the Carabinieri Art Squad. The General's success rate is in the ninetieth percentile. You're a female, in a skirt, who knows antiques. Don't play with me, Ms. Sheppard; it may be hazardous to your health."

"Well then, Enrico, you have nothing to lose, do you? I'll take that as a yes. And, when you arrive back, have the contract in your hand. This female, in a skirt, who knows antiques, will give you and the General your first lesson on how to solve the case. And we'll see how your competent, General Capalli, deals with that."

Sheppard left the room and never turned back. Right now, she needed to get out of Villa Marcella and away from the obnoxious presence of Enrico Brosconni. As she walked down the hall she felt sickened by the vivid images that flashed in her head of the repulsive shipping tycoon. His scrunched up nose, his beady eyes, his down turned mouth, and his dark Italian lips which spit daggers at anyone in his way. Sheppard felt her stomach curl as if she had ingested sour milk. She crossed the threshold to the door of her room, as the phone chirped away. She picked up the handset and braced for more.

"Ms. Sheppard?"

"Yes."

"This is Antonio Capano. Senior Brosconni's car will be waiting out front whenever you wish to leave."

"Thank you Antonio." Christina hung up the phone. She looked out the balcony doors to the endless expanse of ocean which seemed to disappear into the cloudless blue sky. *A female, in a skirt, who knows antiques*, she muttered, *we'll see about that*!

44

CHAPTER 8

Sheppard needed a panoramic view of Brosconni's estate, so they drove above the tiny strips of terraced land where the locals farmed their lemon crops. The Sfusato Amalfitano, the current variety of lemons grown on the Amalfi Coast, was harvested by hand and brought down to market by donkey and cart. The terrain was steep, the road narrow, and the Alfa Romeo looked conspicuously misplaced on the old dirt access road. It bounced in the pot holes and its slow crawl up the cliffs kept it suspended in a constant cloud of dry dust. As he focused on the hairpin turns, Brosconni's driver objected.

"Signora," he insisted, "this road, it was not made for an automobile."

Sheppard ignored his pleas as she peered out her window and studied the landscape below.

"Signora," he said again with his eyes glued to the bending curve ahead, "you don't understand, Signora, this is not safe."

With the entire view of Villa Marcella now visible, she turned her head toward the front seat.

"Stop here," she instructed. She opened the door, and stepped from the back of the four door sedan and scanned Brosconni's estate. She examined the position of the villa suspended on the edge of the two hundred foot cliff, the concrete helicopter pad to the north side carved into the ledge, the long winding road which began at the front entrance and looped around steep inclines and rugged cliffs. Then Christina studied the west side, toward the Tyrrhenian Sea, and within seconds she spotted exactly what she was looking for—a dirt road which straddled the steep declining slope, weaving back and forth as it made its way to the coast. Her premonition, last night, had been right.

The old road confirmed Christina's research from the internet. Dating as far back as the 16th century, lemons had been grown, harvested, and shipped from the little coastal ports of the Amalfi Coast. These fundamentally crude and undisturbed roads were a direct access from the cliffs to the sea. Also aware Villa Marcella was constructed in 1572 by the Bordatelli family, and its strategic location provided protection from hostel invaders, Sheppard had concluded the ancient road would have provided the perfect escape route if the Villa came under attack. She pinpointed its location in her memory and climbed back into the car.

"I'm finished," she said, "turn around and take me back to the villa please."

Brosconni's driver shook his head. He put the car in reverse and started to back down the narrow winding dirt road. Sheppard's head snapped around. With her eyes bulged out of their sockets, she stared out the back window in shear fright.

"What are doing?" She said, her voiced raised almost to a panic.

"Signora," he said peering out his window into the side mirror, "I tried to explain this to you."

"Explain what?" She gasps, now seeing nothing but the trunk of the car.

The driver's head turned to the opposite side mirror. He tried to locate the road through the dust and the ninety degree bend as he replied.

"There is no place to turn around, Signora, we can only go one way."

Sheppard slumped into the seat, grabbed the pull bar on the door, and squeezed her eyes closed, tight.

Arriving back at Villa Marcella, safely, Christina spent the afternoon drawing a footprint of the living room, hall, and adjoining office. She worked off a clip board carefully measuring the length and width of the rooms, the different nooks, and sketched it on the paper to a ¼" scale. Even the exterior doors, balcony, and windows did not escape her detailed blueprint of the Villa. Although it was not to architectural quality, she scratched and scribbled until the drawing was complete.

Sheppard was determined to make Brosconni and Capalli stagger in their egocentric ignorance.

Men that shallow, she had said to her friend Jermaine Arket after an incident involving a Hollywood star, must be strategically assisted in order to fully appreciate their lack of humanistic depth.

The actor, named Bruce Stark, had looked on both coasts for a Chippendale high boy to furnish the renovated bedroom of his town house on 82nd Ave. near the Met. Stark swaggered into her 2nd Ave. showroom and was approached by one of Christina's agents—a woman. Stark demanded a salesman, with the emphasis on "man." And with a half bent grin on his face he said, "it takes a man to know antiques, after all, what gender were all the great masters—you see my point?" Sheppard was called to the floor.

Insult after insult flew as Stark examined each individual piece. Sheppard allowed Stark to uncurl plenty of rope, she figured the further the fall the more dramatic the stop. Then, she said, "I have an extraordinary Chippendale in the back, but I'm afraid it's the most expensive piece in the showroom." Stark bit, and bought, for a hundred forty five but with three more zeros attached. And as he prepared to leave proud as a peacock, Sheppard explained the piece was a fake, made only seventy-five years before. She ripped up his check, and calmly said, "your masculine expertise will be the hit of the Hollywood parties, after all, you are the great Bruce Stark—yes?" She was prepared to assist Brosconni and Capalli in much the same way.

Now, still seething from Brosconni's remark, Sheppard would demonstrate to the shipping tycoon and The General how the Hepplewhite vanished two nights before. So she walked back to her room to complete the final details on the prints, and as she sat on the balcony and checked the scale of the last window for dimensions, Sheppard heard a knock on her bedroom door.

"Come in," she said, "it's unlocked."

Antonio Capano stepped across the threshold with a silver tray which held a glass of Chardonnay.

"I'm sorry to disturb, Ms. Sheppard, I thought you might like a drink."

"Thank you, Antonio," she said still staring at the print, "please put it on the table."

Capano placed the wine glass in front of Sheppard and tucked the silver tray under his arm.

"Ms. Sheppard, I made a reservation for six thirty at the Hotel Caruso in Ravello per your request."

Sheppard looked up. "Thank you Antonio."

"Senior Brosconni's driver will transport you to the Hotel and back."

She gave an appreciative smile to Capano and nodded.

"Anything else, Ms. Sheppard?"

"No, thank you Antonio."

Capano bowed and left the room. Christina locked the bedroom door and went into the bathroom and filled the tub. She lounged in the hot soothing water with the Chardonnay, and envisioned the balcony of the former 11th century palace, now restored into the Hotel Caruso. She had been told, upon leaving New York, the one place you must dine on the Amalfi Coast is in Ravello. The hotel balcony, her friend had said, is perched on the cliffs as if floating on a drifting cloud. And as she placed the warm cloth on her white breasts which bobbed above the water, she savored the last of the California Chardonnay and dreamed of her late husband Ray.

It was as she'd been told: the sensation of being suspended high in the air looking out to nothing but blue endless sea. The waiter in his white coat and black bowtie had pulled out her seat, politely asked if she cared for a drink, and then excused himself in Italian dialect. He arrived a few moments later with her wine and left a menu by her side. And as she sat enjoying the ambiance, the view, and reading through the entree's as she savored her wine, a man's voice startled her and she jumped.

"Excuse me………..Ms. Sheppard?"

Christina jerked her head around and caught a glimpse of the man standing behind her.

"My apologies for startling you, Ms. Sheppard, may I call you Christina?"

He knows my name?

He stepped around so she could look at him directly.

"My name is Randolph Hancock." He said.

Christina had recognized him from his picture on the back of the book jacket. She had read two of his non-fiction works. He was a direct descendent of John Hancock and wrote about his great—times six—grandfather's role in the revolution. The second was also a biography; it dealt with John Langdon's life, also a signer of the Constitution of the United States, and Governor of New Hampshire. *But something about Hancock looked different, the way he wore his hair, the mustache? What is it,* she thought as she found herself mesmerized by his handsome features.

"Yes, I know who you are; I've read two of your novels, and I enjoyed them very much." She said.

"That's sweet of you," he said, "may I sit?"

What? Why? Sheppard was caught off guard. She had intended on spending a quiet evening alone, with her thoughts and her memories of Ray. And now, she felt that uneasy discomfort of having her planned intent interrupted, never the less by a man. Christina Sheppard was an incredibly attractive woman; she had encountered this very same approach many times before, and in the past, she resorted to her infamous retort of a chilling icy stare. It repelled even the most voracious of oncoming advances. But something made her hesitate, and he took advantage of her pause.

"Please." He asked.

Christina tried not to examine him, but found herself surprised by her interest. He wore a white button down oxford, no tie, and blue blazer. His hair, mid-long, mostly straight, but with enough wave and gray that it had a Michael Douglas look. She tried to recover.

"Please, may I sit?"

What?

"Would you mind if I ordered a bottle of wine?" He asked, as he pulled out the chair.

What is he doing?

Hancock sat down.

Tell him to leave, Christina, now!

"I attended your lecture last year in Boston. It coincided with my research. I was fascinated by your presentation on 18th century craftsmanship, particularly the part about getting inside the mind of the master cabinetmaker if you wish to get inside his work."

The waiter arrived at the table, and they both looked up as he spoke. Randolph went off in fluent Italian and ordered a bottle of Chianti. Christina understood the word Chianti, but that was it and then the waiter nodded his head.

"I hope you don't mind; I went ahead and ordered a bottle of red."

Something about him drew her in, but yet, if she hadn't known who he was, and he hadn't had such a respected reputation, Sheppard would have demanded he leave. *Wait and see where he goes with this!*

"Where did you learn to speak Italian like that?" She asked.

"I studied the Roman Empire in Italy for a year when I was a history major at Harvard."

Randolph stopped and tasted the wine.

"Molto bene, grazie!" Randolph said.

The waiter poured Christina a glass and then Randolph.

"Volontà che tutti per ora?" The waiter asked.

"Si, grazie." He said and turned to Christina. "Buona salute," he said as he raised his glass, "here's to good health."

"Salute!" She said.

Then Hancock placed his wine glass on the table and with a dead serious stare looked across to Christina.

"I didn't find you here by accident." He said. "I made some inquiries and learned you were dinning at the Hotel Caruso tonight."

You did what?

CHAPTER 9

In Rome at the Carabinieri headquarters, General Capalli sat at the head of the conference table on the sixth floor suite—center of operations for the crack Carabinieri Art Squad. Capt. Giovanni Penso sat to his left and Capt. Pietro Tinelli (his other aide) to his right. Six officers of the special unit were seated in the remaining high back, leather chairs, with one exception. Detective Stan Mitchell of the metropolitan police of Scotland Yard sat at the other end opposite Capalli. It was 6:05 pm on a Friday evening, two days after the theft, and the general looked clearly irritated. He turned to Capt. Penso and nodded.

"Yes, General." Penso said.

Penso opened a thick black binder which had the blue, red, and gold heraldic symbol of the Carabinieri on the front and flipped over the first thumb tab which had forensics written on it.

"Here's what we have." Penso said "John Miller, a small antique dealer southeast of London, bought the entire contents of an estate outside a small village in Kent. He purchased the items from Laurie Cornwall, the deceased man's daughter, who resides in the United States. We contacted Ms. Cornwall, and she claimed to have no knowledge of the desk that was discovered in her parent's attic. John Miller then sold the piece to Carlo Bennetto. Bennetto, a dealer from Rome, sold it the next day to Brosconni. He drove with the piece in his van to Folkestone, boarded the Eurostar train, unloaded in Calais, France, and drove the approximate 1500 kilometers to the Amalfi Coast. Brosconni then summoned Christina Sheppard, from New York, to examine the piece. Sheppard arrived the next day, and that night the Hepplewhite went missing.

Besides Miller, Bennetto, Sheppard, and Villa Marcella's employees, no one else, we believe thus far, had knowledge of the desk."

"What about Miller and Bennetto?" General Capalli asked.

Capt. Penso looked down the table to the Englishman.

"This is Detective Stan Mitchell of Scotland Yard. I worked with Stan on the Ashmolean Museum's theft of the Cezanne back in ninety eight and then again last year on the artifacts taken from the Etruscan tombs outside of Rome. Stan's been working on the dealer John Miller."

Again Penso looked to the end of the conference table and nodded. "Detective Mitchell," he said.

"Yes, thank you Giovanni," Mitchell said as he addressed the table, "gentlemen. Yesterday I was asked to question John Miller at his antique shop in Kent. When I arrived, the shop was open, but there was no sign of Miller, and his office desk had been ransacked. I investigated further and found Miller in the back room, dead. He had a bullet through his forehead, and he was sprawled out on the floor. I called forensics and then had a look around. There was no evidence of forced entry or of a struggle."

General Capalli leaned back in his chair with a pensive look on his face.

"How long had he been deceased?" Capalli asked.

"Maybe one or two days, it's hard to say. We're waiting on the results of the autopsy, but someone entered that shop for one purpose. There was still cash in the register, the antique jewelry was still in the glass cases, and it's hard to know if any antiques were taken without an inventory, but we think not. Whoever entered that shop was there for one reason—take John Miller out."

"What about his phone records?"

"We checked those, General, we found three calls to antique dealers the day before. One was to Bennetto, one to Arthur Collet a dealer in New York, and one to Francois Rousseau a dealer in Paris. Rousseau confirmed he had done business with Miller before and that Miller tried to sell him the desk. Collet, the New York dealer, claims he'd never conducted business with Miller before, but Miller had called Collet for the same reason--to sell the desk.

Bennetto, we know, bought the piece, but we haven't been able to locate him just yet."

Capalli raised his hand for Mitchell to pause and lifted his head toward the ceiling. He collected his thoughts and then looked back to Mitchell.

"Had Collet or Rousseau spoken to anyone about the desk?" Capalli asked.

"They both confirmed they had not."

The General turned his head left. "Capt. Tinelli, what about............what was the name of the Roman dealer that sold the desk to Brosconni?"

"Carlo Bennetto, General."

"Yes, Bennetto, what about this Carlo Bennetto Captain?"

"General, after Bennetto delivered the Hepplewhite to Brosconni, he returned to his shop in Rome. His secretary confirmed that. She said he briefly worked at his desk, didn't make any phone calls, and then went home. He hasn't been seen since."

"What about the check from Brosconni?" Capalli continued.

"He deposited it, General, that afternoon on his way back to his shop."

"Credit cards?"

"Bennetto stopped in Lyon, France for dinner and stayed the night. Then he gassed up in Florence on his way to the Amalfi Coast and again in Atrani on his way to Rome."

General Capalli rolled his eyes to the end of the table.

"Detective Mitchell," he asked, "how soon before we'll learn of Miller's time of death?"

"Tomorrow."

"And the check from Bennetto?"

"It was still in Miller's office, General. It was never deposited."

"So we can assume he was killed on the same day Bennetto took possession of the desk?"

"That's a reasonable assumption, General."

"Lt. Armone!"

"Yes General?"

Capalli pointed to the blank calendar suspended from the wall.

"Yes General." Armone said. He rolled out of his high back chair and marched over to the board.

"Det. Mitchell what time did Miller call Bennetto?" Capalli asked.

Mitchell thumbed through his notes sitting in front of him. A second later he looked up. "Three in the afternoon on the 6th." He answered

Capalli swept his hand through the air toward Armone. The Lt. wrote down, phone call Miller - Bennetto, 6th, 3pm.

"What was the date on the check from Bennetto?"

"The seventh." Mitchell said.

"What time and day did Bennetto charge his ticket on the Eurostar to cross the channel?"

"The seventh at 11."

"How long, Capt., is the drive from Kent to Folkestone?"

"About forty minutes."

The General turned to Armone.

"That puts Bennetto at Miller's shop around 10:15 on the 7th. Brosconni took possession on the

8th, Sheppard arrived on the 10th, and the desk disappeared sometime between 10 pm on the 10th and 6 am on the 11th. Capt. Tinelli, take a team and find Bennetto. Capt. Penso, I want the cell phone records of every employee at Villa Marcella, and that includes the American, Sheppard."

General Capalli swiveled half way around in his high back chair and looked out the wall of glass onto the Piazza Sant' Lgnazio. His elbow sat on the arm rest of his chair and his fingers propped up his chin. His men sat quietly and waited. They once sat nearly five minutes in silence, while the General organized his thoughts and methodically pieced together the information that had been collected. Capalli was known throughout the Carabinieri for his sharp instincts and his ability to compile a strategy that would ultimately solve the crime, even from the thinnest of leads. His father had honed his young son's mind with tricks and games which forced Alberto to project beyond the hand full of clues the Colonel had shoved in his face. It made Capalli as tough as he was shrewd, and by the time he entered military school, Alberto was recognized as a brilliant campaign strategist and a Bull dog with a Bloodhound's nose. As he rose in the ranks of the Carabinieri, he was handed the most complex crimes and he was expected to solve them. And he did.

The General's high back started to move and circled around and faced the desk. Each buzzed military head came to attention.

"We are no longer looking at just the theft of a Hepplewhite: we are now involved in a homicide."

The General then glanced around the table.

"Capt. Tinelli—find that Roman dealer, Bennetto! Lt. Danato—get on the American dealer Author Collet! Lt. Bianchi—the French dealer Rousseau! I want these men questioned—again! Find out what they know and who they talked to. I want everything there is on these three. Lt. Pisano, go back with Det. Mitchell, dig up everything you can on this English dealer, John Miller, and I want the autopsy report as soon as it's released. Gentlemen, let's get to work!

CHAPTER 10

Christina sat back in her chair, looked across the table, and waited for an explanation. Hancock was swirling the Chianti in his glass and smelling the aroma as the red liquid ran down the inside.

"Well?" She asked.

Her patience had run thin waiting for an answer. The last thing she wanted was a man with romantic ideas sneaking around to find out where she was going and where she had been. In the six years since her husband's death, Sheppard handled her business with professional eloquence, but the minute anyone tried to get too close, she clamped up like a cherrystone plucked from the mud. If that was the reason for his previous statement, it would be a short night for the aspiring Randolph Hancock; Sheppard would see to that.

"I think you owe me an explanation," she said.

Hancock looked over the glass of Chianti. Sheppard's soft facial features had grown strong and cold.

"Well?" She said clearly aggravated now.

"Ok," he said, "relax Christina. I'm not trying to come on to you, that's not why I'm here. I started a new project about a year ago; it's a Biography on Washington. My research had uncovered some fascinating information concerning a desk he commissioned in 1786 that was never delivered. Colonel William Smith, an aide-de-camp to Washington during the Revolution, had been instructed to deliver the piece back to the newly independent states aboard the Lucretia. Washington trusted Smith and knew he could count on The Colonel's loyalty to see that the piece was delivered. Shall I continue?"

"I'm listening," Sheppard said.

"So in May of 86' The Lucretia set sail for America. In digging deep in the bowels of the Harvard library, in an old dock masters manifest of Boston Harbor, I found an inventory of the cargo unloaded in June of 86. Included in that account was a crate which it claimed contained a desk constructed by George Hepplewhite and marked as the property of Colonel William Smith. That would be, according to my research, the desk Smith was to have delivered to Washington."

"That's impossible," she said, "I saw the desk and the receipt from inside the Hepplewhite. That desk was not on board the Lucretia."

"That's correct Christina. I found a claim for the missing desk issued against the crate builders out of London. When Washington arrived at Governor Hancock's mansion where he was to pick up the desk, and they uncrated the piece, the container with the Hepplewhite was empty. It never made the voyage to the states."

"They found the desk in an attic in a crate, southeast of London." She said.

"I understand that, I read the story after the theft. It makes sense now. Someone must have switched the crated desk with an empty crate. The question is why?"

"What do you mean why?"

Hancock paused to allow Sheppard time to distinguish between romantic prey and historical comrade. He had observed her posture, and he noticed her stiffness had begun to let go. Hancock offered a reassuring smile and continued.

"I'll get into that later." He said. "How was the condition of the desk?"

"Pristine, like new."

He nodded. "That's logical, it was never used."

Hancock did a quick inspection of Sheppard's face. Her eyes had softened and looked to be fully engaged. He ran his hand through his hair and continued.

"How far did you get with your examination of the piece?"

Sheppard found herself intrigued by the movement and the way his hair fell back into place. She made an intentional effort to look away as she answered his question.

"Two compartments, I was tired from traveling and needed rest."

"Did you find anything other than the receipt?"

"There were two documents in the back compartment, but I left them until they could be handled properly."

"I see."

"Then the desk disappeared."

Hancock stared out toward the darkened landscaped dotted with sprinkles of light. He thought back to June of 1786, Boston Harbor, when the crate was met at the gangplank by an emissary of the then Governor of Massachusetts, John Hancock. Randolph felt a surreal sense of closeness to his forefather, even though they were separated by centuries. He snapped his attention back to Sheppard.

"So now you understand why I'm here?" He asked.

"I understand what we have in common." She said.

"When the story broke about the theft, and you having been summoned by Brosconni, I had to see you. If you recover the desk, I would like to work with you on the examination of the piece. There could be a treasure trove of information in those two documents. Someone had placed the correspondence inside that desk, which obviously was meant for the future president. Its contents could be of great historical value."

Hancock looked up from his dinner.

"Well?" He said.

"Well, what?"

"Will you allow me to work with you on this?"

"I would be happy to help in your research, only….."

"Only what?"

"You understand the desk, if we recover the piece, does not belong to me. Enrico Brosconni feeds his ego on having what no one else can have. That includes exclusive viewing of my examination and the discovery of any remaining compartments inside the desk. Although, if up to me, I would grant you your wish, I sincerely doubt Brosconni would be so accommodating, particularly after the events of the last few days."

"I see."

"But, I can be persuasive, and I have an idea."

"What's that?"

"Just leave it at that."

CHAPTER 11

General Capalli's helicopter landed on the concrete pad at 11:05 Wednesday morning, with The General and Capt. Penso inside. Capalli had been informed it was urgent; Sheppard had information, Brosconni had said, on how the Hepplewhite had left the Villa, and she suggested that he call forensics and tell them to come along. The General was not amused. The investigation had given up very few clues, and being summoned by a woman, particularly Sheppard, made the ride from Rome to the Amalfi coast almost intolerable. And as the door to the cabin slid open, Capalli marched full stride toward the villa the instant his boots hit the ground.

The General met Brosconni and Sheppard in the living room, and he demanded an immediate explanation. But Sheppard had her own agenda and smiled and raised her hand.

"So good to see you again, General." She said

His eyes, cold as steel, pierced her stare, but she fired back a look of defiance. The General took command.

"Alright Ms. Sheppard, this better be good." The General warned, "do not waste anymore of my time."

"What do you know of the history of Villa Marcella, General?"

"Come, Ms. Sheppard, I've been asked to fly from Rome to the Amalfi Coast for a history lesson—get on with it!"

Brosconni looked puzzled as he stood next to Capalli. Penso, who shadowed the two, had his captain's hat under his arm. It was clear that Sheppard was enjoying herself, which irritated the General even more. Brosconni's face went from puzzled to annoyed.

"Yes," he said, "get on with it Ms. Sheppard, we have no time for your childish games!"

"Did you bring the contracts, Enrico?" Sheppard asked, as if she was a grade school teacher asking the student if he'd brought his homework.

"We'll deal with that later," he said, "after you show us your ground breaking investigative work."

"First the contracts, Enrico, then the show."

Brosconni walked over to the lamp table next to the couch and picked up a packet of papers. He handed them to Sheppard.

"I've already signed them. You can sign them later and return my copy to Capano."

It wouldn't matter. The signature on the contracts was not Brosconni's; he had a servant sign it. It would mean nothing if she tried to enforce it. The shipping tycoon turned with a bent grin on his face.

"Now, get on with it!" He said.

"I have a saying, gentlemen, which has served me well in my profession; get inside the mind of the craftsman and you get inside his work: simply defined that means understand the psychological as well as the physical if you wish to understand the craftsman's art. Thus, the history of Villa Marcella, General, is the key to understanding how that desk left this room. Villa Marcella was built by a noble family who feared attack by foreign invaders—very common back in 1572. As you know, it was strategically placed to allow only one way in and only one way out. So how, General, in the case of an invasion would the Bordatelli family escape, if the only means of attack was also the only means for which to flee?"

Capalli removed his cap and rubbed his buzz cut with the palm of his hand.

"I'm running out of patience, Ms. Sheppard."

"Yes, yes, of course you are, General. Gentlemen, let me show you something, follow me if you would."

Sheppard walked over to the card table and nodded, inviting them to view her drawings.

"Have a look at these."

"What is this?" Brosconni asked.

"These are drawings of the living room and your adjoining office to a scale of one quarter inch. If you wish you can check the measurements."

"Yes, I see that, go on!" Capalli said.

"I'd like you to examine the paneled wall," she pointed to the wall that separated the living room from Brosconni's office, "and the adjoining wall in the office."

"What are we suppose to see, Ms. Sheppard, I see walls that separate two rooms." Brosconni said.

"Pay particular attention to the closet in Enrico's office. That closet, gentlemen, is three feet deep. It starts flush with the office wall and ends at the living room wall. Where the interior side closet wall ends, it leaves a void on the other side of three feet. Thirty-six inches is the standard measurement for a staircase, gentlemen."

Sheppard pulled two white cotton gloves from her red blazer and slipped them on.

"Follow me."

She led them over to the panel wall and stopped them in the center of the partition.

"Here is your answer to how the Hepplewhite left the room. Your surveillance cameras detected no one entering or leaving this room. That is because no one did enter or leave that night, at least not from the opening to the hall."

The wall was divided into three sections of raised panels with a continuous chair rail running the length at thirty inches off the floor. Where each section of panel ended, a decorative roping was carved into the chair rail. Below the rail were matching panels and a continuous baseboard running the length of the partition.

"Observe, gentlemen!"

Sheppard walked to the center panel and, with her protective gloves on, slid her fingers underneath the chair rail. On the underside against the paneled wall, she felt a small impression on each end of the chair rail just inside the two motifs of decorative roping. With both hands, she pushed the two impressions, and the chair rail popped out slightly away from the paneled wall. The decorative roping had been intentionally placed to conceal the joints at each end. Christina then pushed the chair rail down toward the floor, and it swung on some type of hinge flat against the panel. As she did this, the entire upper and lower panel released as a solid door and slid back about an inch—enough to allow the chair rail to miss the wall when the panel slid past it. Sheppard then put her covered hand on the top panel and pushed the door to the left. It revealed a dark open stone stair well that dropped down below the floor."

"There you have it, gentlemen, Bordatelli's escape route."

All three stood with their mouths open as their eyes stared into the darkness.

"General," she said, as she handed him a flashlight she retrieved from her back pocket, "you may want to set your men loose. I believe they'll find this tunnel ends in some obscure location near the dirt road that the locals use to bring their lemons to market. That old road leads down to the sea. The perfect escape route if you have a boat and a Hepplewhite you wish to abscond with."

"Son of a bitch, someone in this Villa knows about this," Brosconni said.

The General let out a loud high pitched whistle. The head of the forensic unit stepped to the entrance to the living room, and the General shook his head. The unit of six Carabinieri rushed into the room with their boxes of equipment. General Capalli snapped his fingers and pointed at the walls and to the inside of the medieval tunnel. Sheppard had walked back over to the card table and was folding up her prints. The General turned to Penso.

"I want the name of every person that has worked in or on this Villa since Senior Brosconni took ownership."

"Yes sir."

"Question every employee again, I want some answers."

"Yes General."

Capalli turned to Brosconni.

"No one is to go in or out of this room, Enrico, with the exception of the forensics team."

The General strolled over to Sheppard.

"I'm curious, Ms. Sheppard, how is it you were able to discover that secret passage and none of my men detected it?"

"What are you implying General?"

"No one would take such a valuable piece and then disclose how they carried it out unless, perhaps, they wished to divert attention."

"General Capalli, I fear you try to amuse yourself with your own intellect. A house, General, is no different than a piece of furniture: it's made by human's hands with a craftsman's mind. Individuals of wealth required security for their valuables and for that they turned to the old master cabinetmakers. Noblemen needed a means to secure their families and for that they turned to the master builders. As I stated before, you get inside the mind of the craftsman, you get inside his work. This, General, was no more of a challenge than finding a shoe in a shoe box. One just needs the expertise required to open up the lid."

Sheppard slipped the papers into her inside coat pocket and started to walk away.

"Ms. Sheppard." Capalli said.

She turned. "Yes General?"

"I've underestimated you; I won't make the same mistake twice."

"I may be mistaken, General, but I think that's a back handed threat."

"Did you know, Ms. Sheppard, the man who first discovered the Hepplewhite is dead? Someone put a forty-five in his forehead. I fear we may have to bring you up to Rome for questioning soon—stay close. You'll be hearing from me."

"Good day, General."

CHAPTER 12

General Capalli stood dazed, as he stared into the dark opening of the secret escape tunnel. Christina Sheppard's aggressive, unflappable attitude had clouded Capalli's intuitive clarity; a position both uncomfortable and unfamiliar to the General's sense of an individual's guilt or innocence in investigating a crime. He was brought up in a household where his father, the Colonel, had not just total command over the young Alberto, but over his docile, obedient wife as well. Alberto observed, learned, and grew accustomed to a woman's subservience and, in fact, had married a woman much like his mom. He treated his wife in the same manor he treated the men and women who served under him. But Sheppard's confident, intentional defiance of proper rank and order unnerved Capalli and dislodged his ability to separate the difference between legitimate suspect and subservient angst.

His two way radio jerked him back into command.

"Si," he said.

"General, we are at the bottom of the stone steps at the beginning of the tunnel. It appears one set of prints is incoming and one set of prints is outgoing. We are making plaster casts of the imprints and then will continue to explore the shaft."

"Keep me informed"

"Yes General, over."

"Capt. Penso!" He said as he clicked the audio button.

"Yes General."

"Where are you?"

"I've set up in the security room, General; I'm examining the ledger of past and present employees."

"Very good." He said and slipped his radio back into the holster. One of the special unit forensics investigators had worked his way around the secret door and was checking for prints.

"General," he said, "the door is operational from the back side as well. There is some type of latch release, but there are no prints on it."

Brosconni had taken a position behind the General and watched and listened as the Carabinieri carried out their crime scene investigation. His hands were clutched behind his back in a tight angry clasp, and he rocked on the soles of his shoes. Some sewer laden vermin had slipped through the walls and violated the great Brosconni. And, it could have happened at any time: the tunnel had been there all along. A passage he knew nothing about, right under his nose, in his sacred Villa Marcella. He took out the fob from his side coat pocket and pressed the Capano button. In a matter of seconds, Antonio appeared at the columned entrance, at attention, and spoke.

"Yes Senior?"

"Tell Ms. Sheppard I want her here—now! Secret doors, secret tunnels, she won't sleep until I know there are no more."

I'm sorry Senior, but Ms. Sheppard asked me to call for a rental car, and she had packed up some of her belongings and left. She said she'd be touring the Amalfi Coast for a few days, and if anyone needed to reach her, they could call her on her mobile phone."

"You get her on the phone—right now—I want her back."

"Yes Senior."

"General!" Capalli's radio blurted out.

Capalli pulled the two way from his belt.

"What is it?"

"General, we're about thirteen meters down the route, and it appears the suspect stopped to rest. There are four spike marks in the dirt; we believe from the legs of the desk."

"Measure the distance between each mark; photograph them, and plaster cast the shape of the holes."

"Yes General, over."

Brosconni turned toward Capalli, his eyes shooting left to right.

"The son of a bitch must have gotten tired from carrying my desk, alone."

The General nodded and then clicked his two way.

"Penso!"

"Yes General?"

"What have you got?"

"I'm still going over the books, General."

Brosconni stomped out onto the balcony patio. He reached with his hands and squeezed the marble railing with such authority it turned his knuckles white. *They took it by fucking boat!* His eyes stared down to the rich blue of the Tyrrhenian Sea. He envisioned a boat with his Hepplewhite on the deck, a man at the helm, and the gurgling of water as the engines revved and sailed off with his prized Hepplewhite on board, *son of a bitch!*

The image reminded him of when he was as a boy and stood on the porch of his mothers little shack. He had watched a stray dog lurking below, rummaging through garbage cans in search of a meal. The same dog who had stolen the steak he had bought on his way home from Pompeii. He had parked his bike under the eaves of the porch, and when he returned, the dog had run off with the paper wrapped steak he had laid on the wooden deck. So he had waited for the dog for two days, and it came scavenging just like he thought. He raised his twenty-two rifle and took careful aim as his elbow rested on the rail. The mutt approached slowly sniffing and weaving looking for the scent of food. He eased the trigger and shot off a round, and as the wounded dog yelped in pain on its side, Brosconni smiled. He slid in a second round and propped up his elbow, took aim, and put a twenty-two slug into the dog's brain.

Brosconni raised his head as he concluded his memory and envisioned the man at the helm of the boat. He felt his finger ease the trigger, and the blast release, and then he pictured an explosion of red blood from his head. The man flew backward and……..

"Enrico, you might want to hear this." The General said.

Brosconni smiled and moved in a deliberate pace toward the open doors with the image still fresh in his brain. He entered the living room.

"What is it?" He asked.

The General picked up his two way.

"Go ahead Penso." He said.

"General, three years ago a local craftsman named Benvennuto Saleno repaired some damage to the raised panels in the living room."

Penso was still talking as Brosconni whipped out his fob and pushed the button.

"It states he worked for six hours and was paid 64.38 Euro's."

"Talk to him." Capalli said.

"Yes Senior?"

Brosconni stared at the opening to the hall and then spoke in a slow, deliberate voice.

"Come…..in…..Capano," Brosconni said, "sit!"

General Capalli moved toward Capano and held his hand up to Brosconni. He then lifted the Chippendale chair Sheppard had sat in to inspect the desk, placed it in front of Antonio, and sat down. Enrico stood to the side of Capalli about to explode. Again the General put his hand up toward Brosconni.

"Antonio, tell me about Benvennuto Saleno?" The General asked.

"He's a local carpenter General."

"How do you know of him?"

"His mother was a friend of my family's."

"You called upon him?"

"Yes, when Senior purchased new furniture for the balcony, the movers damaged the panels when they removed the old pieces from the porch. I called him to repair the panels, General, why?"

"Were you with him when he did the repairs?"

"No General, I showed him into the living room, he set up his work space out on the balcony, and I went about my daily chores."

The radio on Capalli's belt chirped in.

"General?"

The General's eyes didn't leave Capano as he pulled his two way from his holster.

"Go ahead," he said.

"General, we're at the end of the tunnel. It's about fifty meters long and ends in a small scruff of trees. It's hidden from the dirt road by tree cover. We can see where he exited the tunnel, but there are too many tracks in the road to tell which are his. The road travels about thirty meters to the coast. We can see an inlet just below us."

"Bring the casts and equipment back to the van."

"Yes General, over."

Brosconni tried to say something, but Capalli raised his hand.

"Did he tell you that he found a secret door in the panels?" The General asked.

"He found this?" Capano said as he pointed to the opening.

Capalli repeated the question.

"Did he tell you he found a secret door in the panels?"

"No"

"Take a moment, Antonio, you don't want to say anything you might regret."

Capano looked to Brosconni and then to Capalli.

"I swear to you. I hired him, paid him, and he left."

"Why haven't you used him again?"

"He died more than two years ago in a moped accident on the Strada Stalale."

The General paused. He leaned closer to Capano.

"I see.' He said. "Who else saw him working in here?"

"No one, I closed off the room when he worked."

The General looked up to Brosconni and nodded his head as he rose from the chair.

"You may go for now," Capalli said, "but I will have more questions for you later."

Brosconni did a double take to Capalli and then to Capano. Then he froze as it came back to his head of staff.

"Where's Sheppard?" Brosconni asked.

"She's not coming." Capano responded.

"Get out of here!"

As Capano left the room the livid tycoon questioned The General.

"Alberto?" Brosconni asked.

"This Saleno found the escape tunnel." Capalli responded.

Capalli lifted his two way radio to his mouth as the voice sounded out of the speaker.

"General?"

"What is it, Penso?"

"General, Saleno's dead. He died two and a half years ago……"

"I know that."

"There's more." Penso said.

Capalli looked to Brosconni with inquisitive eyes.

"Go ahead," he said.

"Saleno was a convicted felon. He was arrested six times for breaking and entering and in possession of stolen goods."

"Son of a Bitch!" Brosconni shouted and started to pace about the room.

"Hold on Enrico, go ahead Penso."

"He was caught in an art theft sting and spent four years in prison."

"Is his mother alive?"

"Yes, General."

"Talk to her, find out everyone he was associated with, who he met in prison, where he lived after release, get on it"

"Yes General."

Brosconni stared at the columned entrance to the living room. A moment later Antonio appeared and Enrico turned his back to the hall.

"You called Senior?"

Brosconni spoke as he faced the balcony.

"You hired a convicted felon and brought him into my Villa? You ignorant letch—you're fired! I want you, your wretch of a whore, and your brain dead kid out by sunset, or I'll have the three of you dragged out by your hair."

"But Senior, we have no place to go Senior, we......"

"Get out!"

CHAPTER 13

After a day of touring, and nothing else planned, Sheppard called Hancock and asked him to meet her in Amalfi at the Piazza Flavio Gioia's bronze statue of the aforementioned man, who many years ago invented the compass. At 6 pm, she said, and we can stroll the Via del Duomo and look for a place to eat. She drove from Atrani where she had spent the day and maneuvered the Strada Stalale with a death grip on the steering wheel. Cut into the cliffs of the Amalfi Coast, the Strada Stalale seemed more like an amusement park ride than a road for vehicular traffic. And more than once she pictured her demise, as the car jumped off the road, and she plummeted hundreds of meters down the cliffs into the Tyrrhenian Sea. By the time she rounded the last curve and rolled down toward Amalfi, her neck was stiff and her shoulders ached. She rocked her head back and forth to stretch her neck muscles as she slowed to a crawl and turned right into the parking lot at the rear of the Piazza Flavio.

Sheppard walked through the maze of tour buses, loading up their passengers as Amalfi began to settle for the night. When she rounded the last transport and spotted Randolph beneath the monument, her heart began to pound inside her chest. Her legs felt weak, and she stopped to catch her breath. Sheppard understood for the first time since she met Hancock exactly what was going on. It was as if she saw a ghost. Randolph Hancock looked so much like her late husband, Ray, they could have been twins. His finger combed hair and trimmed mustache looked exactly like her last memory of Ray, and the way he dressed and his posture as he stood under the bronze statue was such an exact likeness she had to convince herself it really wasn't Ray. She took two deep breaths, straightened her blazer, and walked over to Hancock at the statue.

As they moved up the Via del Duomo and entered the Piazza, they stopped and stared at the magnificent Cathedral of Amalfi. With its sixty-two steps, it was a commanding structure which rose high above the street. Still trying to calm the throat closing rush streaming up her body, she jumped when Hancock spoke.

"Christina," he said, "are you ok, you seem spooked."

She turned her head slightly toward Hancock with a sheepish smile on her face.

"I'm alright," she said, "it's just the trip from Atrani; I've never driven on a road like the Strada Stalale before."

Hancock shook his head in agreement and then gently nudged her back with his hand encouraging her to move on.

They continued passed pottery shops and small quaint stores, and Christina kept her revelation to herself. Sheppard never talked to anyone about her husband; it brought back too much pain. But in her head, she must have been lost somewhere in memories, because she felt Randolph yank her to the side of the street. An Italian stud, with his shirt open, cigarette hanging from his mouth, smiled as he barreled past and almost nailed her with his blue and white motor scooter.

"I didn't even see him." She said.

"They like to get your attention," he said, "particularly when you're very attractive."

Sheppard nodded rolling her eyes in a sarcastic gesture.

"Let's just find a place to eat," she said, "I need a glass of wine."

They agreed on a restaurant called La Pesce dal Mare. Hancock explained that meant "the fish from the sea," but Sheppard neither cared nor heard a word he said. They were seated, ordered the vino, and Sheppard kept her gaze from Hancock. She was spooked, but not for the reason she had told Hancock. So she looked down to her glass as she started a conversation, trying to take her mind off the haunting apparition sitting across from her at the table.

"General Capalli, the man in charge of the investigation, told me the gentleman who first discovered the desk was shot in the head. He inferred it has something to do with the Hepplewhite. I don't see how but nothing has made much sense since Brosconni flew me in from New York."

Hancock was silent. His brows scrunched down toward his nose, and he looked deep in thought.

"What?" she asked.

"I'm afraid there's more to my research than I've told you, Christina."

"What do you mean?" She said now clearly shaken out of her past.

Randolph took a slug of his wine and looked up to the waiter as he handed the menus out. *I need to be careful,* he thought, *too much, too soon, would definitely scare her off.*

"Randolph?"

Hancock turned to Sheppard.

"Were the two documents you viewed inside the desk still sealed with wax or were the seals broken?"

"They were intact."

"Are you sure?"

"Do you know what eidetic recall is, Hancock?"

"No."

"It's a photographic memory: I can recall every piece of furniture I've ever examined and all the contents I've discovered inside. Yes, I'm sure. What's so important about the seals?"

The waiter approached and asked if they were ready to order. Christina said she was starved, so they opened the menus, dictated their choices, and waiter left.

"What's so important about the seals?" She asked again.

"In my research, both in Europe and the United States, I've uncovered bits of information which pieced together formulated a theory which I yet cannot prove. The essence of that information is this: George Washington, who had used couriers during the war carrying false information to trick the enemy when it was intercepted, was well aware of the power of documents being breached. When he was informed two documents would be sent from Great Britain in 1786, the contents of which was so sensitive it could re-spark the war, Washington came up with a plan. With the understanding it must be under the tightest security and with the least amount of attention, he sent word to a Colonel William Smith."

Sheppard's looked surprised.

"That was the name stenciled on the crate the desk was discovered in."

"That's correct," he responded. "Washington had seen plates of a Hepplewhite design and wished to purchase a desk for his beloved Mount Vernon now that the war was over, and he spent a great deal of time at home. The desk would become not only a prized piece for Washington's collection, but crated for transport home, it would act like a safe. Colonel Smith, on sending the piece to the United States, had the correspondence hidden in the secret compartment in the desk. When the desk was found over two centuries later, and you claimed the two wax seals were still intact, that verified that the classified information had never been breached."

Sheppard processed Hancock's information as she watched the bustle of human traffic up and down the street. Then her focus turned to Hancock.

"What was so important about the letters?" She asked in a questioning tone.

"They were addressed to two of the wealthiest men in America, Governor John Langdon of New Hampshire, and Massachusetts Governor John Hancock, my great grandfather times six. Upon arrival at Boston Harbor, the crate was met at the gang plank by an emissary of Governor Hancock's. It was escorted to the Governor's mansion where it stayed overnight. Washington, already in route to Beacon Hill, arrived late the next morning. Sent by Hepplewhite to Washington three weeks before was a detailed plate on the twelve secret compartments and the methodology used to access the hidden space.

Washington, upon arrival at the Governor's mansion, was to retrieve the sealed correspondence and hand it over to Hancock. The pine box was brought to Hancock's office in the mansion where one of his carpenters proceeded to uncrate the piece. But as you know now, when the crate was opened the desk was not inside."

The waiter brought their dinners to the table. Sheppard gazed back again to the human traffic walking up and down the Via del Duomo and thought about what Hancock had said. It was now dusk, and the street lights cast shadows of the moving pedestrians along the sides of the shops. Deep in thought, her head snapped up at the sound of the waiter.

"Will that be all for now sir?" The waiter asked in English.

"Yes, thank you." Hancock answered.

Christina tried her fresh grilled local catch with cherry tomatoes and then raised her eyes to Hancock.

"This is very good," she said as she wiped her mouth with her napkin. "Tell me more about the letters."

"Washington above ground followed the normal protocol: he filed a claim against the crate company and had the theft investigated abroad. Below ground, however, Hancock and Washington sent word to Smith to investigate the theft and find the piece. They were afraid if the desk fell into the wrong hands, and the letters were discovered, it would commence a chain of events which could re-ignite the war and this time without the help of France."

"And you can document all of this?"

"I cannot without the letters, which is why I contacted you in the first place. Even though you've proven those letters exist, without them, this is all just theory not fact."

Sheppard looked up from her dinner.

"How do you know all this?" She asked.

"I told you, my research."

"So what does this have to do with murder?"

Hancock took a hit of wine and laid the glass on the table as his eyes rolled to Sheppard.

"I have no idea, yet."

"Who wrote the letters?"

"I'm working on that."

Hancock paused and took a bite of his food. *Time to change the subject,* he thought, *too much, too soon, could backfire.*

"How did you know the secret escape route was there in the living room at Brosconni's Villa?"

"I sensed it as I always do. Then, when I stood on my bedroom balcony, reviewing the images of the room, I saw the hair line cracks in the paint on the paneled wall at the baseboard and crown molding. That confirmed my instincts: the panel had indeed moved

CHAPTER 14

The call from Capt. Tinelli came into General Capalli's office at 11:25 am, Rome time. The investigation at Villa Marcella had continued well into the afternoon the day before, and besides the plaster casts of a size nine and a half Sperry Docksiders, and four square casts of the Hepplewhite's legs, forensics struck out. The Docksiders explained the reason no dirt tracks were found on the living room floor: the shoes slip off and on with ease. The tunnel confirmed the desk was taken by boat. Lt. Pisano in England with Scotland Yard's Det. Mitchell had found nothing on Miller to indicate he'd end up with a blank look on his face and a hole in his forehead. And the General had three men combing through Benvennuto Saleno's short life. He believed the deceased carpenter was the best lead they had, and he was.

Capalli had anticipated the call from Tinelli and the information on the missing antique dealer Carlo Bennetto. Bennetto had been reported missing by his family the day after he sold the desk to Brosconni. And as General Capalli picked up the phone, Capt. Penso walked into his office, saluted, and sat in one of the winged back chairs facing his desk.

"Go ahead, Capt. Tinelli." Capalli said.

Capt. Penso seated opposite General Capalli, in front of the General's desk, listened to one side of the conversation.

"I see.....yes.....how long? I want you to complete the investigation and then return to the command center." Capalli said. "We'll have a staff meeting tomorrow morning, 8am."

Capalli hung up the phone and stared across the desk to Penso.

"General?"

"Bennetto's dead. He was found with a forty-five popped through his forehead."

"It seems someone is working their way up the ladder." Penso said.

"Where's Brosconni?"

"He's flying back to the Villa; he had a meeting with his attorneys early this morning. He should be back there by now."

"And the American?"

"She's still touring the coast."

The General swiped his military buzz cut with the palm of his hand.

"Call the Campania unit," he said, "and have them post a man at Villa Marcella around the clock."

"Yes General."

Capalli hesitated and collected his thoughts. He turned his head, squinted his eyes, and then looked back to Penso.

"Did Enrico have the steel door installed at the end of the escape tunnel?"

"They completed it this morning. The only way it can be unlocked is from the inside."

"Good, get Sheppard and warn her she'd be safer with Brosconni."

"She's pretty pig headed, General. What if she refuses?"

"Then she's on her own."

General Capalli reached for a folder and opened it up. He pulled out a packet of papers and slid them across to Penso.

"It's the autopsy report on Miller. He died only hours after Carlo Bennetto bought the Hepplewhite. We can safely rule out Bennetto, unless he decided to pop a slug in his own forehead the same way Miller got it—not likely. According to Miller's phone records, he talked to three dealers, no more. With Bennetto cold, that leaves Collet and Rousseau as the only other two who had knowledge of the desk."

Capt. Penso looked up from the file folder.

"General, they appear clean."

"Dig deeper, I want half the staff on Collet and Rousseau and half the staff on the Saleno investigation."

"Yes General."

Capalli swiveled around and stared out his window as Penso opened the autopsy papers and began to sort through the report. The General's instincts were buzzing his brain and something didn't feel right inside. He worked a case in 01 that brought up the same uneasy quiver in his gut, and he never solved the crime: five paintings taken from the residence of the famed Italian actor Marcelino Deluchi Fabrichio. Two Giorgio Morandi's, two Amedeo Modigliani's and one, the prize of the five, Da Vinci, all valued at over twenty million American dollars. The General concluded Fabrichio, a man who loved his women, his wine, and his Ferraris, staged the theft to collect the insurance claims on the treasured art. Marcelino dumped his cash as fast as he dumped his women, and no director would touch him after several drunken episodes on the set. The why was obvious to Capalli, but the how and with whom failed to materialize. The lack of evidence forced the General to let Fabrichio go; a blemish not forgotten by Capalli and an investigative misstep not to happen again. As he swiveled back around to the desk, Penso pulled his eyes from the report and looked up at his commander.

"Talk to Tinelli," Capalli said. "I want the ballistic report on the rounds from Miller and Bennetto analyzed by tomorrow morning."

"Yes sir."

"We have a disconnect here, Capt., which now complicates the investigation. Why kill Miller and Bennetto, to track down the desk? If Bennetto told his killer that Enrico purchased the piece, then how does the shooter learn of the secret escape route at Villa Marcella? Saleno's been dead for over two years. If Collet and Rousseau are the only two besides

Bennetto to have knowledge of the Hepplewhite, of which they had the opportunity to buy the piece, what interest would they have in dropping Miller and Bennetto? And what about this Benvennuto Saleno, if he discovered the tunnel, why didn't he use it when he was alive? The man was a convicted felon; Brosconni's Villa was filled with expensive works of art. Did Saleno have a plan, and he died before he had a chance to carry it out? No, Capt., we are looking at this from the wrong end!"

General Capalli's phone rang and he picked it up.

"Si."

Penso looked confused as he sat thinking about the General's statements.

"Did you talk to Senior Brosconni and inform him of the danger? I see………yes……………what time……….." Capalli looked at his watch. "I want him followed, and I don't want him to know he's being watched. Tail him until you can get some of your plain clothes men there and then back off." Capalli hung up and looked up toward the ceiling.

"General?" Penso asked.

"Enrico had his driver bring his car around, and he left in a hurry—after he was told about Bennetto."

"Did he say where he was going?"

"No, he refused to answer the officer's questions."

Capalli sat and searched with his eyes. *What's he up too?*

"General," Penso said, "you were saying about the investigation?"

"I want Antonio Capano brought in for questioning. Use the Campania headquarters."

"Yes General."

"I want a polygraph performed on Capano; we'll see what he knew of the escape tunnel and who's responsible for the missing Hepplewhite."

CHAPTER 15

Earlier at Villa Marcella:

Brosconni sat on the balcony, off the living room, in a large cushioned chair and stared at the plain white envelope in his hand. Antonio's replacement, Lorenzo Pietro, had delivered the mail to Enrico only moments before. To his right, scattered on the terracotta tile next to his chair, was the rest of the correspondence strewn in a chaotic pile on the floor. Brosconni raised the envelope into the air and up to his eyes to examine it further. On the front, addressed to Senior Enrico Brosconni, was written, "confidential, open immediately." But that's not what caught his attention. What challenged his interest was the top left hand corner, printed in black ink—the return address.

George Hepplewhite
Red Cross Street
London, England

Brosconni looked at the postmark: May 14, 2010, London, England. He reached for the gold letter opener on the table to his left and turned the envelope over. The knife seared a path at the top of the fold and cut a clean slit end to end. Brosconni pulled out the one page letter, type written, and read the opening line. "If you want your Hepplewhite back, you will follow my instructions precisely." He shifted his position in the chair, looked out over the Amalfi cliffs, and then refocused on the printed words on the white sheet of paper.

"If you speak to anyone, Carabinieri, Polizia, Sheppard, you will never lay eyes on the piece again. You do as instructed, and you will re-unite with your missing desk. Fail, and you will lose your prized Hepplewhite—forever."

Go to the Cathedral of Amalfi. When inside, walk to the fifth pew on the right and sit at the end next to the exterior wall of the church. Reach underneath and you will find taped to the wood another envelope. Inside, you will receive further instructions."

Brosconni folded up the letter and stuffed it in his right side blazer pocket. He had already pushed the button on the fob in his hand. Pietro stood behind him at the doors to the living room.

"Yes, Senior?"

"My car—now!"

"Yes, Senior."

As the Alfa Romeo stopped at the balustraded steps to the Villa, Brosconni raced past the Carabinieri guard he had spoken to moments before. The driver opened and closed the rear door, circled around to the driver side, and climbed behind the wheel with commands being fired from Brosconni.

"La Cathedral di Amalfi—veloce!"

"Si."

"Ora! Dannazione, ora!"

"Si."

Brosconni looked at his watch, 11:45 am.

"Fretta si idiota!"

He verbally pushed the driver down the steep inclines, around the sharp s-curves, and along the jagged cliffs of the Amalfi Coast. The wheels screeched, as they tried to hold the narrow road. Brosconni went quiet. He slid back into the soft leather and stared out the window as his rage festered to a feverish pitch. *No one gives Enrico Brosconni fucking orders—no one!*

"Più veloce," he shouted, "move it!"

His hand squeezed the grab bar on the car door as his veins thumped in his neck. Only once before had Enrico Brosconni found himself on the receiving end of a leveraged scheme. An American ship owner, Stephen McCord, attempted to purchase the same shipping company Brosconni had his sights on. McCord believed he held an advantage over the Italian competitor—proof Brosconni had lined the pockets of an American politician out of New York. He threatened Brosconni. "Back off or face the consequences," he said—a fatal mistake. No one backs Enrico Brosconni against the wall and walks away with their financial empire intact. One of McCord's freighters mysteriously went down. His overseas orders dropped twenty percent. And, back home, McCord was indicted for selling and delivering military weapons to the Iranians. Brosconni's onslaught had not only succeeded in destroying McCord and his International cargo company, but sent a strong, acknowledged message throughout the shipping world.

As he looked out the window toward the city of Amalfi, and whatever was stuck to that pew, only one thought raced through Brosconni's head—revenge.

"Faster!" He said.

The driver looked into the rear view mirror.

"Senior, we are being followed by the Carabinieri."

Brosconni looked through the back window, as they sped down the Strada Statale.

"Pull into the Piazza Flavio. Drop me off amongst the tour buses and then continue down 163. I'll call you when I'm ready to be picked up."

"Yes, Senior."

Brosconni studied the Piazza as they approached the congested parking lot. He waited until they reached a group of six buses.

"Stop!" Brosconni shouted.

He jumped out the back door and quickly scanned the horizon.

"Vai, go!"

The Romeo sped off, and Brosconni disappeared in the chaos of tourists which loaded and unloaded from the eighteen wheeled transports. He waited until he spotted his car head up the Statale, checked for the Carabinieri, and then quickly shuffled across 163 onto the Via del Duomo. He glanced over his shoulder as he slid along the left side of the

Duomo, and when he reached the cafes directly across from the Cathedral, he located an empty table and sat down. Brosconni surveyed the landscape, gazing up and down the Duomo and then onto the sixty two steps of the Cathedral. All was clear. He got up, and in a quick, steady gait he headed toward the steep, wide steps.

As he climbed the incline, his blood began to boil once again. He knew if he wanted his prized desk back, he would have to play along—at least until he could get an edge. But being led on a leash like a dog went against Brosconni's twisted makeup, and if he was to get the advantage, he'd have to put aside his violent rage. For Brosconni, that was like telling a stalking cat not to kill. Brosconni lived to feel the dominance in conquest, and the power relinquished in defeat. He loved the hunt, and he loved the kill, and ascending the last few steps, he felt the rush of adrenalin that pervades the body as the battle is about to begin.

Brosconni stepped between the pews and sat down. He reached under the wooden seat and felt for the envelope. Just as the letter had said, it was taped to the underside of the pew. He pulled the tape lose and raised the sealed envelope above his knees in order to see the front. Like before, typed in black ink, was the name Enrico Brosconni. He pulled out the gold letter opener from his inside blazer pocket, slipped the knife under the flap, and cut a seam across the top. As he slid the letter opener back into his pocket, he glanced around the church, nothing unusual caught his eye. He focused back onto the envelope and pulled the crease apart, then, he looked inside.

The first item he slipped out was a photograph of the desk. He examined it and determined it was indeed his prized Hepplewhite. He removed the letter, opened it up, and felt his face go flush upon reading the first line.

"Enrico Brosconni in the house of God; what an oxymoron that is! I bet you feel like a squid out of water squirming for a breath of air."

Brosconni scanned the church a second time and then returned to the note.

"I know what you're thinking, but don't. You must clear your mind of all thoughts of retaliation, strategic scheming, or reversing the predator to the prey. At the first sign of aggression, I quit, and your precious piece disappears—forever! We're just getting warmed up, Brosconni, and if you follow my instructions to the "T," you just might touch your Hepplewhite again."

Act one: Return to your Villa. Send an email with your cell phone number and instructions for texting to debbieb@hotmail.com. You will receive further instructions via a text message. I've already warned you about aggressive behavior, Brosconni. The email address is a slave. I've hacked into her computer and can read, send, or erase any correspondence I wish to intercept. So ends lesson #1.

Brosconni slipped the paper and picture into the envelope and put it in his inside coat pocket. He removed himself from the Cathedral, stood on the top step high above the piazza, and called his driver. As he descended down the sixty two steps, he thought about Stephen McCord; his cockiness in the beginning, and his demolished spirit in the end. Now, Enrico Brosconni had another bug to crush, and as he stepped back onto the street, Brosconni's extermination would begin with a single call. A man called Salvador Tomassi Anachello, who once broke into one of the most secured networks in the world— The Pentagon. *Anachello*, Brosconni smiled, *would hack the hacker by noon the next day, and then,* he said to himself, *"we'll see who's the predator, and who's the prey.*

Brosconni strutted down Via del Duomo, across Strada Statale, and over to his awaiting car. The driver opened the back door, and Brosconni slid in. He studied the Carabinieri guard in the patrol car through his back door window and amused himself with the confused look on the guard's face. The driver climbed in, and Brosconni again barked his orders.

"Villa Marcella!" He said.

"Yes, Senior."

As the driver turned left onto 163, Brosconni stared out his window to the beach below and a crooked grin cracked the lines of his face. *Enrico Brosconni, è sempre vittoriosa, sempre*!

.

CHAPTER 16

Sheppard had been disturbed all day. She worked her way up the Strada Statale to Positano in her rented Jetta and thought about what Capt. Penso had said: "Bennetto like Miller is deceased, and you may want to consider the safety of Villa Marcella; we have a guard posted 24/7." Christina reacted exactly as Penso had predicted and proceeded to drive up the coast. Being involved in a situation surrounded by death had ignited the old wounds of her family's passing, complete with the horrid memories of endless, painful nights alone in the cold grip of darkness. She had considered for a moment calling Hancock, but resisted the temptation and, like in the past, persuaded herself it would pass. But as she sat in the little café at the water's edge sipping a strong espresso, Christina Sheppard wrestled with the surging emotion of wanting companionship with another man. And it caught her off guard, laced with an onslaught of gut wrenching guilt.

As she looked up at the cliffs of Positano, to the houses and shops carved into the rock, she thought about Jermaine Arket. He had wanted much more than she could give, and as time progressed, Arket could no longer handle the emotional backlash of being pushed away. Christina realized that now; she had been emotionally dead. Her awareness started at the Caruso as she sat across from Hancock and questioned him about his real intentions. Then the haunting image of Hancock as he stood by the statue of Flavio, and her knees buckled at the likened image of her deceased husband, Ray. And although she perceived herself as a kind and caring person, what she saw in Brosconni rattled her insides; it was like looking in a mirror and seeing a part of herself she hadn't, for six years, wanted to acknowledge— detached, unemotional, and cold. Now, sitting in the romance of the Positano coast, Sheppard felt for the first time in six years the stranglehold loosen on her breathless emotions, and she acknowledged that she missed Jermaine Arket.

But recognition is different from action, and for Christina Sheppard, it was one step at a time. Besides, she found herself in the midst of a theft / murder mystery, and it spiked her investigative instincts to a high resonated pitch. After all, that's what Sheppard did for a living, unlock the unknown, and the added sense of danger excited her now. Her life, particularly the last six years, operated in the safety of cracking long held secrets of old inanimate objects. But this was the ambiguity of anonymous real people, human beings who could think, scheme, and even murder. And as she finished the espresso from the miniature cup, she knew what she needed to do. It hit her like a rush of cool morning air on a late September morning.

She drove down Strada Statale, toward the city of Amalfi, like her senses had just escaped a dense London fog. It had been many years since she felt an inkling of emotional clarity, and she raced the Jetta around the s-curves as if the smoky haze had tried to catch up. As she navigated the narrow coast road, Christina recalled the image of Hancock's face. She dialed in to when she had told him about the murder of Miller; the dealer who had found the desk. The expression was curious to her now. Her sixth sense told her Hancock had held something back; he knew more, but what and why? As she pondered the question, Sheppard's foot shifted to the brake and pressed it hard toward the floor. The Jetta came to an abrupt stop.

In front of her was a line of six cars and at the front a tour bus. Heading north, another tour bus sat headlight to headlight with the one heading south. Behind it was a line of eight cars. Two groups of men had abandoned their vehicles and stood opposite the other group—the ones going northbound facing the ones going southbound. They screamed in a chorus of Italian chaos as their hands cut violently through the air. Sheppard stepped out of the car and approached the melee in the middle of the road.

After a moment, she realized what the argument was about yet couldn't believe it was the behavior of grown men. Neither bus could pass the other on the narrow Strada Statale, so they fought valiantly, macho y macho, until one group gave in and backed down—literally! One group of cars and one bus had to back up until each vehicle found a niche in the rock wall to park against. When all the traffic had found an alcove, then the other bus and row of cars could continue on their merry way. The only glitch in the Italian traffic control system was a lack of referee and, of course, Italian DNA.

After a half an hour, the road was cleared for the southbound traffic, and Sheppard continued toward the city of Amalfi having witnessed her first display of gang style Italian road rage. Having lived in New York City, she had seen plenty of street incidents that were loud, ridiculous, and on public display but never with such passion and determination to uphold one's right of way. She shook it off as she sailed by the Hotel San Pietro, constructed on a peninsula cliff, and tried to refocus on Hancock's expressions, searching for anything unusual as he related the results of his research.

CHAPTER 17

8am, Thursday morning, General Capalli sat at the head of the conference table staring at his men. The caverns under his eyes were black, and recessed, and wrinkled. When ensconced in a complicated and perplexing case, Capalli rarely slept. He had always been a driven man, his father the Colonel saw to that, but after the unsolved Fabrichio theft, he became obsessed with every detail, every suspect, and every clue. Consequently, Capalli had to survive on the two to three hours of sleep his mind would allow each night, and it would remain that way until the case was solved. And, he would ride his men as hard as he pushed himself.

He looked to Capt. Penso and nodded.

"Yes General!" Penso opened a file and lifted the first page attached to a clip at the top. "They picked up Antonio Capano last night. He, his wife, and his son had taken refuge at an old friend of the families in Minori."

"And the polygraph?"

"As we speak, General, we should have the results this morning."

Capalli nodded his head.

"The guard at Villa Marcella lost Brosconni somewhere in Amalfi." Penso explained. "He said Brosconni's driver pulled in amongst the tour buses, and Brosconni must have slipped out."

"What was he doing in Amalfi, and why did he leave his Villa in such a rush?"

"We're not sure yet, we're still working on that; Brosconni refuses to talk to the guard."

Capalli held his hand up toward Penso and turned his head in disgust. He had known Brosconni almost sixteen years, and yet he was not surprised. Capalli, soon enough, would question Brosconni himself. He lowered his hand.

"What about the driver?" He asked.

"He knows nothing. He dropped Brosconni off, and then picked him up when he was called."

"I want to know where he went and why!"

"Yes General."

Capalli looked to Capt. Tinelli.

"What about this carpenter—Saleno?" He asked.

"We've questioned Benvennuto Saleno's wife, family, cellmate, and all the known associates he befriended on the outside. His wife recalls the day Saleno went to Villa Marcella; Benvennuto was excited about the opportunity to work at such a prestigious place. She said when he came home that afternoon, Benvennuto told her things were going to change. He was beaming ear to ear and said, "they'd own a house of their own, soon." She assumed that meant he would be working full time at Villa Marcella, but he never went back. She asked Saleno what he had meant by his remark, and he told her he had a plan and soon they'd be rich. But nothing became of his promise, she said, and after his death, she was broke and had to move in with her mother."

The General shook his head.

"So, he did know of the tunnel. Continue Capt."

"His cellmate never talked to Saleno after his release. He claims he didn't even know Saleno had died. He worked as a dishwasher at an upscale restaurant in Naples. I checked his phone records and talked to the owner of the restaurant: he's clean. That's all we have so far."

"I want to know who he told, Capt., get me a name!"

"Yes, General."

Capalli scanned the table and then stopped at Tinelli.

"What about Bennetto?"

"Ballistics said the bullet recovered from Bennetto was fired from the same weapon that killed Miller"

"Go on!"

"After extensive interviews with family, employees, and friends, the evidence supports only one conclusion: the homicides were an attempt to locate and secure the priceless desk. Both homicides occurred prior to the theft at Villa Marcella, and, in a time line that coincides with the hand off of the desk. Clearly, as suspected, someone learned of John Miller's discovery and paid the antique dealer a visit only hours after Bennetto purchased the piece, and, likewise, after Bennetto sold the piece to Brosconni. I believe, General, whoever murdered Miller and Bennetto also learned of the escape tunnel and took possession of the desk."

The General swiveled around toward Rome and rested his chin onto both of his interlocked hands. Insistent on vigilant investigative protocol, Capalli was clearly enraged. He believed the Fabrichio investigation failed because his then aide, Capt. Carru, in his overzealous eagerness to solve the crime and obtain a promotion, overlooked the one piece of evidence which would have nailed Fabrichio stone cold.

Carru, like Tinelli, had opted to formulate a conclusive opinion based on preliminary findings and articulated a theory that would have solved the crime—so he thought. But because of this errant supposition, Carru dismissed information from a heroin addict who claimed he had seen Fabrichio meet with mobster, Carlo "the artist" Compinno, whose nickname mimicked his passion for art. By the time the General learned of the informant and the information he had, weeks had passed, and the art work, likely passed through Compinno, was long gone. Capalli blamed himself. He failed to recognize Carru's reckless investigative behavior, and he swore it would never happen under his watch again. Now, as his chair stopped its rotation at the mahogany desk, the General turned to Tinelli. The Captain froze in his chair.

The Captain knew without Capalli saying a word he had crossed the line. The authoritative intensity of his stare was more than words could demand, and Tinelli squirmed in the silence. Capalli held him in his grip a few moments more and then addressed the rest of his staff.

"This case will demand every ounce of your attention, gentlemen, I will not tolerate speculative postulation. You follow leads, and you look at the facts. The next one of my staff that wishes to amuse their egos at the expense of this investigation will find themselves relieved of service on the Carabinieri Art Squad!"

The General looked to the left side of the table.

"Lt. Armone."

"Yes sir?"

"The board."

"Yes sir."

"Time line number one—Miller – Bennetto – Brosconni."

"Yes sir."

"Over Miller—Collet – Rousseau."

"Yes sir."

" Over Brosconni – Sheppard."

"Yes General."

"Time line number…………"

The phone next to Capalli's general's cap rang, and the General picked it up.

"General Capalli," he said as he answered the call……."yes major………yes………I see…..is there any possibility of inaccuracies?……………..I'm well aware the test is infallible, Major, answer my question………yes……………..yes…….all of them? Release him. I want your report faxed to my office—now!"

The General scanned the table and landed his eyes on each individual member of his staff, one by one. After he looked to Tinelli, his head went slightly back, and he looked down to the top of the mahogany table.

"Antonio Capano passed the polygraph; he knew nothing of the escape tunnel, or who was behind the theft of the desk."

Capalli raised his General's cap to his chin.

"Benvennuto Saleno told someone," he said, "I want to know who!"

CHAPTER 18

Salvador Tomassi Anachello had worked for Brosconni in the past. Anachello was a computer programmer for Microsoft for a number of years and had secure access to the foundation upon which software platforms were written. Tired of the long hours and exhaustive mental crunch from the billionaires running the firm, Salvador turned to corporate hacking, and Anachello soon learned the benefits of working as an independent contractor. Depending on the sophistication of the network and the significance of the information he took, Anachello's one day paycheck accounted for three months worth of Window's work.

Anachello proved invaluable to Brosconni, intercepting contract bids from major shipping lines throughout the world. Brosconni's empire and its ability to secure major freight contracts (others seemed to constantly loose) was built upon Anachello expertise. And now, Brosconni called upon the hacker's skills to electronically track down the son of a bitch who stole his desk. And Brosconni believed, as he always did, it was only a matter of time.

Brosconni had executed the directive spelled out in the letter taped to the pew. The instructions were sent to the email address after Anachello confirmed he was on board and had completed his preliminary ground work. Anachello labored from his computer lab in his basement thousands of miles away. Intellectual espionage, he told Brosconni, required knowledge and a few strokes of the keys. By daybreak he would have the necessary information Brosconni needed to indentify the thief. And as he sat in front of the screen, with Led Zeppelin's Stairway to Heaven blasting in his ears, Anachello pounded away screaming out the words, "and as we walk on down the road...."

It was 9 pm in Seattle, Washington as Anachello worked his magic in his lab: 6 am in Rome, Italy as Brosconni's limo pulled up outside the Carabinieri headquarters and stopped at the front double doors. Capalli, incensed that Brosconni refused to talk to the Carabinieri guard about his visit to Amalfi, demanded Brosconni come to his office and have a talk. Capalli chose the early morning meeting to appease Brosconni, after Brosconni insisted the meeting take place at his lawyer's office instead.

The international media, intrigued by the historical find and fascinated by who commissioned the desk, had multiplied exponentially each passing day. Even at this early hour of the morning the news crews were parked outside Brosconni's lawyer's office waiting for breaking news. To arrive in a Carabinieri cruiser, and step out in front of the press, would give the wrong impression to the world of just who was in charge. The General recognized that. And as Brosconni rode the elevator to the sixth floor, and walked through the inner office to Capalli's door, Brosconni didn't bother to knock.

The General looked up from his desk.

"Enrico, thank you for coming."

"Alberto."

"Please, have a seat."

Brosconni sat in one of the winged back chairs in front of the desk, impeccably dressed as always. He unbuttoned his black silk blazer, settled in, and crossed his leg. Capalli swiveled his chair parallel to his desk and leaned back. His eyes rose toward the ceiling.

"Why the meeting, Alberto, have you found my desk?"

Capalli shook his head no. He lifted his right hand and placed his first finger around his mouth.

"Do you have something significant to tell me about the investigation?"

Again The General answered with a shake of his head. Brosconni pushed back in the chair and clasp his hands together. All emotion had drained from his face.

"I'm a busy man, Alberto!"

The General swiveled back and faced Brosconni and connected with his dark brown opaque eyes.

"Enrico, I am told you traveled to Amalfi yesterday."

Brosconni didn't move.

"The guard stated you intentionally slipped away from him."

Brosconni said nothing. His elbow rested on the arm of the chair, and his hand was raised to his face as he inspected his finger nails in his left hand.

"What was so important in Amalfi, Enrico?"

Again nothing.

"Enrico, we go back a long ways; I would not like to think you would intentionally deceive me."

Brosconni clutched his hands in front of his chin and remained unresponsive to Capalli's questions. The General had seen Brosconni like this only once before. Back in 95 Alberto Capalli had just reached full Colonel and was assigned commander of the regional Campania unit. One of Brosconni's cargo ships, the Annamarie, was delivering a load of South American rare timber into the port of Naples. It was suspected, that along with the legal lumber, the Annamarie was carrying artifacts looted from ancient tombs in Brazil. Because of their association, Capalli questioned Brosconni personally. What The Colonel observed in Brosconni eyes never left his memory. It was the presence of pure evil, and Enrico, without saying a word made his message loud and clear: I could end your career with the snap of my finger!

Capalli took a breath and continued.

"Enrico, let's be frank, you want your desk, I want the arrest. It appears to me we want the same thing."

Brosconni dropped his hands to his lap.

"I, will, get my desk back," he said, "you can count on that. You want to be ring master to that circus out there, that's your business. I recommend, however, not at the expense of my piece. Your quest for celebrity will become your downfall if that's the case."

"Are you threatening me Enrico?"

Brosconni's face went stone cold. He stood up, buttoned his blazer, and walked over to the mirror on the wall. He angled his head to the left, then to the right, and then he adjusted the knot on his silk tie, sliding it back and forth. As he opened the office door and stepped into the outer office, he neither turned nor spoke a word, and he didn't bother to close the door.

The driver sped off with Brosconni in the back busy on his Smart phone. He looked at his watch, 6:45 am Rome time, 9:45 pm Washington time. He studied the coliseum as his driver circled around the ruins on the Via Giovanni Giolitti. *Rome*, he thought, *in its glory, as it should have been forever*. Brosconni could taste it now. As Anachello pecked away in Seattle, Brosconni envisioned how he would crush the cocky little vermin like a worm on the side of the road. And he'd watch in sardonic ecstasy as he had his legs broken piece by piece. As the driver cruised along the Roman Aqueduct, a crooked grin emerged on Brosconni's face, and he whispered his creed he devised decades before.

Enrico Brosconni è sempre vittoriosa, sempre!

CHAPTER 19

Sheppard walked through the front entrance and strolled over to the desk.

"Welcome to the Hotel Caruso, signora, how may I help you?"

"I have an appointment with one of your guests, Randolph Hancock."

"Very good, madam, I will ring his room."

"Would you be kind enough to tell him I'm on the balcony: I'll be staying for lunch."

"Very good, madam."

Sheppard had called Hancock from her mobile on the ride from Positano. She insisted on meeting him upon her arrival. Hancock knew more than he was saying, she had concluded, and she wanted to know what it was and why he held it back. Between her gifted memory, her sixth sense, and her female intuition, the truth stuck out like a Chippendale in a pawn shop. There was more to Hancock than just his research; Sheppard was certain of that. And as she moved in front of the chair held back by the Italian waiter, Sheppard was determined to find out what was behind the famed historian and what his real purpose was on the Italian coast.

"Christina, why the urgency, have you news of the Hepplewhite?"

She turned her head and looked up at Hancock. He shuffled around the table and pulled out the chair.

"Why are you here?" She asked.

Hancock looked miffed. He sat down and smiled at Sheppard from across the table.

"I explained that to you, Christina, I'm researching material on George Washington."

"Why are you really here?"

Hancock's eyes turned toward the hotel doors, then into her eyes, and then out to the rippling water shimmering in the sun. He had seen the determination in Sheppard's stare. She wanted the truth, but how far could he go, how much could he tell? He looked back to Sheppard.

"I'm not sure where to start." He said.

His gaze grew distant, and Christina studied the expressionless trance on his face. He lifted his hand and ran his fingers through his hair. She cringed at the move, lifted her brows and took a breath, and then got back to the reason she had come to the Hotel in the first place.

"Hancock," she said, "I'm waiting."

The life seeped slowly back into the deep brown of his pupils. He caught her eyes in his as the visual tug of war lasted only seconds. He turned and waved to the waiter. When the waiter arrived at the table, Hancock ordered a bottle of Chianti and again locked onto her persistent stare. He needed her confidence, and there was only one way to gain her trust. If he strayed from the truth, he would never get near the desk or its contents. He couldn't risk that. Yet what he was about to tell Sheppard could be conceived as outrageous, too far from historical fact to be believed. But he had no choice now. If he wished to complete his life's work, he had to convince Sheppard that it was the truth. And, he had to tell it all.

"All right," he said, "but are you sure you can handle the truth?"

"Try me," she said.

Hancock turned his head away for a split second and then slowly brought it back to Sheppard.

"Alright," he said again, "when Washington and Hancock opened the crate, and found the desk missing, they summoned Governor Langdon of New Hampshire to the Governor's mansion in Boston. There, the three men organized a team of four individuals, whose investigative skills trumped some of the finest examiners of that time. They traveled to London to meet with Smith for one purpose: to locate the missing desk and personally escort the piece back to Boston and hand deliver it to Governor Hancock at his mansion on Hall Street."

"How do you know this?"

"I'll get into that later."

Hancock was interrupted by the delivery of the Chianti. After he had tasted and accepted the bottle, and the waiter had poured the glasses, Hancock hesitated until the two of them were once again alone.

"It was imperative they take possession of that desk, and the four men that traveled to London had express orders to resort to whatever means it took to retrieve the piece. So they sailed to England.

Washington had believed the secret compartment was secure and the safest place for the letters to remain on their trip to the states. The significance of the correspondence, someone learned, could be worth an equally significant amount of ransom if they had the desk as leverage. What the four men learned was Smith had been betrayed by one of his own confidants, an aide named Lamar, and that individual had switched the crates."

Hancock lifted his glass.

"So if they knew who betrayed Smith, why didn't they get the desk back?"

"Because the man who switched the crates was dead." Hancock said and as his peered over his glass at the confused look on Sheppard's face.

"Dead, how?"

"He was tortured in the tower of London under the directive of the troubled King George. King George, in one of his sane moments, believed the unrest in the Thirteen Colonies had been driven by an underground source in his own homeland. Lamar, because of his association with Colonel Smith who was aide-de-camp to Washington, was believed by His Majesty to be an American spy. King George had no way of knowing how close he was to finding out the truth. Lamar had a relapse of loyalty to Smith and chose death over giving up the desk. As you now know he stowed the Hepplewhite, still in the crate, in a farm house attic southeast of London, where it hid in obscurity for over two hundred years."

Sheppard turned and looked out over the steep cliffs. Without moving her head her eyes rolled to Hancock's face. Convinced by his expression he was telling the truth, she turned her head back toward the table. Hancock remained silent.

"Why would King George torture the suspect, the war was over?"

"King George never got over the loss of the colonies; some theorists believe that's what made him go mad. Others suspect he knew the truth but couldn't prove it."

Sheppard pondered Hancock's premise for a second. But what kept popping in her head was the one question that had been nagging at her since Hancock made his bold statement, "it could re-ignite the war," so she got right to the point.

"What was in the correspondence that was so important?" She asked.

"Before you can comprehend the content of the correspondence, Christina, you must understand the story behind it."

"Go on."

"The four investigators returned to Boston empty handed. Washington, Langdon, and Hancock now understood how the desk disappeared, but they also knew it would not be lost forever. And, when it was found, so too would the correspondence."

"But no one ever discovered the desk."

"Correction, Christina, a man named Miller stumbled upon the desk."

"Why would it matter now?"

"That, Ms. Sheppard, is where we begin our story."

CHAPTER 20

I'm listening," she said.

The tables of the Belvedere Restaurant were half full as Hancock studied the crowd and then looked back to Sheppard.

"Have you read a book called Pedagogy of the Oppressed, Ms. Sheppard?"

"No," she said as she leaned in toward Hancock. He spoke in a soft tone, just above a whisper.

"It theorizes that change will never come from the oppressor, it will only come from within the ranks of the oppressed: oppressor being an operative word meaning in this case to rule over—to govern or to dictate. And, as we know, what can start with good intentions, does in time become inept, self serving, and even corrupt. One only needs to look at history to acknowledge civilizations only last, and dominate, until the masses are educated and bring this change about."

"You're boring me, Hancock. It appears you are setting the foundation to defend what you are about to say. How does this have anything to do with me, the desk, or the two documents inside the piece?"

"Many of the "educators," if you will, Ben Franklin, Paul Revere, Sam Adams, John Adams, Langdon, Hancock, and Washington to name a few, not only had vested financial interests in becoming an independent nation, but a determined interest in governing this new nation as well. Hancock, for example, recognized his shipping fleets would benefit greatly without the constraints placed upon his merchant ships by England and, to have political clout, along with fortune, assured Hancock and others of a dominating role in the construction of a new government and the conventions that structure would follow."

Sheppard picked up her wine, stood up, and took two steps to the brass rail of the balcony. She leaned her arms on the metal, with her hands clasp to the glass and studied the houses below. Hancock felt her presence just behind him but stayed silent. He was losing her, and he knew it, but he feared jumping too far ahead without a solid explanation would scare her off for sure. He slugged his wine as he explored his options, but before he finished his mental debate, she clarified her position.

"Hancock, I consider myself a good judge of character, and I sense you are an honorable man, however, your intentions are completely unclear to me, and I feel you're avoiding telling me the truth. Either you give me something I can grab onto, or I'm afraid I will have to leave!"

"Please, Christina, have a seat, I'll try not to bore you further."

Christina walked around to the back of her chair and stared at Hancock. He motioned with his hand asking her to sit. She placed her wine on the table and pulled out her chair and stopped.

"Get to the point, Hancock."

"Please, sit."

Sheppard, hesitant, eased around the chair and slipped her legs beneath the table. She sat without removing her eyes from his. Hancock nodded a look as to say thank you and took a breath and continued.

"The premise that the Revolutionary war was fought to free the thirteen colonies from Britain's suffocating control is only half the truth, Christina. That's what the forefathers wanted you to believe."

She stared at Hancock behind a strand of blonde hair with her brows scrunched around the deep blue of her eyes.

"What?" She said.

Hancock scanned the balcony as if someone could be listening. He hesitated for a moment then turned back to Sheppard.

"The revolution," he said in almost a whisper, "was conceived by an organization which had its roots in the mother land."

Sheppard smiled sarcastically.

"You're a conspiracy theorist, Hancock. You surprise me, I thought of you as a non-fictionist."

"I find the facts," Hancock responded, "and I follow them, Christina."

Sheppard studied the landscape and thought about Hancock's statement. When her eyes reached the blue water which sparkled in the mid-day sun like crystals floating on top of the sea, she stared into its beauty and contemplated if Hancock had become hypnotized by his own historical fantasy or really believed he had stumbled upon classified historical fact. Sheppard had made a living, and a life, based upon verifiable fact. Even Arket, frustrated by her pragmatic attitude, respected her ability to approach history, and its relics, with a sense of empirical knowledge which neither clouded nor embellished the truth. Hancock's comments did both, and it made no sense why he would risk his hard earned reputation on such an irrational premise so far from the documented truth. Sheppard turned back to the table and was surprised by the serious look on his face, and the commitment she read in his eyes.

"Which facts are those, Hancock?"

"Christina, I am not a crack pot, hear me out."

"I'll listen, Randolph, but, I already have one foot out the door."

Hancock continued.

"The colonies, they believed, presented a unique and unprecedented opportunity to develop a continent rich in resources with the necessary infrastructure already in place. Think of the possibilities given the financing and complete governmental control that it offered to those in a position to organize and win the confidence of the illiterate masses. The visual representatives, i.e. the

Langdon's the Hancock's would take the commands of this distant organization with the understanding that they would be a part of, and the extended arm to, this invisible group which would now exist on both continents under one united but covert rule."

The waiter, now at the table, took their selections for lunch. Christina excused herself and walked half dazed to the rest room. She needed a break. Hancock's insistence on continuing his supposition at first irritated Sheppard, but yet she found herself compelled to stay. Now, as she stood at the mirror brushing her shoulder length blonde hair, she recognized the reason why.

A number of years ago Sheppard was called to investigate a John Townsend Fall-Front desk built in 1765. The furniture makers, Townsend and Goddard, were located in Newport, Rhode Island. The piece was believed to be commissioned by the famous Revolutionary war general Nathanael Greene. It was in fact authenticated by the letters she found in one of the three secret compartments inside the desk. But the real discovery came in the form of dispelling a now century's old myth.

Sheppard had read and been instructed by classroom professors that John Adams, lawyer and future president, was a magnificent oratorical speaker able to persuade politicians on both sides of the fence. But the real truth, written in correspondence from Samuel Ward, a delegate of Rhode Island to the Continental Congress, was that Adams spoke with a pronounced lisp. His meaning was misplaced as his fellow compatriots focused on his speech disorder not the content of his words. What stuck with Sheppard then, and influenced her now, was how often historical fact is bent or omitted to present an image other than the truth. And, if that was the case, which Hancock now pleaded, she owed it to herself to hear him out.

Sheppard returned to the table as the waiter delivered their meals. They both took a short reprieve from the conversation and focused on their food. Halfway through Sheppard's salad, Hancock continued.

"The dissension found its roots with the conspiring members of the Continental Congress. Like any revolt, it started with only a few but soon grew as selected members came on board. With the help of their counterparts in Great Britain, the society multiplied rapidly, and by the time Peyton Randolph was elected the first president of the Continental Congress (and some consider him the first President of the United States as General Washington addressed him in a letter) the die had been cast—war was on the horizon."

Hancock paused to clear his throat with a gulp of Chianti. The waiter cleared the table and Hancock insisted on paying the bill. As he looked at his watch he realized he had to go.

"I'm afraid I must cut our conversation short, Ms. Sheppard, I have previous business to attend to."

"This society you refer to, does it have a name?"

Hancock again scanned the balcony and then leaned in toward Sheppard.

"I have business for a day in Rome. While I'm gone, research Prince Henry, Duke of Cumberland.

He was head of this organization from 1782 until the time of his death in 1790. And, here's your first nugget: his older brother was George III—that's the mad King George by the way. On the American side check out Peyton Randolph. You may discover an interesting connection. My great grandfather six times out, John Hancock, followed Randolph as second president of the Continental Congress—look him up too! George Washington, Ben Franklin, you get the idea. Once you get started on the first few, the rest will fall in place."

"When can we speak again?"

"I'll call you when I finish my business, and I would hope if you hear any word on the Hepplewhite you would not hesitate to inform me of the news."

CHAPTER 21

Brosconni was back at Villa Marcella when the call came in. He was in his office, adjacent to the living room, sitting at his desk staring at the Amalfi coast. Enrico picked up the phone.

"Brosconni," He said.

"Senior Brosconni, Salvador Anachello, how are you sir?"

Brosconni eased his high back leather chair toward the mahogany paneled wall and leaned back.

"Cut the small shit," Brosconni said, "tell me what you have!"

"Senior, I've never seen anything quite like this, whoever is responsible is a 1337."

"What the fuck does that mean?"

"He is what's referred to as an elite—an innovator. He writes his own programs, develops his own security, and uses a line of slave computers to cover his tracks. He took over the computer I investigated with what's called a rootkit: the compromise of the computer is undetectable by its owner. He replaced the system's binaries with codes of his own. It intercepts crackers like myself from stringing the line by using a series of networks protected by viruses written by his own hand."

"Enough!" Brosconni said, as his chair swiveled toward the open French doors facing the coast. "Can you identify him?"

"Not as of yet, and I believe he might have detected an intruder."

"You ignorant ass, if you've compromised my ability to rescue my piece, I'll see to it you spend the rest of your days as a bitch in prison stripes."

"But Senior........."

Brosconni hung up the phone. He jumped from his chair and raced to the balcony and leaned against the marble balustraded rail. *Son of a Bitch!* He turned and rested his backside against the rail as the sound of a ping chimed in his pocket which indicated a text message had arrived. *Shit!* The Smartphone slid from his side blazer pocket and hung in the air at his chest, and he touched the icon and brought up the message.

*You're an inept fool, Brosconni, dressed up in a business man's suit.

I warned you!

Now God will decide the fate of your precious Hepplewhite.

Act two: Go to your place of birth—Naples—and to the cathedral Duomo di San Gennaro. When inside, walk to the fifth pew on the right and sit at the end next to the interior marble column of the church.

Ask the lord for forgiveness and then reach underneath the pew to learn if repentance is granted."Every idle word that men shall speak, they shall give account thereof in the day of' Judgment!" Matthew 12:36." So endeth lesson #2.

Brosconni's hands fell to his side with his Smartphone hanging from his right. He reached in his left side pocket, pulled out his fob, pushed the button, and retreated back inside. Pietro arrived and opened the door to the office.

"I want the Bell ready to fly in ten minutes." Brosconni ordered.

"Yes, Senior, will that be all?"

"Have a car waiting for me at the Naples airport—now!"

"Yes senior."

Brosconni fell back into his chair and stared wide eyed out the doors. Anachello had never been outgunned, and it baffled Brosconni how this wretch of a human being continued to have the expertise to outsmart his every move. Brosconni had always maintained control and yet, somehow, someone had circumvented his grip from the start.

He pounded out the sequence of events in his head. *The son of a bitch knew the Hepplewhite was in Villa Marcella, he knew how to access the room, he knew he could escape by sea, and he knew I would turn to Anachello to track him down. I'll roast that arrogant punk on a spit—son of a bitch—and now this, the Duomo di San Gennaro. How did he know*?

Brosconni loathed religion. His mother forced him to attend the Duomo di San Gennaro on Sundays. And he would be forced to look at the very same men that entered his house during the week and paid his mother as she lay naked on her bed. By age six, he refused to attend and was forced to be counseled by one of the very men who violated his mother. He was a member of the rectory, a respected member of the church, and young Enrico was repulsed by having to listen to his lies.

But worse, he was made to succumb to the man's appetite for young boys. For two years, twice a week, Brosconni was forced to perform and be a victim to various acts of sexual abuse in a back room not far from where the congregation would sit on Sundays. And now, he was headed back to the very place where foul men washed away their vile sins, and he felt the same gut wrenching sickness he felt as a little boy.

The helicopter rose, banked north, and headed up the coast. A minute passed and the Smartphone in his pocket rattled its ring. Brosconni looked at the caller id—Capalli. Brosconni had refused to talk to the guard at Villa Marcella, and the Carabinieri officer immediately called Rome. Brosconni smiled and slid the phone back into his pocket.

The flight lasted only minutes. A car waited on the tarmac, with the back door opened, and a driver in a black suit standing at its side. Brosconni slid in and ordered the driver to the Via Duomo and to the Duomo di San Gennaro.

"Hurry," he said.

"Si," said the driver.

The driver took the Via Don Bosco to Foria and turned left on Via Duomo. He pulled up to the cathedral and stopped.

"Wait here." Brosconni ordered.

Brosconni moved quickly from the car to the steps and with each marble tread his Ferragamo suede loafers touched, the saliva in his mouth became more pronounced. His stomach churned as he opened the heavy wooden door and entered. He pulled the silk handkerchief from his front blazer pocket, bolted back out the door to the platform at the top of the stairs and vomited on the marble steps to the cathedral. He wiped his mouth, retained the silk cloth to his face and raced to the fifth pew. The cathedral was empty except for a few patrons in the front, praying. He scanned the interior as he slid to the end and reached underneath the bench—nothing! *What?* Brosconni leaned toward the alter and checked a wider region of the wooden pew, but again, nothing. He slid off the pew and onto his knee and looked under the seat. Then he checked the pews in front of him and in back. *You son of bitch!*

Enrico Brosconni raced out of the cathedral, down the steps, across the Duomo di San Gennaro and into the awaiting car.

CHAPTER 22

Capalli paced the parquet floor seething at Brosconni's arrogance. *Your quest for celebrity will be your downfall if that's the case!* He stopped at the window and looked down to the Piazza di Sant'Ignazio and felt his face flush with anger. The eyes of the world had descended upon Rome, to the General's briefings, as the Carabinieri crack art squad toiled to recover the missing desk of an American President, while Brosconni, who had the audacity to threaten the General, seemed now to be sabotaging the investigation as well. Capalli pulled his sight from the church of San Lgnazio and locked his eyes onto the pile of investigative files stacked on his desk. Capalli knew, if he had any chance of cracking the theft of the Hepplewhite, he'd have to get a grip on Brosconni.

The General strolled to the files and dropped into the swivel chair parked parallel to his desk. He turned the chair toward the window. It was clear to him what Brosconni was up to, and why he kept it to himself. And, he knew Brosconni all too well; he would play both sides—sharing information, to Brosconni, was a one way street. Capalli reached over to the folders and slid the Brosconni file in front of him and opened it up. He thumbed through the papers and read through the unsuccessful attempts to monitor his activities, track his movements, and collect information from his phone conversations: Brosconni used the Skype internet phone system and on the road, windows mobile Smartphone. The encrypted software made it impossible to crack. Capalli closed the file and swiveled back to the window. *1995, the Annmarie,* he thought, *God damn it!*

"General Capalli?"

Capalli swiveled back around to his desk and pushed the button on his intercom.

"What is it Caprina?"

"General, Capt. Penso would like to speak with you."

He looked back at Brosconni's file.

"Send him in," he said, "and locate Capt. Tinelli; I want him in my office right away."

"Yes General."

Still staring at Brosconni's file on his desk, Capalli responded to the two knocks at the door.

"Come in, Capt." He said.

Capt. Penso walked through the door with his briefcase in his hand, stood at attention, and saluted The General.

"At ease, Capt., have a seat."

"General Capalli?"

"Yes Caprina."

"General, Capt. Tinelli is on the phone with Naples airport; he said he'll be a few minutes."

"Send him in when he arrives!"

"Yes General."

Capt. Penso sat in the wing back chair opposite Capalli and opened his briefcase sitting on the floor beside him. He pulled out a thick file and placed it on the desk and opened it up. Capalli looked to Penso.

"You wanted to speak with me Capt.?"

"General, I think we may be on to something concerning that New York dealer, Arthur Collet."

"Continue!"

Penso had been working with a Detective Stanno out of the midtown south precinct in Manhattan. Detective Stanno was Penso's contact in Manhattan and had conducted the original interview with Collet after they learned John Miller (the dealer who found the desk at the farm house in Horsemonden) had contacted him about purchasing the piece. Detective Stanno, upon further investigation, questioned Collet a second time at the precinct's interrogation room and had faxed a transcript of the conversation to Penso. The transcripts were accompanied by Stanno's notes and the background checks on Collet.

"General, it appears from my contact in New York that Collet's professional history is in conflict with his actions. Miller's contacting Collet was not a random act taken from an internet directory: Arthur

Collet had spent most of his professional career searching and contacting dealers, particularly small time small town dealers, throughout the English country side in search of one particular item—a Carlton House desk, but more specifically a desk circa 1786."

"And?"

"General, 1786 was the year Washington commissioned the piece and the same year it was supposed to make the journey to Boston Harbor."

"How could Collet know Washington had commissioned a Hepplewhite?"

"That's the same question Detective Stanno had. So he brought Collet into the station for questioning. Collet claims while researching Hepplewhite in London, he met an old furniture restorer who attested to an ancestry of descendents deeply ingrained in eighteenth century furniture. Passed along with that tradition was a long held family lore that one member actually worked for Hepplewhite himself. And, that George Washington had commissioned Hepplewhite to construct a, as Hepplewhite called it, a gentlemen's writing table."

"So why search Europe on the premise this story may be true?"

"Because the second half of this family saga claims, Colonel Smith, with a group of investigators from overseas, had questioned everyone in Hepplewhite's firm. The desk had disappeared, and they were searching for information that would result in the recovery of the piece. But to the family's knowledge, it was never recovered."

Capalli swiveled his leather chair and faced the window with his fingers propped under his nose. The General contemplated Collet's story, riveting through the facts like a hard drive on a dell computer. Penso picked up the file, knowing The General's introspection could take time, and rifled through the papers. They both looked up at the sound of a woman's voice.

"General, Capt. Tinelli's here."

"Send him in, Caprina, and we are not to be disturbed, understood?"

"Yes, General."

After the Capt. stood at attention and saluted Capalli, he burst out with the news.

"General, Enrico Brosconni flew to Naples and hired a car, but we learned of it too late."

Capalli folded his hands on the top of his desk, and his eyes lifted toward the ceiling. His head shook up and down. Then he turned to Penso.

"Capt. Penso, brief Capt. Tinelli later."

"Yes sir."

"That's quite a story Collet told Detective Stanno, Capt. Penso, but his credibility is suspect. Why, if Collet believed the story, and his enthusiasm blanketed the English country side, did he not hop the first plane to England and purchase the piece?"

"Detective Stanno asked Collet the same question."

"And?"

"Collet stated the following: Miller's expertise on authenticating Carlton House Desks was severely flawed. Collet had previously traveled to Miller's shop on an earlier lead, and it turned out to be a reproduction made in the early 1900's. Collet dismissed the phone call, which he now says he regrets."

"What about travel?" Capalli asked.

"Nothing, Collet had alibis, and his passport had not been used to travel abroad. He personally could not have killed Miller or Bennetto, we checked the dates. Besides, he may have wanted the desk, but he had no motive for murder."

Capalli stood up and walked over to the window and stared down to the Piazza with his hands clasp behind his back. Without turning around he asked Penso,

"What else did Detective Stanno say?"

"He said in his twenty years on the force he has never seen anyone so smooth or unflappable; it made his investigative hairs stand up."

Capalli knew the type all too well—Marcelino Deluchi Fabrichio, the Italian actor whose art disappeared. Fabrichio could convince a person he was wearing red when he had on green with such a charming sincerity one would walk away believing he was color blind. And Capalli, who processed every failed investigation into a useable formula, had postulated this: honed deceit, at its core, is constructed around a genuine truth. Decipher the fact in the fraud, he had told his men, and the perpetrators trail will follow.

He turned toward Penso and Tinelli.

"Collet knew the desk existed," he said. "That's the nugget of truth in his lie. No dealer, particularly Collet who's obsessed in obtaining Washington's Hepplewhite, would dismiss a lead like that without asking for a picture of the piece faxed to his office. In which case, after viewing the photograph, he would catch the first flight to Europe. He's good, but he's not that good! Capt. Penso, find out how he knew of the existence of the desk, and why he wanted to obtain the piece so bad he would scour the country side of England. Fill in the gap between that and his failure to travel to London to purchase the piece, Capt. Penso, make me understand the why! "

"Yes, General."

"Capt. Tinelli, Brosconni is up to something, and I want to know what. His field trips have a meaning, and, I suspect, it has a direct connection to whoever stole the desk. Get a grip on Brosconni; I don't care how!"

CHAPTER 23

The Windows Smartphone sat on the night table next to Brosconni as he slept. At exactly one thirty two in the morning it pinged, and the light on the screen turned on. The radiance of the beam reflected off the wall just above the touch pad, and Brosconni, who lay on his side asleep, opened his eyes. Still half unconscious he reached over, picked up the phone, rolled onto his back, placed it on his chest, and stared upward to the gilded panel ceiling illuminated by the soft light of the three quarter moon. His right arm, covered by the brown silk sleeve of his pajama top, rested on his forehead as his brain clicked on, and Brosconni mode drifted to the surface.

He lifted the device above his head and studied the screen. On the upper middle top of the touch pad was the little notation indicating a text message had arrived. Brosconni slipped out of bed and put on the brown silk bathrobe laid out at the end of the mattress. On the chest of the robe, underneath a yellow coat of arms embossed in bright red silk thread were the initials—EFB—Enrico Filipo Brosconni. The custom made Ferragamo slippers beneath the robe garnished the same three letters. As he stumbled through the cobwebs to the deep cushioned chair in front of the stone sculpted fireplace, Brosconni switched on the wrought iron floor lamp and dropped down into the chair.

After the episode at Duomo di San Gennaro, in Naples, Brosconni's attitude had changed. "No one plays games with Enrico Brosconni," he had whispered on the ride back to the airport, "no one who lives to tell." A man this powerful, with unlimited funds at his disposal, and, a predisposition to deal with obstacles in any way he saw fit, has resources—people who get things done. And as much as he was determined to recover his desk, having to walk into that church was not something Brosconni would let go. So as the Bell 429 lifted off, Brosconni sat with his Smartphone and punched in the letters with his thumbs, hit send, and thought about the last time he had sent that text. And a crooked grin cracked Brosconni's face as he recalled the final results.

For years, Brosconni had been shipping illegal hardwoods out of Indonesia's Papua province. It fed China's voracious appetite for forest products, most of which ended up as exotic hardwood floors in the homes of Americans throughout the United States. The smuggling operation raked in hundreds of millions a year. It had its expenses though. Each ship had to pay hundreds of thousands in bribes just to get the illegal logs free of the Indonesia coast. The currency delivered was the U.S. dollar: groceries in a bag were the code words used, and it was personally exchanged by the captain of the ship.

On two occasions the money was intercepted before the bribe changed hands. The loss amounted to four hundred thousand dollars, that's when Brosconni sent the text. The thief turned out to be a cousin of one of the dock workers. When the authorities stumbled upon the scene at the thief's slum of a home, his wife, and two children were all dead in their ransacked metal shed. Outside, hanging from two trees, was the thief and his cousin the dockworker. Brosconni's bribes were never hit again.

But this was different, and Brosconni knew it. Finding a petty thief confined to a known location in a poverty stricken country was simple in comparison to what he now faced. The Carabinieri, after all, had so far come up empty. Even with the cooperation of investigators on three separate continents, General Capalli had yet to have a single suspect. But Brosconni would rather be dead than be controlled by another human being, and sitting idle, while some letch spewed out commands, wasn't in the tycoon's DNA. Besides, Brosconni never lost; he afforded setbacks but never defeat.

As he sat in the chair, he looked up from the Smartphone and out the French doors to the water with the moon reflecting off its surface. He rubbed his cheek with his fingers and thumb, and the sound of his skin scraping the thick black whiskers broke the silence of the night. And as his hand stopped, Brosconni wondered if it had been a mistake sending the text. After all, he had other assets at his disposal, and he questioned, as good as they are, would they remain undetected. So as he stared at the screen, Brosconni understood the risk he'd taken. It seemed acceptable at the time considering his rage after Naples: revenge seemed an almost acceptable exchange.

But now, as happens in the clarity after sleep in the middle of the night, his state of mind was different. Brosconni had searched the globe to obtain what Antiquarian experts would consider mankind's priceless art. And he did it for no reason other than his own pompous exclusivity. Brosconni had no intentions of sharing the Hepplewhite, or its contents, with the international community of scholars. That was Brosconni's definition of power. And this, the Hepplewhite, was the ultimate prize. As historians hungered to learn of its contents, Brosconni would feast upon their famine and nourish his demented ego for years.

As he sat there in the dim light of the lamp, his right hand rose to his forehead and massaged his eyes as the Smartphone sat on his lap in his left hand. Brosconni rubbed his thumb on the screen and the touch pad lit up. He looked at the time on the bottom right—1:40 AM. Then he slid his pointing finger up the pad and opened up the text.

*Proposal accepted—Skype me details in the morning.

CHAPTER 24

"Do you know Arthur Collet?" The General asked.

Aggravated by having to make the trip from Pompeii to Rome, she stared at Capalli from across the interrogation table with disgust. Touring the ancient Roman City had been on her to do list for the past six years; she just never made the time, not since Raymond died. They had planned a trip that spring, had booked the airline tickets with intentions to start in Rome and work their way down the Amalfi coast to Pompeii. After the plane crash, Sheppard abandoned the tickets, hotel reservation payments, and avoided any thoughts of Pompeii.

Then, in Positano, recognizing her emotions and her personal life had died along side her husband, she chose to confront her demons and visit Pompeii. General Capalli's request to travel to Rome, particularly to the Carabinieri headquarters in the middle of her private guided tour, was an inconvenience she contemplated forgoing, but the General made it clear she could come on her own free will, or under duress. She chose the prior.

"We crossed paths with our work." Sheppard said.

The General wanted to question Sheppard personally. Besides finding out how much Sheppard knew of Collet, he had a secondary motive, and he reasoned if he had any chance of gaining Sheppard's trust, he needed to treat her with respect. Putting her in the hands of Penso or Tinelli would have sent the wrong message; Capalli had witnessed her will at Villa Marcella, and he wanted her to cooperate, not obstruct. So he tempered the authority in his voice.

"Your interests coincide, yes?"

"We both have expertise dealing with the Carlton House Desk." She said. "Did you bring me here, General, to question me about Arthur Collet?"

"Ms. Sheppard, Arthur Collet is a person of interest. You coincidently live and work in New York City, have a common fascination with a particular desk, and your names have somehow surfaced, although thousands of miles apart, in the mysterious disappearance of Senior Brosconni's Hepplewhite. We are trying to piece together everything we can on Mr. Collet and your cooperation would go a long ways in proving you have nothing to hide."

Sheppard turned her head slightly and looked at Capalli through the sides of her eyes.

"Am I a suspect, General?"

"Ms. Sheppard, we are merely trying to establish your relationship with Mr. Collet, and gain information…………"

"Am I a suspect, General?"

Capalli raised his head slightly, and his eyes rolled toward the ceiling. He took a breath and exhaled.

"No, Ms. Sheppard, we've found nothing to indicate you're involved in this case."

"Then why am I here?"

"We need your help." He said.

Capalli leaned back in his swivel chair. It killed him to say that, particularly to a woman. He believed she wasn't involved in the disappearance of the desk, and he had nothing to hold her on, but he needed her as an expert on the Carlton House desk. As hard as it was for the General to admit, her skill at detecting and opening the secret escape tunnel impressed him. Her being involved with Brosconni could prove an asset when it came to his whereabouts, and having knowledge of Collet, their first real suspect in the case, sealed Capalli's decision to try and bring Sheppard on board. But The General gave orders, he didn't ask, and the prospect of having to curtail to a woman made his Italian blood boil.

Sheppard, with a hint of suspicion in her eyes, watched Capalli rise from his chair and walk over to the small one way mirror cut into the wall. He kept his back to her as he spoke.

"How well do you know Arthur Collet?" He asked.

"I know he's obsessed with the Carlton House Desk."

Capalli turned and faced Sheppard, maintaining his macho stance yet symbolically projecting his appreciation for her lack of resistance.

"Please, continue Ms. Sheppard."

"It's a known fact among my colleagues that Collet has an interest in any new discoveries of that style desk produced in the late eighteenth century. It appears he is looking for a particular piece, perhaps as many of us are, a genuine Hepplewhite. The difference, however, between Collet and my fellow Antiquarian collectors is his obsession: he has spent most of his career looking for this one specific cabinetmaker—George Hepplewhite. As a dealer, he had little interest in anything else. I found that odd."

"How so, Ms. Sheppard?"

"A dealer is in business to buy and sell antiques: he did neither."

Recognizing Sheppard had engaged with his questions he strolled back to his chair. He rested his hands on the back.

"Perhaps he was a collector instead."

"Collet had a small showroom with overpriced furniture which did not sell. He made it a point to attend the major shows and connect with the appropriate dealers. My colleagues knew what he was looking for."

"And it's unusual for a dealer to seek out one particular piece?"

Sheppard recalled an incident with Collet, at her 2nd Ave. showroom, concerning a 1786 Sheraton desk.

"A few years back, I purchased an eighteenth century desk from the estate of a family in

Bedfordshire, England. It had been purchased when the country mansion was under construction and remained in that Bedfordshire residence until 2008 when a friend informed me the family was selling the piece. The morning the desk arrived, I was in the back room having the piece uncrated when Collet came in. When he recognized the piece as a Sheraton, he thanked me for my time and excused himself. He had no interest in the desk, or my examination of the piece, even though it was a rare find—very strange."

With his finger across his lip, he stared at the florescent light recessed in the ceiling panels above his head. Then his eyes rolled back to Sheppard.

"Why do you consider that strange, Ms. Sheppard, if his only interest was in finding a Hepplewhite?"

"Because either Arthur Collet is telepathic, or his bizarre behavior has an explanation far beyond that which any of us understand."

"You've lost me, Ms. Sheppard."

"General, I have the ability to recall images, conversations, situations, with remarkable detail. Events which took place twenty years ago are as fresh as our conversation today. Arthur Collet is not a dealer looking for a one of a kind masterpiece. I can still see his face in the back room of my shop, the look of disappointment, an odd sense of destiny or mission derailed once more. I make a living with my instincts and my memory, which fused together solve mysteries others cannot. Arthur Collect's life's work is not about owning a mahogany desk constructed by the eighteenth century master craftsman, George Hepplewhite. I'll bet my career on it."

Again, Capalli walked over to the mirror cut into the wall. This time he turned and faced Sheppard rubbing his forehead with his left hand.

"Can you prove it?" He asked.

"I did not invite Arthur Collet to my showroom that morning, and I had not told anyone the piece was arriving that day. So you tell me, General, how Collet knew an eighteenth century Carlton House Desk was purchased by me and was to arrive in my showroom office that very day?"

CHAPTER 25

Brosconni was contemplating the text message when the second ping arrived. He scanned the text and then checked the time, 1:41 am. He recognized the address, and his hand holding the Smartphone dropped to his lap. He looked out toward the balcony lit by the moon, as the soft breeze shook the bottom of his silk robe. He hadn't heard a word from the Mr. X since before the church in Naples, and he feared he may not hear from him again. He looked back down at the touch pad, and rubbed the icon, and the text opened up.

*You haven't disappointed me, Brosconni, your arrogance, insolence, and inability to play by the rules remain intact. You have exactly thirty seconds in which to text your goons and call off the "proposal" or this will be the last instruction you will receive. Time starts now!

Brosconni replied to the text.

*What proposal?

*You now have twenty seconds.

*Disregard text message, Brosconni typed in, proposal cancelled! He pushed send.

*Very good, Brosconni, have a pleasant night!

Brosconni looked at the time at the bottom right of the screen, 1:43 am, 10:43 pm California time—Salvador Anachello would be hacking up a storm. Brosconni wrote the text.

*Anachello, text me—now!

Brosconni laid the Smartphone on his lap and rubbed his eyes with his hands. He pulled the fob out of his bathrobe pocket and pushed the button. After he slid the device back into his pocket, he flipped the phone over in his lap, nothing. A few seconds later, the screen lit up and the ping sounded. He opened it up.

*Yes Senior Brosconni, what is it?

Two knocks at the bedroom door, and then it slowly opened, and Pietro peered through.

"You called sir?" He asked.

"Get me a brandy!"

"Yes sir."

Brosconni picked up the phone and typed.

*Anachello, what the hell is going on, he knows I sent a text?"

Anachello's response came back.

*Your software is encrypted: the CIA hasn't even been able to crack the code.

*Bullshit, he knows!"

Again two knocks at the door, and Pietro walked in with a silver platter and a snifter half full of Remy Martin Louis Xlll. Brosconni read the incoming text as Pietro placed the brandy on the table beside him.

"Will that be all sir?"

Brosconni nodded.

*Have you opened a text message from him?

Brosconni answered.

*Yes, several.

*It couldn't be, no one to my knowledge has the capability of ......

*Of what?

*Of hacking into Skype. The only explanation is he's in your phone and computer.

*What the fuck are you talking about?

Brosconni reached over and lifted the snifter, inhaled the expensive aroma of vintage brandy, and swallowed a slug. The text continued.

*Remember our last conversation?

Brosconni agitated replied.

*Get to the point!

*When you opened his text, he must have had a program which took over your phone and computer. He knows everything you read, talk, and text the second you write it, but I still think that's impossible.

*Is it, Anachello?

Brosconni looked at the screen confused and typed.

*Who the hell is that?

The mysterious texter continued.

*Freeze—your—fingers—Brosconni.

Is it, Anachello, for an elite, an innovator?

*So you're the 1337?

*And you're the amateur who tries to play with the big boys?

Brosconni watched as the two shot text back and forth, terms he didn't understand as he drank his brandy and watched the linguistic war pound Anachello into a technological licking. It was two ten in the morning before the final blows were launched, and Anachello, who was clearly staggering, never saw the knockout punch coming.

*I have other business to attend to, Anachello, I'm finished playing touch pad with you. Can you count down from five?

*What's that supposed to mean?

*It means, when you reach zero, your screen will go black, and your hard drive will go blank—adios!

Brosconni waited for a reply from Anachello, but it didn't come. The hacker from California had been infectiously destroyed. He took another swig of the brandy and watched as more text appeared.

*And so ends lesson number three! School is over, Brosconni, let's see if you've learned enough to survive your journey. If, by the time it's over you haven't struck out, you will meet your precious Hepplewhite face to face. But remember, three strikes and you're out, and I mean out!

The text stopped. Brosconni sat in his cushioned chair with all expression drained from his face. His eyes rolled down to the Smartphone lying on his lap, the words frozen on the screen, and he scanned to the clock, 2:13 am. The 1337, as Anachello had called him, was not only a thief, but he had the expertise to wipe out the California hacker. His intentions since the robbery, with the field trips and the text, were to kick Brosconni in line--

demonstrate with absolute clarity that he was in charge. And as Brosconni sat there under the cover of the night, he got the message loud and clear. Whatever game 1337 was playing, the road to the Hepplewhite was paved with rules whose conventions would be imposed by him. Brosconni felt the rage rush up through his body and turn his face afire.

Then, the next text appeared.

*We start now! First you must cleanse your soul and seek forgiveness to the heavenly father on your quest to regain control of the Hepplewhite. Go to the holy city in Rome................................

CHAPTER 26

The day after her meeting with Capalli, Christina Sheppard was still in Rome. Her professional interest in finding and examining the desk, and the commitment to hear out Hancock, had been, up until now, the only reason she delayed her return to the states. But that had now changed. After speaking with her close friend, Nancy, the manager at her 2nd Ave. showroom, and strolling through the Roman Forum like a lifeless drone, the emotional void of a six year shut down had taken its toll. So much so, she was beginning to feel depressed.

She moved through the Forum, through the columns and the crowds, with an intense guilt eating at her insides for wanting to move out from under her catastrophic past. She walked down the Via Sacra (the sacred road) symbolically embracing the once great structures which now lay in a sea of ruin. Stopping in front of the space which contained the ruined House of the Vestal Virgins, Christina's gaze dropped toward the marbled columns which lay strewn across the ancient site. *Live or die,* she challenged her tormented soul, *pick one or the other but not both!*

She dinned in a local café, strolled the Piazza Trinta dei Monti, and sat on the marble treads of the Spanish Steps and watched the young Italian studs court the swooning giovani donne. For hours Christina gazed at the Fontana della Barcaccia, ("Fountain of the old boat") which stood at the base of the steps in the Piazza di Spagna and became mesmerized by the streams of water cascading through the air. She studied the 1627 masterpiece and tried to remember how it felt to be held in the arms of a man; it seemed so long ago.

The steps were lined on each side with blooming, burgundy azaleas. As the crowds streamed up the historic steps, Christina descended down to the Piazza below, around the fountain, and toward the north side to the street. Her pace slowed as she entered Via del Babuino and stopped at the shops and restaurant facades. At times she stood and stared into the glass storefronts, but she saw nothing of what was inside. At a small café' she studied the reflection: her face seemed to float on the glass, and she felt a surreal detachment from the person staring back.

The metro ride back to the hotel brought back thoughts of Washington's desk. She scanned the images of Hancock sitting at the lunch table at the Hotel Caruso. His likeness, which reminded her of Raymond, had a meaning she thought. *Was it coincidence?* Summoned to Italy for the most astounding opportunity of her career, and out of nowhere walks a man that looks like, and has mannerisms similar to, her deceased husband, Ray. *Was it an omen? Could it have been a portent, one of those significant moments mysteriously offered to signal change?* Jermaine Arket, in their last conversation together, had said, "you will find your way out of your darkness through the light of your work, but only if you are open to its message." *Could he have been right?* She stared out the window at the crowd awaiting the metro as it approached the Lepanto station, and she thought about what Arket had said.

The metro pulled away, and for 9:00 pm on a Saturday night, Christina was surprised that the car was only half full as it picked up speed and rumbled through the tunnels. She straightened her blazer with one hand and ran her fingers through her hair with her other and noticed a young Italian man watching her as she did. The metro rattled along, and she clutched her small hand bag slung over her shoulder under her arm. *Arket was right, he was right about a lot of things.* Her eyes locked onto the window across the isle—black with a sprinkle of occasional light. *Look at the series of events, it all makes sense.* The metro slowed, as it approached Ottaviano *San Pietro* station, and she moved her legs to the side, as a group lined up by the door.

If the Hepplewhite had not been stolen, I would have finished my examination a week ago and never met Hancock. I would have been back in the states instead of riding the subway in Rome. Think about it, I would have never have allowed myself the time to tour the Forum, contemplate at the Spanish steps, or spend personal time in Rome. Listen to Arket, listen to yourself for Christ Sake, Christina, you're a walking cadaver. The doors closed and the metro took off. Valle Aurelia was stop number five, she recalled that now, as she pictured the stations in her mind—*two more.*

Christina turned back to the window. *What do you think Raymond would say to you: I'm dead, I want you dead? I don't think so. What about mom and dad? Get out there and live, Christina, live for us, live for your husband, live for yourself!* She spotted movement in the glass. The Italian man who had watched her brush her hair with her hand was coming toward her. Oh please!

"Mi scusi signora, do you mind if I sit?" He said in a thick Italian accent.

The metro slowed. Cipro *Musei Vaticani* appeared on a sign out the window. *One more stop.* Christina looked up. He was attractive, perhaps in his late thirties, and had a brown leather jacket unzipped with a collarless black t-shirt underneath.

"Signora?" he asked, "may I sit?"

Her head rolled back down toward the floor as she answered.

"I get off at the next station."

"Me too, how long have you been in Rome, signora?"

The doors opened and people shuffled off the metro and in turn shuffled on. The disturbance gave Christina time to think. The doors closed, and the metro left the station.

She watched him in the window across the aisle, as he waited for an answer. Without turning her head she spoke.

"Two days."

"Rome is a very beautiful city, no?"

"Yes."

"Mi scusi, signora, you are a very beautiful woman. I could not help notice you when you embarked at Spagna, did you not see the Spanish Steps? They are where lovers meet."

Oh Christ, the Italian stud is making his move.

Christina turned to the man. The metro slowed and without saying a word she stood and held the pole to steady herself. He stood up next to her.

"I'm sorry, signora, I'm afraid I upset you. Please forgive me."

Christina said nothing.

"Signora, there is a little café a short walk from the station, may I buy you a glass of wine?"

Sheppard had made an appointment to meet Hancock tomorrow at noon. She had planned on leaving Rome for the Amalfi coast early in the morning.

"Signora, please!"

"I'm leaving Rome early tomorrow, no thank you."

The metro stopped, the doors opened, and they walked to the steps and onto the street. Christina had said no for six years, and she was surprised when she let him sit down on the metro. Now he insisted on showing her the café. "A very public place," he said, "you would be safe." And, she could not believe she went in.

They drank the first glass talking about the Spanish steps, which he recited like a tour guide, and she found herself intrigued. As she drank the second, she could feel a buzz tingling through her body. She noticed something else, down below, which had been turned off and the circuit breaker pulled for three quarters of a decade. He touched her hand, and Christina felt her dried up love cave dampen. Halfway through the third glass, she looked him in the eyes, feeling the effects of the liquor, and realized she better go. She turned away.

"Signora?"

"I have to go."

"Signora?"

"Thank you for the wine," she said and stood up with the Italian stud still sitting at the table. Then, before he could say another word, Christina bolted out the door, down the sidewalk, and was gone.

CHAPTER 27

Sheppard had agreed to meet Hancock at Fiordo Di Furore, a small village carved into the steep cliffs just below Praiano. Its location and size were almost undetectable by the average traveler, and Christina, having no recall of Furore on her previous excursions, picked up a guide book on her drive from Rome. Hancock had insisted on the isolated fishing village and gave no explanation for the change. Sheppard arrived at 11:45 and parked in the small allocated lot just above town. Standing by her car, she looked out over a handful of structures that made up the village and spotted the restaurant at the end of the street, dug into the sands of a curved beach strewn with overturned wooden boats. Hancock sat at a table on the patio overlooking the colored row boats. When she arrived at the table, Hancock detected a puzzled look on her face.

"Christina," he said as he scanned the landscape, "I'll explain, please sit down."

"Hancock are you playing secret agent now?"

"Christina it's no joke. Listen to me," he said as he followed a villager walking to his boat, "something's happened, and I think I'm being followed."

Sheppard looked away from Hancock and gazed out toward the water. She contemplated the drama for a moment and then turned her head back to Hancock.

"Go on, I'm listening."

"Have you spoken to anyone about our conversations?"

"No."

"Does anyone know of our meetings?"

"I told you, no. Get to the point Hancock."

The waiter arrived at the table. Christina ordered a diet coke, Randolph ordered an ice tea. He handed them each a menu and left. Hancock continued.

"My research and my premise must be spot on. It's more important than ever we locate and read the correspondence in that desk. It is imperative you tell no one of our meetings or the information I've shared with you. It could mean the difference between life and death."

Surprised by Hancock's theatrics, Sheppard studied his eyes as they moved side to side. *Was that fear or the nervous reaction which followed a lie?* Hancock picked up his glass of ice tea as Sheppard laid her arm on the wrought iron rail, leaned forward, and spoke in a very soft tone.

"Life and death, Hancock, what do you mean?"

"Before I left for Rome, my room was ransacked and my laptop was stolen. All my research was on that hard drive."

"Was it backed up?

"Of course, I keep a flash drive in my pocket, and I have an online service which I pay for the storage space. My laptop is password protected; it would be unlikely who ever stole it had the expertise to unlock it."

"It sounds like an ordinary theft to me."

"Right, except for the note they left behind. It said, stop the research now. Destroy your back up and return to the states!"

"Or what?"

Hancock jerked his head up. The waiter had surprised him. Christina glanced at the menu and made a snap decision on the salad with a piece of local fish. Hancock took a minute more to study the choices. The air was still thick with the suspense of their conversation, and Sheppard turned toward the beach. She thought about the two dead dealers that had been shot in the head and realized Hancock could be next. Hancock placed his order, and the waiter turned and strolled back inside. Christina waited until he disappeared behind the door and then looked to Hancock.

"Or what?" She said.

"The murders of those two dealers……..."

"Miller and Bennetto."

"Yes, Miller and Bennetto, the note said, or you'll end up like Miller and Bennetto."

"Did you go to the police?"

"I can't."

"Why?"

Hancock's head fell toward the table as his hand caught his forehead, and it sat in the palm of his hand. Ray used to make the same move when faced with a painful choice. Sheppard glanced left to the water to regain her focus and then back toward Hancock.

"Why?" She asked.

"I've been married twenty eight years, and I love my wife. The note said, if I go to the police they would," Hancock paused and tried to collect his emotions, "they would kill Martha."

Hancock pulled his head up.

"I can't take the chance," he said looking at Sheppard, "I couldn't go on if they hurt Martha: I wouldn't want to go on."

Christina picked up her soda and gulped a slug. Hancock had just plunged Sheppard back to 2004, to the Meadow Lands, and the horrific carnage of twisted metal and burned bodies. She rubbed her forehead with her fingers as she faced the Tyrrhenian Sea. The blood drained from her face, and her eyes squinted half closed making her forehead wrinkle. The abrupt halt to the conversation, and the eerie silence, alerted Hancock that something he said had leveled Sheppard.

"Are you ok?" He asked.

Sheppard said nothing, didn't move or blink an eye.

"Christina………..Christina, are you ok?"

She turned in slow motion and looked at Hancock.

Yes," she said as the color returned to her skin, "I'll be alright." Sheppard took another gulp of her coke and then took a deep breath.

"What do you propose to do?" She asked still struggling to regain her composure.

Hancock scanned the restaurant and spotted the waiter with the tray of food. He fell back in his chair, folded his arms, and looked to the winding road carved into the cliffs. The sun traced the lines of the curved pavement. Sheppard recognized his pause and did the same. As their meals were placed in front of them, each gave a smile and a nod.

"Is there anything else I can bring you?" He asked

"No, thank you," Hancock said.

Randolph studied the waiter's movements over his shoulder and waited until he went inside. Then he leaned in toward Sheppard.

"I plan to continue; I've obviously struck an historical nerve. Miller and Bennetto were murdered because they had had possession of the piece and although they no longer did, they knew where it went and to whom. But, more importantly, they had seen the face of the person who would kill in order to obtain the Hepplewhite. That sealed their fates."

"But your wife?"

"I instructed her to stay with her sister in California. She'll be safe there."

"Then go to the police."

"No, I won't risk my wife's safety, and, I can't allow my research to become public just yet. If it did, and the correspondence was not recovered, I would be recognized as another Oliver Stone. My reputation as a renowned historian would never recover. That is why you must tell no one. Our meetings are to be random, spread out in different locations, and you must never be followed. I'm going underground—going to disappear. We must find that desk and capture that correspondence. What I have to say is meaningless without those letters, and, perhaps, it is my only ticket to safety. I want you to promise me if anything happens to me you'll make sure my wife is safe—promise me!"

"Yes, of course."

"Thank you! Here is the address." Hancock handed her a piece of paper. She took the address and placed it in her side blazer pocket.

"Will Brosconni call you when he finds the desk?" He asked.

"Yes, he cares about only one thing, his Hepplewhite. He will want to know the contents hidden inside the desk, and for that, he will come to me."

"Good! When he does, will you insist that I be present?"

"I can arrange that."

"Excellent!"

Sheppard pulled a strand of hair from her face as she lifted her fork. She cut a piece of fish on top of her salad and bundled it with the butter lettuce and fresh tomato. As it rose to her mouth, the bite of lunch stopped dead in mid air. She looked to Hancock.

"Who's behind this?" She asked. "Who would want the desk so bad they would murder two people?"

"Did you do the research on the names I gave you and the organization they belong to?"

"Yes—are you saying...........................?"

Hancock nodded yes.

CHAPTER 28

Capalli had gathered his team in his sixth floor office, and they were seated around the rectangular, mahogany conference table. As always, The General sat at the head flanked on one side by Capt. Penso and on the other by Capt. Tinelli. Sheppard's perspective on Arthur Collet had reinforced Capalli's suspicions and with two dealers dead, the press wanting answers, and Brosconni disappearing every other day, Capalli pushed his team to the brink. Needless to say, with the investigation covering London, New York, and half the Italian peninsula, processing the inflow of information became a near impossible task. But General Capalli expected no less than miracles from his men, or they wouldn't be on the crack Carabinieri Art Squad—at least not for long.

"Capt. Penso," Capalli said, "is Scotland Yard cooperating?"

"Yes, General, Detective Mitchell had a team question dealers throughout the countryside. In his report, Mitchell states that Arthur Collet had organized, over a number of years, the ability to detect any new eighteenth century Carlton house Desk discovered at any time, and, at any place in England. Through a network of small town and world renowned dealers, Collet received information the moment a new piece surfaced. That positioned Collet at the top of the antique food chain; he had first access to any new piece before it hit the market. But here's the disconnect, with the vast amount of energy the New York dealer expended on instantaneous intelligence, he purchased not a single piece. It appears Arthur Collet was after something specific, crafted between the years 1785-1786, and according to Mitchell's investigation, Collet never found what he was looking for."

The General leaned back in his leather swivel chair and rubbed his fingers on his chin. Then he turned to Penso.

"What about..............."

"General!"

Capalli looked down to the desk and picked up his phone transmitting as a two way radio.

"Go ahead," he commanded.

"General, we got him."

"Where?"

"Brosconni just landed in Rome. He went from his helicopter to an awaiting car and sped from the airport. We're tailing him now, and we have two copters in the air."

"Let me know the minute he arrives at his destination, Lt. Don't lose him!"

"Yes General."

Capalli laid his phone on the desk and lifted his head. His eyes rolled down toward the table top, and he reached with his hand, turned the phone half way around, slid it in front of him, and then positioned it just to the right. He turned to Penso.

"What about specific contacts, did he have any?"

"None that we know of yet. It seems the individuals in his network only knew Collet as a dealer from New York, who kept the connection fresh with periodic calls, but he didn't forge a relationship with any of them specifically. Most dealers prefer to have a working relationship with a colleague overseas. They can share information and depend upon each other's expertise—not Collet."

Capalli stood up and walked to the window and look down to the Piazza Sant' Lgnazio. As Penso continued, a clear picture had already been painted in Capalli's mind, and as Penso finished, he turned from the window and looked to Tinelli.

"Capt. what about New York?"

"General, Detective....................."

"General!"

Capalli held up his hand to Tinelli and picked up his phone. He pressed the button, as he stood behind his chair.

"Yes?"

"General, they are on Piazzetta del Bel Respiro. They are headed in your direction."

"Keep on him Lt." He turned back to the Tinelli, "Capt."

"General, Detective Stanno has completed a similar investigation in New York. From the dealers, he received much the same information. Detective Stanno examined five years of Collet's tax returns, and there was no reported income from his showroom."

"None?" Capalli asked.

"That's correct nothing in five years. He lives in a very expensive town house near the Metropolitan Museum, had reported income of half a billion last year from investments and doesn't have a family or a wife."

Capalli stood up and walked to the window. With his back to his men he continued.

"What about his personal life?" He asked.

"We know very little so far. However, there is one piece of information Detective Stanno thought relevant to our investigation."

"What's that?" Capalli asked as he turned from the window and faced Tinelli.

"General, Arthur Collet is the Grand Master of the Masonic hall on 23rd Street in Manhattan. He has been for the past ten years."

"And why did Stanno think that relevant?"

"General, Washington was………………"

Again the two way radio.

"Yes?"

"General, they're headed into the Holy City, what should I do?"

"Follow them! If he stops, and gets out, shadow him. Before you do, remove your weapon, I don't want any security breaches to alert Brosconni. How are you transmitting to me?"

"Everything is under cover, General. Hold on, the car is stopping."

"Get out and follow, keep me posted but do not blow your cover, understood?"

"Yes General."

"Capt. Tinelli."

"General, according to Detective Stanno, George Washington was a devote Freemason. He was one of the most significant figures in the Revolution and, the first President of the United States."

Capalli studied the Piazza as he contemplated the connection to Collet. He knew very little American history, and he hadn't understood Stanno's point. Capalli turned toward the table.

"Capt. Tinelli, why would Detective Stanno think this relevant?"

"According to Detective Mitchell, in London, Collet was searching for a desk crafted between 1785 and 1786. That was the time period Washington commissioned the desk, and as we know it was destined to sail on the Lucretia, but it didn't. The head of the premier Grand Lodge of all New York is searching for a desk which matches the date and description of Washington's desk. Is it coincidence? Perhaps, but something about Collet, and his "professional behavior" doesn't make sense. Is the possibility of a connection bizarre, yes, but nothing to date about this case has been ordinary or followed normal protocol. I agree with Detective Stanno—it's worth looking into."

Capalli turned back toward the window and stared down at the Church of Sant' Lgnazio. His pragmatic intellect wrestled with his investigative instincts. *A connection over hundreds of years, for what? A desk crafted in the eighteenth century was stolen in 2010: was it the theft of a priceless antique—nothing more?* The premise Stanno offered violated every strand of Capalli's investigative DNA, but he couldn't ignore the possibility, or that his strict analytical discipline and military training could be wrong. He turned.

"I want everything you can dig up on this Grand Lodge in New York, on Arthur Collet as Grand Master, and why the Masons would be involved with Washington's desk—everyone out except Captains Penso and Tinelli!"

The room cleared, and Capalli stood at the window with his back to Penso and Tinelli. Without turning he spoke.

"As farfetched as this seems, Captains, this could be our first real break—work it!"

"General!"

Capalli picked up his two way and stood at the window.

"Yes?"

"Sir, you're not going to believe this, but, Brosconni is entering St. Peters Basilica."

Capalli turned to Penso and Tinelli with a confused look.

"Follow him!" He said.

"Inside, General?"

"Yes, inside!"

The communication from the Lt. had lowered to an almost undetectable whisper.

"General, he walked over to the stoup, made the cross with the water, and he's saying Hail Mary's."

"What?"

"He's repeating Hail Mary's over and over!"

CHAPTER 29

Brosconni stepped aboard the Bell 429 resigned to play whatever game the mysterious letch had concocted. Patience, he had learned, provides opportunity; no one is infallible and neither is their planned intent. And he had a formula for when the opening arose. Wait, prepare, and strike as if Lucifer were inside your soul. It worked on the streets of Naples, and it worked as he built an unscrupulous shipping empire. So he'd wait, and somewhere between St. Peters Basilica and his prized Hepplewhite, the crack would rear its head, and when it did, the fires of hell would rain down upon Mr. X.

Brosconni snapped his fingers and the rotors began to spin. As the roar chopped through the air, the ground let go its grip, and the Bell rose above the Da Vinci airport. When it finished its ascent, the Bell banked hard left hugging the coast. As it raced over the water, Brosconni reached into his pocket and slid out Lorenzo Pietro's cell phone. He had taken it from his head of staff before he left for Rome. As the town of Anzio breezed by on the left side window, Enrico reached into his inside pocket and pulled out a piece of paper with numbers written in ink. He punched them in.

"Ciao," he said, 'did you receive my Fed Ex? Yes, good. You do exactly as I instructed. What? The proposal was canceled because my Smartphone was not secure. You are never to call, text, or email me; I will contact you at the appropriate time."

Brosconni flipped the phone closed and slid it back into his side pocket and studied the landscape as they zoomed down the coast. As the 429 approached Monte di Procida, he instructed the pilot to fly over the outcrop of land and swing in toward Naples. He commanded the pilot to slow down and descend lower, and they crawled over the city as Brosconni searched for his old neighborhood.

"Vi," he shouted over the pounding of the rotors, "there, over there!"

A crooked grin cracked his lips as they flew over the slum where he had spent his youth, and he thought of Nico Sparanzo whom all the kids had feared. Nico was fourteen and Enrico was twelve. Sparanzo had shaken down the young Brosconni and had taken the money Enrico had picked from the pockets of the tourists at Pompeii. The next day, Enrico waited in the alley behind Giovanni's grocery store, the route Sparanzo took home to his house. Hiding under a stair well, he spotted Sparanzo a few feet away. When he reached Brosconni, the first thing to break was both his legs below the knees. Lying on the ground, Sparanzo held up his hand to protect his head, and as he did, Brosconni whaled the cut in half two by four around and proceeded to break his arm. That's how the equation wait, prepare, and strike first came to be. And as Brosconni turned from the window with the smirk still on his face, he mumbled his decades old mantra: *Enrico Brosconni è sempre vittoriosa, sempre!* He took one last look and he shouted to his pilot.

"Go!" Brosconni ordered. "Vai, vai.

The Bell hugged the Amalfi Coast as Brosconni sat in the back reviewing his strategy in his head. He now had support in place, trained covert professionals, and with each text instruction on the road to the Hepplewhite, the noose would slowly tighten. *The son of a bitch,* Brosconni whispered, *will get whacked when he least expects it.*

They were just over Positano when the ping sounded. Brosconni pulled out his Smartphone and looked at the screen. He opened up the text.

*Strike one, Brosconni, you let the plain clothes Carabinieri follow you into the church—two left!

Brosconni clicked reply and typed.

*Wait, what do you want, money?

Brosconni typed again.

*I'll give you half a million Euros to stop this nonsense, no questions asked.

Nothing. Brosconni waited another minute, nothing. *Shit!* The Bell banked hard left and turned inland as its rotors chopped through the air. It approached Villa Marcella, hovered briefly, and then descended as if on a string to the pad. Brosconni had already unbuckled his seat belt and prepared to disembark. The 429 touched the concrete, and the anxious tycoon flipped the latch, pushed the door, and jumped out. He barreled down the terracotta paver path brushing his short hair back with his hand. As the side oak door swung open, and Pietro stood with the panels to his back, Brosconni flew through the kitchen adjusting the knot of his tie, raced into the main hall, flung his office door aside, and fell into the leather chair at his desk. He picked up the phone and dialed.

"General Capalli," he said. "You know God damn well who this is. Put Capalli on— now!"

"Fuck you, Capalli, I told you not to interfere, you son of a bitch: you can kiss your storied career goodbye................................No, you listen, when I'm done there won't be a hole big enough for you to crawl into......................shut the fuck up, you dumb son of a bitch, start packing up your desk!"

Brosconni took a breath and slammed the hand set onto the carriage. He swiveled his leather chair half way around and stared out to the sea.

CHAPTER 30

General Capalli took a breath and slammed the handset onto the carriage. He swiveled his leather chair half way around and stared down to the piazza. He knew this day would come; it hung over him for fifteen years like the smell of death. Capalli's life and reputation had been impeccable, and he was highly respected by both the citizens of the Italian peninsula and the men who served under him, but he was human, and the strict military discipline demanded upon him in youth had a lapse of rebellion in middle age. And who was there to witness and exploit his darkest hour—Enrico Brosconni.

Capalli raised both hands to his chin and made a church steeple at his lips as his eyes sunk downward, and he thought back to ninety five. The summer of 95, Alberto Capalli surprised his wife on her fortieth birthday with a cruise to Lisbon through the straits of Gibraltar. At forty one Capalli's career had seen one promotion after another, and he'd reached the rank of Full Colonel. He was head of the regional unit of the Carabinieri in Naples, and his discipline and long hours of dedication left little time for the personal pleasures most rising Italian men enjoyed. Dinner was often a sandwich at his desk. He lived the stringent work ethic his father, the colonel, had instilled in him. And it had its price.

Alberto Capalli had never learned to relax. Even as a teenager at military school when others took to the movies on a Saturday night, Alberto was buried in the stacks researching military strategies until the library closed, and the librarian had to throw him out. That same dedication, years later, expedited his rise in the Carabinieri, but did little for his social skills or his ability to cultivate a healthy marriage. Although his wife, Carlota, knew better than complain, Alberto was not blind. He sensed the unhappiness and discontent in her demeanor when he arrived home after 9:30 on a Saturday night. So Capalli booked the trip to Portugal in hopes of re-firing his marriage but the luxury cruise backfired instead

On the boat Capalli was restless, bored, and had trouble sleeping at night. He felt trapped by the confinement, and the crowds irritated his intensely private personality. By twelve thirty the second night, he lay in the bed staring at the ceiling ready to crawl out of his skin. He climbed out from under the covers, got dressed, and left Carlota alone sound asleep in the room. That's when something in Alberto Capalli snapped.

Alcohol normally didn't fit with his rigid lifestyle, but he found himself at the bar, then the slots, then the black jack table, and Alberto Capalli was hooked. He had never gambled before in his life, and he found himself winning, and the free money became as intoxicating as the gin. As much as he tried to stay away from the tables the next few nights, the prospect of a windfall lured him in by midnight. For the first time in his life, Alberto Capalli had lost control, and he began a three month binge into the darkness of addiction and, like any other obsession, it had to be fed—a perfect mark for a man like Brosconni.

Brosconni made it his business to collect information on individuals, in prominent positions, which could be used to gain an advantage when his ships pulled into port. It didn't take Brosconni's cronies long to learn, Alberto had traveled and gambled in Monaco on a number of secret weekend jaunts and in so doing, racked up a pile of debt. Soon, Capalli became desperate. His credit was cut off, and he needed his fix. Capalli was ripe to be picked.

Colonel Capalli's regional unit inspected all arriving ships that sailed into the port of Naples, and Brosconni, whose ships carried as much smuggled contraband as it did legal cargo, set the colonel up. A ship captain, who worked for the tycoon, financed a jaunt to Monaco with airfare, a room, and twenty thousand American dollars to entertain his obsession. In return, Capalli was to overlook a shipment of stolen artifacts arriving from Brazil. Unable to control his addiction, Alberto Capalli crossed the very boundaries he was sworn to protect. When he realized what he had done, Capalli was sick. He quit the Black jack table's cold turkey, but Brosconni had documented the entire event, and although Capalli refused to cooperate again and allow contraband into his port, Brosconni held the silver bullet which could end Capalli's career, and his finger was now on the trigger.

The General's hands dropped from his lips to his lap. His head slowly rose, and he swiveled the chair back around to his desk. It made him nauseous when he thought of ninety five and how he could have been so pathetically weak. Free falling into the grip of a self deprecating addiction had haunted his soul for fifteen years, but allowing smuggled artifacts into his country, national treasures which he had given most of his life to protect, was an act he could never forgive. It was a cancerous sore on a distinguished career and tantamount to the fatal flaw. And he knew, as he looked across his desk at the two empty chairs, his days as commander of the Carabinieri Art Squad was about to come to an end.

CHAPTER 31

"Are you saying that freemasons were behind the start of the American Revolution?" She said, with the fork of salad still suspended in the air.

"I'm not saying it, I'm stating it, its a fact."

She dropped her fork into her salad and turned her head away from Hancock and stared at the rocky cliffs. Sheppard didn't move as Hancock continued.

"That's the tip of the iceberg, Christina, hold on to your chair. Before I go into the specifics, let me give you some information you can use along the way to back up the facts. Here is the simplest form of the equation: masons in Britain organize mason brothers in the thirteen colonies, who denounce British rule and fight for their independence. Remember now, this is the simple form; I'll get as specific as you want later on. Covertly, with the help of their British counterparts, they organize the movement, become prominent activist, and place their fellow masons in positions of power. With the Revolution won, and a country in need of a new government, these visible and well respected individuals (after all they did birth and win a war) are not only a shoe in to establish, but to run, the new political system of the United States."

Sheppard turned back toward Hancock with a half smirk on her lips.

"Who killed Kennedy, Hancock, Richard Nixon? Not only are you a conspiracy theorist gone amuck, but your attempt to befoul the forefathers of our great nation will have you symbolically hung by the American people and their press."

"You miss the point, Christina, I'm not trying to assassinate reputations; I'm attempting to disclose the facts. When there is a void in leadership, many forms of power fill the gap: Dictators, Prime Ministers, Emperors, call them whatever you like. The Masonic order was based in principle on sound beliefs, brought together to form, what they believed, was a just and fair government. The founding of the Premier Grand Lodge of England in 1714 gave all masons on that continent a central seat of power. And, as their organization matured, the Sovereign Grand Inspector General (the highest level of the 33 degrees in the hierarchy of the lodge) in collusion with other select members, developed a master plan to transpose the Masonic order on a scale unprecedented in its past. This theory is not new, Christina. The speculation of Masonic control in the seat of our government has circulated for years. The difference between conspiracy theory and my thesis is the correspondence in Washington's desk—it dispels all doubt."

Her stare thawed, her eyes moved down to her lunch, where she lifted the fork and consumed the first bite prepared almost ten minutes before. Sheppard was aware of the Masonic conspiracy theories, who wasn't? The Masonic symbol of the eye in the pyramid on the one dollar bill, the Washington monument, a tribute by the masons to the first President of the United States, fellow brother mason, George Washington, mason, Ben Franklin on the hundred dollar bill, the corner stone of the capital laid by the Grand Lodge of Maryland, the list is infinite. But Sheppard, being a realist, was never prone to such speculative reasoning, and as she sipped her coke, and reloaded her fork, she listened with a tentative ear as Hancock articulated his theory.

"One of the basic principles of Masonic belief was to create a new world order. What better place to begin than an established collection of states, on a continent rich in resources, with the wealthiest of their citizens fellow brother masons. Successful colonists like Hancock, Langdon, and Franklin, to name a few, were receptive to the prospect of independence, particularly when it meant their profits would exponentially increase without the constraints and taxes of the British rule."

"Why would British citizens betray their own country?"

"Great Britain was a Monarch whose rule was absolute; any attempt to reduce the king's stronghold would be met by certain death. The master masons of the Grand Lodge, and their plan to expand their secret society into a functioning governing force, acknowledged that and recognized the need to look abroad. The thirteen colonies, thousands of miles from the British coast, proved ideal.

A miniscule piece of the British Empire far from the reach of the king's grip, the colonies, the Master Masons believed, would become independent with little resistance from The Monarch's troops. And, if King George III decided to retaliate with force, the Master Masons had the assurance through secret correspondence from fellow mason, General Lafayette, that King Louis XVI would support the Colonists in a war. That signaled for the Sovereign Grand Inspector General that the infrastructure was now in place."

Hancock paused, and Sheppard looked up from her salad. They had been sitting on the portico for more than an hour, and he had observed by Sheppard's posture and her methodical gathering of the food on her plate, she had grown restless with his talk. What he assumed, however, was far from the truth. Christina, fascinated by the images Hancock's story had conjured up, plunged her imagination into an historical feast of eighteenth century London, Red Cross Street, and Hepplewhite's shop. She pictured George Hepplewhite instructing Colonel Smith on how to access the hidden compartments. And as Smith reached to the back secret shelves, and slid in the sealed correspondence, she felt her body quiver. It was the very same compartment she had reached her hand into two hundred and twenty four years later.

"Christina," Hancock said, "am I boring you?"

Sheppard brought her vision back to Hancock.

"I asked if you were bored?"

"No, Hancock, continue."

Hancock scanned the beach and then looked left to the access road.

"I can't, I must go: we've been here too long. What if you were followed?"

Sheppard rolled her eyes.

"If I had been followed you would have known by now. Look around you," she said, as she pointed toward the winding road traversing the incline, "there hasn't been a car since I drove down to the village. We've seen one local fisherman attending to his boat. Unless someone's sitting up there in the cliffs with some high tech listening device, I think you're safe."

"No, I must go!" He said as he placed fifty Euros on the table. "Please excuse my abrupt departure, Christina, but we must be careful, you don't fully understand what's at stake. They will stop at nothing to assure the information I have is never released."

CHAPTER 32

Capalli decided after a long sleepless night if he was going out, he was going out with a bang. He sat at his desk, at six in the morning, resigned to his fate and at peace with the consequences for his unconscionable behavior. But as long as he was commander, The General would use every asset at his disposal to solve the case. And, he knew he had time. Brosconni was busy running around trying to retrieve the Hepplewhite—Capalli believed that—and until the shipping tycoon stopped, Capalli's secret was safe.

As he leaned back in his leather chair, he took a long breath, scanned the room, and his gaze stopped at the citations which hung on the wall behind the Brescia leather couch. He read the gold framed document centered among the ten black frames.

*General Alberto Giuseppe Capalli
Commander of the Carabinieri Art squad
In recognition of his excellence in the
recovery after forty years of Caravaggio's master
piece, "The Nativity"
Signed this 17th day of January in the year
two thousand and five
Prime Minister of Italy
Silvio Berlusconi*

He exhaled, and his eyes rolled down to the computer screen already alive on his desk. And in the early morning hours as the offices of the Carabinieri Art Squad remained empty, Capalli worked the files on Arthur Collet.

By 7am Capalli was in the conference room surrounded by his men. Capt. Penso had been working on the Arthur Collet investigation with New York Detective Mike Stanno. Capt. Tinelli had been assigned to Brosconni. The Lieutenants were split fifty – fifty: Armone and Danato with Penso, Bianchi and Pisano with Tinelli. General Capalli looked to Penso first.

"General, Detective Stanno has unearthed some interesting facts about the Grand Lodge of New York. After his initial examination, Stanno's instincts compelled him to dig further into its history and its long line of Grand Masters. The results, he states, had captivated his full investigative attention having an esoteric connection between the present and the past."

"What the hell does that mean, Capt. Penso?" Capalli said as he lifted his espresso toward his mouth.

"General, I must first qualify what I am about to report, by assuring you, Det. Stanno is not some renegade nut case grasping at invisible straws. His reputation with the New York City Police Department is renowned for his investigative work involving unsolved, complex crimes with seemingly untraceable connections. He thinks outside the box, General, and that strategy has produced some of the finest detective work in the state of New York."

"Get to the point, Capt."

"Stanno believes Arthur Collet is directly involved with the murders of Miller and Bennetto and the motive is tied to the desk."

The General rose and walked over to the window and turned his back to the table. The other officers were frozen in their chairs, glued to Penso's words. They waited with the flat screens lit up in front of them as Penso clicked on the mouse. He continued.

"Stanno states: in order to prove Collet's involvement, it is paramount to look at the historical time line of facts with some speculative imagination, otherwise, one cannot proceed to prove a motive, his guilt, or how he committed the crime."

Capalli spoke but didn't move.

"You've prepared us, Capt. Penso; we're all braced on the arms of our chairs, get to the point!"

"The Grand Lodge of New York was established in 1787—one year after Washington's desk was to make its journey to the United States, and the same year the Americans ratified their constitution and formed a new government. The first Grand Master was a Robert R Livingston: one of five who wrote the Declaration of Independence—the other four, Benjamin Franklin, Roger Sherman, John Adams, and Thomas Jefferson all had evidence of membership or affiliations with freemasons. The first individual to be sworn in as president of the United States in New York was George Washington, a zealous mason for forty seven years. He was given the oath of office by, none other than, Robert R Livingston, the head mason of the Grand Lodge of New York. John Adams was the first vice president under Washington. He, along.................."

"Capt. Penso," Capalli said turning now toward the table, "spare us the American history lesson, what does this have to do with the murders of Miller and Bennetto or the missing desk?"

The General again turned his focus to the window and picked up the little espresso cup from the saucer. All eyes looked to Penso.

"General, freemasons established their lodges and beliefs under a cloak of secrecy. No one really understands who or what they are or what purpose they serve."

"Capt.?"

"The construction of the new American government, and its soon to be government officials, were filled with fellow masons. Stanno believes this was no coincidence, and that there is something about Washington's desk that is of extreme interest to Collet, and the officers directly under him in the Grand Lodge of New York."

"And this is?" Capalli replied with his hand now wrapped around his chin.

"He thinks there may be something hidden in the desk that the lodge has for centuries tried to recover."

"And what is that, Capt.?

"Perhaps the two documents Sheppard and Brosconni mentioned, but he says, unless you can crack the infrastructure of the Grand Lodge and decipher its closest held secrets, you'll never be able to connect Collet to the two murders or prove the motive was centered upon the desk."

Capalli looked down to the bustling piazza and felt a sense of urgency in his gut. The time he had left as commander was in direct confrontation with an investigation more complex and geographically diverse than any he had ever encountered. He rubbed his forehead with the fingers of his right hand as he tried to comprehend the farfetched premise of Detective Stanno. If what he proposed was credible, how could he possibly infiltrate a two hundred and twenty year old organization out of the state of New York, whose foundations were built in the shadows of the American Revolution, and, had the capacity to keep their organization so secretive for over two centuries the general population had no idea what the Masonic lodge was about? Capalli eased his body toward the table with the recognition that Stanno's theory could be right but yet impossible to prove.

He reached his chair and placed his hands at the top of the back. He scanned the table and looked into the eyes of each of his men. In the silence, Pisano wiggled his pen between his fingers. The others sat at attention in their chairs. Capalli's demeanor outwardly had not changed since the officers entered the room, but internally, his heart raced. In a calm commanding voice he spoke to Tinelli.

"What about Brosconni?"

"General, Senior Brosconni at the moment is parked in Villa Marcella. He is being monitored twenty four seven, and we will be notified if there is any change. As you requested, we have spoken with Da Vinci Airport. Senior Brosconni's pilot has filed a flight plan for tomorrow."

The General perked up, and his stare intensified as he looked to Tinelli.

"And?"

"Sir, the flight plan is to JFK, in New York."

Penso looked up from his flat screen.

"What time?" The General asked.

"Nine tomorrow morning."

"Capt. Penso, contact Detective Stanno and tell him you will be arriving in New York by morning. Brief the detective on Brosconni's plans and have him set up the needed support with the proper assets. I want to know where he goes, who he sees, and what business he has in New York."

"Yes sir!"

"You and Capt. Tinelli book a flight to New York tonight. I'll call Commissioner Kelly and ask for his full cooperation on both ends of this investigation. Capt. Penso, I want you on Brosconni. Capt. Tinelli, I want this Masonic thing cracked, understood, and you ask Detective Stanno to pull this Collet in for a polygraph and any other men directly under him."

"Yes sir.

"Lieutenants, work the phones! No one sleeps. Retrace every step of this investigation to see what we've missed, talk to the Detectives in charge of the Miller and Bennetto murder investigations—find me something we can tie to New York and this Arthur Collet!"

CHAPTER 33

"Wait," Sheppard said.

Hancock turned around.

"I need to ask you something."

He had just cleared his chair and started to walk away and now stood two steps from the table. He looked to Sheppard for a brief second and responded. "I have to go."

"This won't take but a minute."

"Are you staying in Italy or flying back to the states?" He asked.

"What?"

"I said, are you staying in Italy or flying back to the states?"

Caught off guard, she thought about that, about what Hancock had asked. She knew the investigation could take time, or worse, come up empty. But she had too much already invested not to see it through. Besides, the way she felt about flying, and the fear and anxiety which rushed through her body for the long eight hour flight, left Christina Sheppard no choice. If she traveled home and they found the Hepplewhite, she'd have to repeat the insanity twice. She looked up at Hancock standing behind his chair.

"No," she said, "I'm not leaving just yet."

"Good, then we can discuss your question the next time we meet."

"No, Hancock, I'm not continuing this charade unless you answer one question."

Hancock searched the road behind him, scanned down to the beach, looked back to the eight buildings which was considered town, and then turned back to Sheppard.

"What?"

"From where did the facts of your premise come? Either you have an incredible imagination backed up by the gift of narration, or you have an inside source which you have not disclosed. The details are way too specific and far too abundant to be the product of years of research. How do you know what you know?"

Hancock's head went back, and his eyes shot side to side. His lips puckered too. He scanned the landscape a second time, pulled his chair out, and sat down.

"You've already sworn me to secrecy, Hancock, so let it go."

Sheppard continued her stare. Hancock hadn't expected the question, and he wasn't sure if he was prepared to answer it, truthfully at least. He trusted her. He believed she would keep her word, her vow of silence, and he pondered both sides as he looked to the water.

"I mean it, Hancock!"

He finally responded.

"Why is that so important to you now?"

"Answer my question!"

He took a hit of the watered down ice tea in his glass as he thought it out. His only chance to get to Washington's desk was through Sheppard, and he couldn't afford to lose her now. But what about the vow he took? Was it betrayal, or a means to fulfill a mission he had sworn to complete? *If the truth led to the Hepplewhite then what would it matter?* Hancock placed the glass on the table as his eyes rose up to hers.

"Alright," he said, "I'll tell you the truth, but it may cost you your life. Are you prepared for that?"

If he only knew how many times she wished she was dead. Sheppard turned her eyes away and looked down to the tiled floor of the patio. Her memory flashed back to New York, 2nd Ave, six months after the death of her husband and parents. Christina had lost all will to live. She dragged her lifeless body to the showroom day after day in hope she'd somehow climb out of her darkness. But it didn't work. The image was crystal clear in her mind now.

She stood in the bathroom in the back of the shop staring into the antique mirror as an empty image stared back. The bottle of Valium the doctor had prescribed for bedtime, only when needed, sat in her hand. And without hesitation, she popped the top and swallowed twenty-five pills. Then Sheppard walked to her office, sat in the winged back chair behind her desk, and waited for her long awaited peace.

Jermaine Arket, in town on business, stopped by the showroom to look at a Chippendale piece he was told she had on the floor. He found Christina in her chair. The doctor at the ER said another hour and she would have been dead. She ended up at a swank country psychiatric hospital in Connecticut for three weeks, and Arket visited Sheppard every other day. The scene in the chair was the first time they'd met. Arket looked to buy an antique high back dresser, and Sheppard looked to take an eternal rest. Arket had saved her life, yet more often than not she wished he hadn't entered the showroom that day, because she still hadn't found any peace.

Sheppard arose from the photo shoot of her suicidal nightmare and returned her eyes to his.

"I'll take the chance." She said.

"Alright," Hancock said, "but if I'm going to stay, with the risk of being found, I'm going to enjoy it with a bottle of Chianti."

He pushed out his chair and went inside, and as he did, Sheppard stood and walked over to the end of the portico and leaned on the rail and stared past the sand to the rippling water. She hadn't thought about that day in her office, at least not with such detailed imagery, and it made her feel almost like vomiting.

"Christina?"

She turned to see Hancock placing a bottle on the café table while balancing two wine glasses between his fingers.

"Would you care for a glass of wine?" He asked.

She moved slowly toward the table. Hancock filled her glass. He poured his glass and sat down. Sheppard looked across the table.

"Well," she said, "how do you know what you know?"

CHAPTER 34

Just sixteen miles southwest of Rome, at the Leonardo Da Vinci airport, the Gulfstream's landing gear lifted off the tarmac at exactly 9:03am. Lt. Pisano confirmed Brosconni had arrived in the helicopter, walked into the hanger, and the G550 taxied to the runway and awaited take off. Pisano now stood behind an air traffic controller and watched the screen as the jet turned west, rose to forty two thousand feet, and headed over the Atlantic toward the US. He radioed General Capalli and acknowledged the surveillance on this end was complete.

It was now up to Capt. Penso, in New York, to pick up the tail on the other end. At mach .85 the Gulfstream's cruise time was under nine hours. That would put Brosconni on the ground around 11:30 am New York time, and Commissioner Kelly had given his word the NYPD would cooperate fully with Capt. Penso's investigation. All they need now do is wait.

Over on 357 west 35th street, at the midtown south precinct, Capt. Tinelli, Detective Mike Stanno, and his partner, Steve Deluchi—considered one of the best interrogators south of Central Park—had asked Collet to come in voluntarily for a third round of routine questions. He did, but not alone. Strolling along side the Grand Master was brother mason Briggs Barket, of Barket, Thomson, and Tulane. The firm's reputation as one of the top litigators in Manhattan, and perhaps the eastern United States, was not an unknown fact to Stanno and Deluchi. They lost a big one because of Barket, and they weren't happy to see him walk through the door.

Back in two thousand and three, the two detectives had finally made an arrest on the one year investigation of the very visible Dr Trent McCord case. Dr. McCord was curator at the Metropolitan Museum on 5th Ave. and 82nd Street, and lectured as a guest professor once a year on his doctoral specialty, Egyptian design: the royal tombs and their intrinsic secrets. The firm of Barket, Thomson, and Tulane defended Dr. McCord on first degree murder in the homicide of New York University Senior, Catherine Duquet. Barket led the defense and dismantled Stanno and Deluchi's investigation piece by piece. In the end, McCord was acquitted and Stanno and Deluchi hoped they'd seen the last of Barket, but that proved wrong. Barket marched through the security door with his client, Arthur Collet, and totted an arrogant half smile which brought the foul smell of the Dr. McCord trial back to life, again.

Deluchi opened the door to the interrogation room and Stanno followed them in.

"What is the purpose of this," Barket asked.

"Please, have a seat, we'd just like to ask your client a few questions." Deluchi said.

"Questions you asked in the previous two sessions, detective. Let's get to the point. You've brought in Mr. Collet because some antique dealer called my client and asked if he was interested in purchasing a desk?"

Capt. Penso stood behind the glass in the observation room listening to the speaker which hung on the wall. His hand was on his forehead; he knew where this was headed already.

"That dealer was murdered, Mr. Barket, we're questioning anyone who had contact with Mr. Miller. That's standard procedure." Deluchi said.

"Three times, detective; is my client a suspect?"

"We're still unclear why your client has built a network of dealers throughout Europe with the intention of locating a Carlton House Desk crafted between 1785 and 1786, and yet, has not purchased one single piece of furniture from any dealers we've contacted overseas. Why he has a showroom which has not sold, according to his tax returns, one item in five years. And why, if Mr. Collet has gone to such lengths to locate this specific desk, he did not travel to Europe and examine or purchase Washington's desk? Perhaps he could clear that up!" Stanno said.

Barket held his hand up to Collet.

"Is Mr. Collet a suspect, Detective?"

Deluchi looked to Stanno and gave the answer without turning back.

"Not as of yet."

"My client has nothing more to say. He has voluntarily answered your questions twice in the past. I fear you're throwing darts with a blindfold, detectives, and it's approaching the threshold of harassment."

Deluchi seemed unimpressed by Barket's advance. He continued.

"What are your duties as Grand Master of the lodge on 23rd street, Mr. Collet?"

"Don't answer that Arthur!"

"Is it true, Mr. Collet, Robert Livingston, as first Grand Master of your lodge, swore in President Washington?"

Again Barket raised his hand to Collet.

"That's common knowledge, detective, what could that possibly have to do with a homicide and a stolen desk?"

Deluchi forged ahead.

"Mr. Collet, what exactly is your interest in Washington's desk, and why have you searched for years to locate the piece?"

"Detective!"

"It seems, Arthur, your obsession with obtaining this particular desk is as mysterious as the Masonic Lodge you head. Why is your craft, that's what you call it, craft, isn't it, why is it cloaked behind a wall of secret oaths, symbols, and puzzling names?"

Stanno chimed in, "like Knight of the Brazen Serpent and Prince of Mercy? There are thirty three, am I correct?"

"I believe we've heard enough, detectives, you're grasping at straws when you should be solving a crime." Barket said.

"Am I," Stanno said. "What if you had some dark secret you were trying to protect—something inside that desk. I understand from the news reports that desk survived in an attic for over two centuries, and then, suddenly appeared. The dealer who found it ends up with a forty five through his forehead, a second dealer ends up with an identical manhole above his eyes, and then the desk disappears. What if I said to you, Mr. Collet, my instincts are lit up like a Christmas tree, and you're supplying the power."

Collet put his hand up this time and backed off Barket. He looked to Stanno from across the table and responded.

"Then your instincts would be misguided, detective, and your investigation would be generously off course."

Tinelli walked out of the observation room and over to the coffee station. He had seen enough. Tinelli, Stanno, and Deluchi had nothing on Collet, and Barket sensed it the moment he walked into the precinct. Tinelli acknowledged that as he poured the mud into a Styrofoam cup and dropped two big hunks of white powder into the abyss. As he moved in the direction of the observation door, stirring his mixture with a stick, he dreaded the idea of giving his report to General Capalli, and he was already braced for his response.

207

The observation door opened to the sound of Stanno's voice crackling through the wall speaker as he attempted a comeback to the offensive.

"If Mr. Collet has nothing to hide, counselor, why not erase all doubt: have your client agree to a polygraph test."

"Not buying or selling furniture, detective, is not a crime, it is a personal choice. So, too, is subjecting my client to an unwarranted test, of which, I will have no part. I assume my client is free to go?"

Meanwhile, eighteen miles from the midtown precinct, on the other side of the East River and FDR, Capt. Penso stood behind an air traffic controller listening as Brosconni's pilot received clearance to land. Two plain clothes cops, in an unmarked Ford Explorer, waited for Penso's instructions by the exit to the Airport. Two additional cops with an unmarked car waited outside the International arrivals building. As soon as Brosconni checked through customs, he would be tailed by a detective waiting inside. And Capt. Penso had checked the private air services to see if Brosconni had charter one. He had not.

The Gulfstream approached runway H3 and smoked the tarmac at exactly 11:22 am New York time. Its engines roared, and the reversal slowed its speed on the runway to a lazy glide as Penso stared into the Swarovski high powered binoculars through the tall reinforced glass window of the control tower. He spoke into the mike attached to his epaulet and then returned his concentration to the G550 as it turned off H3 and taxied toward international arrivals. It moved toward the smaller terminal which accommodated the rich and the powerful as they jumped continent to continent in their expensive private jets. Common folk disembark with the other two hundred passengers and headed to the customs corral for inspection, not the ten digit bank account types; they were greeted pleasantly and privately with their own border patrol in a well kept exclusive building. And as Brosconni's Gulfstream turned to the directions of the ground personal's lights, the wheels came to a halt, and the roar of the engines reduced to the hissing of air, as the turbine's slowly stopped.

CHAPTER 35

Disguised as security, the detective inside the small arrival terminal waited as he spoke into the sleeve of his blue blazer. He studied the Gulfstream parked on the tarmac as he moved from the window to the door.

"It's been five minutes and nothing has changed. The jet's door is still locked." He communicated to Penso.

"Patience," Penso said in a thick Italian accent, "he'll come out!"

The detective moved toward customs as he summoned the unmarked car out front.

"Has any transportation arrived yet?"

"Negative, we're the only car out here."

He peered back out the window—nothing—the door to the jet was still closed."

"Is there any sign of transportation arriving by air?" He asked Penso still in the control tower observing with the high powered binoculars.

"Negative." Penso responded.

"What's he up to?" The detective asked.

"We'll know soon enough." Penso said.

Ten minutes had passed, and the disguised security guard grew restless. He strolled over to the cooler and poured a paper cup of water, gulped it down, crushed the cup, and tossed it in the metal can sitting to the right. He adjusted the knot on his tie as the speaker in his ear barked Penso's broken English.

"Anything?"

"Nothing, what should I do?"

Penso raised the glasses from his chest and began a meticulous sweep of the outside of the terminal building. He studied the Gulfstream, scanned around to the left side of the small arrivals building to the unmarked car, the front parking lot, then back around the other side of the building. He put the glasses back on his chest and did a visual sweep of the airport. His right hand moved up to his face, and he rubbed his lips with his first two fingers and shook his head.

"I don't like it." He said into the mike on his epaulet. "Has there been any communication with the cockpit?"

"None."

The disguised security guard looked at his watch—11:45.

"It's been twenty minutes since he landed." He said. "Wait, the door is opening. The pilot and co-pilot have stepped out of the plane."

"What about Brosconni?" Penso asked.

"Just the two pilots. One closed and locked the Gulfstream door and now they're approaching the terminal."

"Shit!"

"What's that Capt. Penso?"

"Nothing, the door's shut and there's no sign of Brosconni?"

"That's correct." He said as he watched the pilots approach. "What do you want me to do?"

"Act like a security guard and question the pilots, find out who's on board!"

"Will do."

The pilots entered the building rolling their bags behind them. The disguised guard pulled them aside and flashed his badge. Penso waited in the tower. He walked over to the coffee station and poured the black slop into the paper cup and diluted the mud with a little container of fake cream and then strolled nervously back to the control tower window. Penso took a slug of the hours old coffee gazing over the top of the cup at the Gulfstream parked on the tarmac. Three men approached the G550—two in pilot's uniforms and the one disguised security guard. Penso placed the cup on the window sill and brought the binoculars up to his eyes. The detective boarded the plane, the pilots waited outside. A few minutes later, the detective maneuvered the steps, landed on the tarmac, and then walked away from the plane as the pilots closed it up. Penso dropped the glasses to his chest.

"Capt. Penso."

"Yes detective."

"Brosconni is not on board."

"Say that again."

"He's not on the plane, he didn't make the flight. The pilots said he arrived at the hanger at Da Vinci airport and instructed them to follow the flight plan, spend the night in New York, and file a flight plan the next morning for the return trip to Rome. They said they left Brosconni in the hanger."

Thirty minutes after his Gulfstream departed the Leonardo Da Vinci Airport, a Cadillac Escalade approached the hanger, pulled inside, and stopped. A driver dressed in a black suit, white shirt, black tie and hat stepped out and opened the rear door. Brosconni slid into the back, and the driver closed the door. The black polished Escalade sped out of the hanger and onto the inner airport road and made a fifty mile an hour sweep of the airport. At the other end of the runways, it stopped at a small but distinguished terminal with the name Private Jet in blue letters on the front door. The driver slipped out, opened the back door, and Brosconni walked into the building, through the lobby, out the back door to the tarmac, and boarded a G550 chartered Gulfstream with the pilots waiting in the cockpit already having done their pre-flight check. The Jets door was closed and locked.

At 9:56 am Rome time the Gulfstream lifted off, rose to twelve thousand feet, and made its turn eastward toward France. As the G550 began its climb to forty two thousand feet, Brosconni sat on the soft leather couch and looked to his watch—9:59. His head fell back, and he calculated his lead time: *eight hours before it lands in New York, half hour before they discover the plane's empty, two hours thirty minute flight time—perfect.* His mathematics deducted when his chartered jet landed he had a six hour head start. Brosconni laid his finger around his mouth, which had a cocked grin on its lips, and closed his eyes. Within two minutes, he was asleep.

"Detective, run the pilots through customs and bring them to the precinct—use the unmarked car out front. Pick me up at the tower."

"Right."

Penso looked at his watch, 11:56. Brosconni's had almost ten hours—*shit!*

It was six in the morning back in Rome, but he had to make the call. Penso slipped out his phone and looked at the numbers. He punched in The General's cell phone and braced his hand on the wall. It rang three times and Capalli picked up.

"General, Capt. Penso.............yes I know it's six in the morning there, but I'm afraid I have bad news, Brosconni wasn't on the plane.................I said, he stayed in the hanger in Rome.................I have no idea, General......what's that.....he could be anywhere..........................I haven't spoken with Capt. Tinelli yet.................yes I'll call as soon as I get off the phone..........................Yes and I'll wake up Lt. Pisano and tell him to call you.........I'll get the next flight out................................Yes, sir, Capt. Tinelli is to stay in New York and work on Collet, I understand General...........................I know this is unfortunate, General, I have no idea how Lt. Pisano could have missed.....................Yes, General,................ yes, General, goodbye—*shit!*"

CHAPTER 36

He had to force himself to talk, to divulge the information he was about discuss. It had been guarded for so many years it felt unnatural, and he sensed a hint of betrayal in his heart. Even though there was a purpose behind the disclosure, and what mattered was its means to its end, it snapped every fiber of the interwoven cloak he had used to protect his secret. And as he peered across the table, Sheppard prodded him again.

"Well?" Sheppard said.

He rose from his seat, and with his wine in his hand, he shuffled over to the wrought iron railing. Hancock leaned against the rail about a foot from where Sheppard sat and took a deep breath, exhaled, and spoke.

"What do you know of the internal structure which comprises the hierarchy of the Masonic Lodge?" He asked.

Sheppard responded shaking her head. "Nothing."

Hancock searched the winding road, the beach, the water, the secluded restaurant. It was an instinctual response to him now.

"You make me nervous," Sheppard said, "sit down."

He strolled back to his chair and fell into the seat. He leaned forward with his arms on the table.

"There are thirty three degrees to the Masonic craft; each degree imparts certain lessons from which you are conferred to the next level. The first seventeen are considered, by those who reach the final sixteen, as the general population. They are granted no access to the centuries old secrets which bond and seal the craft. Very few rise to the eighteenth degree. Those that do are the elite, the protectors of the beliefs and structures upon which the Masonic craft was constructed.

Think of it like the stratum of governments: first the common folk who know only what information they are given to know, and they are content because they believe they know all. The next level is the mayors, the governors, and the necessary infrastructure which guide the states. Each level believing they are privy to the internal mechanisms which run the communal machine. But they are not. Only those at the top understand the true foundations and beliefs from which this complex organization was built. And they alone pass the torch, to only those who are honored with the highest degrees of the Masonic craft."

Hancock paused and gulped a good slug of his wine. He looked up and met Christina's eyes and held her stare in his visual grip, and without looking away, he continued.

"The Masonic lodges have the same hierarchy of structure as the craft's degrees. The Grand Lodge of New York, on 23rd Street, is the center of the Masonic universe. It is the hub from which all lodges respond and are given permission to practice the craft and from where the most sacred truths are housed. Given permission to establish in 1782 from the center seat of Masonic power, The Premier Grand Lodge of England, it now has jurisdiction over more the sixty thousand Freemasons organized in more than eight hundred separate lodges. It is considered the largest and oldest in the states."

Sheppard looked puzzled.

"I don't need a dissertation on freemasonry, Hancock; just tell me how you know what you know."

"Giving you a name, Christina, would be meaningless without the understanding of the sophisticated power structure behind it. Ex-presidents, kings, prominent evangelists and clergy, high ranking government officials, some of the wealthiest individuals in the country have filled these ranks of sixteen degrees over the centuries. Each degree has a specific purpose, and the initiation ceremony to each level is a complex series of centuries old rituals filled with symbolism, rites, and incarnations. And, its enigmatic rituals are firmly entrenched throughout the history of this country. Did you know every prominent building in Washington,

The Capital, The White House, The Smithsonian just to name a few, had a Masonic ceremony where the first stone—the corner stone—was put in place by a Grand Master."

"Alright, Hancock, get to the point." She demanded, disturbed by the direction of the conversation.

Sheppard had little tolerance for anything on the dark side of creepy. The talk of rituals and incantations raised feelings and emotions which had haunted her since the Lear Jet crashed in the wet marsh of the Meadowlands. Her parents and Husband had purchased a Louis XV purple wood desk in California from the estate of famed actor Eric McAlister. His life, like that of the French Count who originally owned the desk, ended by his own hand, both on Christmas Eve, both had written their suicide notes on the purple wood top of the desk. After McAlister's tragic passing, particularly on the same day as the count, the curse of the Louis XV desk circulated throughout the Antique world. And when The Louis XV desk accompanied Sheppard's parents and husband on the doomed flight to New Jersey, its reputation seemed justified, and Christina was swept away in the reported speculation of the curse. Sheppard, like most left behind, tried to make sense out of an event that made no sense, and the dark power of the Louis XV desk became the perfect explanation. And now, Hancock's story of the Masonic craft had driven her emotions back into that darkness.

"I'm sorry," Hancock said, "did I upset you?"
"It's not your fault."

"You asked.'

"I did."

"Would you like me to stop?"

"No, I'll be fine," she said, getting a grip on her emotions, "please continue."

By now Hancock had forgotten about his surroundings. The Alcohol had loosened his tongue and made him less jittery or at least made him forget to look around. He continued where he left off.

"The thirty third degree is an honorary position: it is not earned, it is appointed. Thus the thirty second is the highest conferred degree. It is called, The Sublime Prince of the Royal Secret. Its function is exactly that. All knowledge of the most sacred rites, Masonic influence, and historical fact are passed generation to generation through the thirty second degree, and yes, Christina, Washington's desk and the sealed correspondence are included in that. The significance of that sealed correspondence, and the damage it could unleash to past and present day government, had been kept a secret for two hundred and twenty four years, kept locked behind the oath of The Sublime Prince of the Royal Secret.

Six degrees down, in the hierarchy of the craft, is the Prince of Mercy, mercy being an oxymoron. At the command of the Sublime Prince, and sworn to protect its secrets, The Prince of Mercy's role is to extinguish threats to those coveted truths by any means necessary--hence the two dealers who fell upon an unfortunate antique.

Just above the twenty seventh degree is the Knight Commander of the Temple. His role is to oversee The Prince of Mercy, and to coordinate, issue, and arrange any and all strategies, finances, and transportation and accommodations the Prince will need to carry out his mission.

The Knight Commander of the Temple is a man I have known since birth. We went to college together, graduate school together, and he introduced me to my wife. He came to me a while back wishing to leave the craft, but he knew too much. He believed if the truth was told, via historical nonfiction written by me, the information would be so visible, he and his family would be safe. Unfortunately, prior to the completion of my work, he died of a heart attack. If the book was published today, without his word to back it up, it would simply be considered a speculative conspiratorial fiction without basis or fact."

CHAPTER 37

Brosconni looked at his watch, 12:10 pm. He unbuckled the leather strap, lifted the Cartier up toward his eyes, reset the time to 11:10 am, and then refastened the watch to his wrist. By the passing landscape, Brosconni calculated the G550 had descended to twelve thousand feet and was making its approach to the airport. His head turned up at the sound of a voice coming over the fuselage speaker.

"Senior Brosconni, this is Captain Stephen Mitchell. We are making our final approach and have been given clearance to land. We should be on the ground in approximately six minutes. The Hummer you requested will be waiting for you at the international arrivals building. Our liaison on the ground, Ms. Thomson, will lead you through customs and escort you to the vehicle. I hope you had a pleasant flight and thank you for choosing Private Jet."

He looked to his watch again, 11:13.

As the Gulfstream hit six thousand feet, Brosconni pulled his Smartphone from the side pocket of his blue Armani blazer. He slid his finger on the text message box and opened up the latest communication from Mr. X. His eyes scrolled across the words.

*Remember, Brosconni, you have only two strikes left, rehearsal is now over. Here are your instructions: Fly to City Airport in London and rent a car. Leave the airport on A101. At route A102 turn on the entrance ramp and head south. Continue until you receive your next set of instructions.

He slid the Smartphone into his pocket as the landing gear smoked the runway. His watch said 11:18. His Gulfstream was somewhere over the Atlantic five and a half hours from New York. And as the Carabinieri waited for the empty 550 to hit the tarmac at JFK, Brosconni would be on his way to recovering his prized Hepplewhite.

His men on the ground in London, the covert ops guys, had already put a U2 satellite tracer on the inside of the Hummer underneath the steering wheel and were waiting in two SUV's at a rest stop off A102. The instructions from Brosconni were clear, "stay well behind and out of sight until I signal I have reached the destination chosen by Mr. X. I will put the tracer in my pocket before I leave the truck. When I make visual contact with the desk, I will shut off the tracking device and then turn it back on which will signal for you to move in."

The Gulfstream came to a halt in front of the terminal, and Brosconni broke his stare from the brown Berber carpet at the sound of the fuselage door clicking and opening. A woman appeared at the steps and introduced herself as Ms. Thomson. Brosconni disembarked the Gulfstream, went into the terminal, politely had his passport stamped by a customs agent, and received the keys to the Hummer as Thomson opened the driver side door.

Brosconni looked seriously misplaced behind the wheel of the Hummer. Not just his small stature against a reinforced tank of a truck, but as Enrico Brosconni, shipping tycoon, alone in a vehicle about to drive away. He couldn't remember the last time he had navigated a car on his own, and he scanned the interior and looked to install the ignition key. It seemed more like the cockpit of his Gulfstream, than a means of transportation for the open road. Even the shift lever looked like a throttle. He turned the key, fired up the Hummer, and stepped on the gas and ran up the curb onto the sidewalk. A uniformed cop turned and watched as Brosconni tried to gain control the massive truck, finally bouncing off the embankment used to keep car bombers away at the end of the terminal. Brosconni pushed down on the gas and almost lost control again as the tank headed for A101.

As he connected to 201, a second set of instructions pinged his Smartphone. Brosconni pulled over. He opened up the text and read the message.

*Turn east on 205. Follow the signs for M3 toward Sunbury. You will receive further instruction then.

Brosconni followed 201 and turned onto 205 which skirted the city of London heading east.

Instinctually, he started to steer to the right side of the road and was immediately met by flashing headlights. He swerved back to the left, not accustomed to England's traffic flow, and two vehicles, which he cut off, had to slam on their brakes.

The driver's seat was pulled three quarters of the way forward and raised the same height as he drove the Hummer at half the speed limit listed on the signs. A line of cars honked behind him. Like everything else Brosconni did, he continued oblivious to everything around him, and when he violated a stop sign, he caused another driver to spin out.

Brosconni slowed as he read the street sign which pointed the way to Sunbury. He became confused. The sign said take A316 to Sunbury, he was told M3. He almost came to a complete stop. The horns screeched a chorus of angry discontent, but Brosconni was unimpressed by the intolerant rage of those driving behind him. He sat behind the wheel of the large black tank and made a quick turn onto A316. Again his cell phone indicated a message. He pulled over and brought up the text.

*At the Hospital Bridge roundabout, circle onto Hospital Bridge Road going north. Continue to Twickenham Cemetery and take the first entrance and drive to the first roundabout. Go halfway around, pass the parked vehicle, and stop four feet from the car trunk to trunk. Get out, stand in back of your vehicle, and wait for instructions.

Brosconni drove down 316 and felt the pulse in his neck start to pound. He knew his covert ops guys were probably ten to twelve minutes behind him. He wouldn't signal them unless he made visual contact with the desk. *Whoever this son of a bitch was,* Brosconni thought as he passed the endless neighborhoods of row housing, *he'll regret he ever heard the name Enrico Brosconni.* And it didn't matter if Mr. X chose a public place to meet, not with the crew Brosconni had in place.

As he passed the Twickenham Rugby stadium on his right, his grip on the steering wheel tightened. In his head, Brosconni planned his second act of retribution—Alberto Capalli. He would castrate The General, like Mussolini, in front of the entire Italian peninsula, and he would separate himself from the reported crime. Although the ship captain who set up the Monaco trip was under Brosconni's direct orders, no one could ever prove or connect Brosconni to the bribe. And Brosconni had a plan: first, he would fire the Captain, after he just learned, he'd say, that some years before he bribed Capalli for his own personal gains. Then he'd make public the video of a desperate Capalli reaching out his hand as the captain made it clear that the cash was payment to overlook the stolen artifacts on the ship. And as Colonel Capalli agreed to the terms, his present fate would then be sealed.

Brosconni slowed and focused on the roundabout just up ahead. The drivers behind him had lost their aggression, and no longer honked as he crawled around the circle. They realized it would do no good. Brosconni turned left onto Hospital Bridge Road. About sixty one meters ahead was the main entrance to Twickenham Cemetery, and he slowed some more. Even though it was futile, the car behind him laid on the horn and didn't let up. Brosconni turned into the Twickenham cemetery, and the Hummer eased slowly ahead.

He passed by the building which serviced the grounds and drove up ahead to the roundabout mentioned in the text. The Hummer stayed to the left and crawled around the circle. With three quarters of the loop behind him, he spotted a green Ford Taurus parked underneath two towering English Elm trees. He passed the Taurus and then stopped the black tank four to five feet from its trunk as instructed. Brosconni opened the driver side door, reached under the steering column and detached the U2 tracer, placed it in his side coat pocket, climbed out onto the running board, stepped down to the ground and walked around to the back and waited. He scanned the landscape, the tombstones, and the mausoleums and waited some more—nothing. Then after a minute or two the silence was broken by the eerie ping of his Microsoft Smartphone. Brosconni's eyes rolled down to the side pocket of his blue Armani blazer and froze.

CHAPTER 38

Capalli paced the floor with his hands clutched like a vice behind his back. Irate over Lt. Pisano's incompetence and Brosconni's scheme to avoid surveillance, the General felt squeezed by the massive loss of time. He stopped at the window, released his hands, and raised his watch toward his face, 8:30 am Rome time. *Six hours,* he thought, as he waited for Lt. Pisano to arrive, *we wasted six God Damn hours!*

He turned and dropped into his high back leather chair and stared at the screen of his computer. His left hand was clasped to his forehead as he read Capt. Tinelli's documentation of the interrogation with Collet. He scrolled through the notes using the wheel on the mouse, and his eyes scanned Tinelli's report. As he reduced the text and swiveled his chair around to the window, Capalli now realized that the investigation had not just stalled but fallen off a cliff. And time was ticking toward the end of his career which made the knot is his stomach even worse.

His head went back against the chair, and he recalled the conversation with his wife the night before. He had told her everything. Of course she knew about the gambling trips to Monaco, the debt he incurred, and his month long spiral into the abyss, but she hadn't known of the money he took from Brosconni nor the unforgiveable act of allowing illegal artifacts onto the Italian peninsula. Carlota, a name given to his wife at birth meaning small, and small she was, five foot two, broke down when Alberto disclosed the seriousness of his violations and the possible punishment for his crimes. The press was brutal when it came to Italian leadership's abuse of governmental powers, particularly when it involved wealthy business men. There would be a public outcry for an immediate indictment and full prosecution of his crime.

She was frightened by both the prospect of humiliation and the possibility of reprisal. If Brosconni had the proof Capalli feared, her husband would be convicted and incarcerated at a maximum security prison. That, for a member of law enforcement, never mind the general at the top of Carabinieri, would be considered an instant death sentence. Carlota had choked that out as she gasped in her tears, and Alberto, who was well aware of the facts, tried to consul her. But in his gut he knew, he'd be lucky to live out the year.

Capalli lifted his head and swiveled his chair back around to his desk. He cleared his mind and tried to refocus on the missing Brosconni, the stolen Hepplewhite, and the unsolved homicides. He needed a break in the case, some unexpected lead to pop up and as he put his hand to his forehead and massaged his brows, Caprina's voice chirped in.

"General?"

Without moving his head, his eyes turned to the intercom.

"Yes?"

"General Lt. Pisano's here."

"Send him in Caprina!"

Capalli's head swiveled toward the door at the sound of a knock.

"Enter," he said.

Pisano stood at attention, saluted, and waited on Capalli. The General paused a moment as Pisano felt beads of sweat forming above his top lip. Then, in a commander's voice, he ordered the Lieutenant to sit down.

The Lieutenant responded and gave a silent sigh. "Yes sir."

Lt. Pisano walked around one of the winged back chairs and sat down. He waited for The General to unleash his hell. Capalli faced the window, and Pisano stared at the back of his leather chair. There was a long silence. The Lieutenant had prepared an explanation for the events at the airport, but that all seemed useless to him now. His shined black tie boots moved in at the toes, and his heels pivoted on the floor. The Lieutenant's cap lay on his lap, and his hands grasped the arm rests at the end of the cloth. He looked up at the sound of Capalli's voice.

"Lieutenant," The General said, "the loss of time is inexcusable."

"Yes sir."

"I expect you've learned from your mistake, Lieutenant, if not, your career with Carabinieri Art Squad is over."

"Yes General."

Capalli's chair swiveled back around to the desk. He stared at Pisano.

"What have you found out, Lieutenant?"

Pisano cleared his throat.

"General, Brosconni charted a Gulfstream 550 from a company called Private Jet at the Da Vinci Airport."

"And the flight plan?"

"London."

Capalli turned slightly in his chair, still in view of Pisano, and put his finger to his lips.

"London?"

"Yes sir. Detective Mitchell, of Scotland Yard, confirms he passed through customs at 11:37 London time. Mitchell says he rented a Hummer and left the airport alone. A liaison of Private Jet, Ms. Thomson, escorted him to the vehicle and was the last to see Brosconni before he drove off in the Hummer."

"And, of course, this Ms. Thomson has no idea where he was headed or in what direction?"

"No sir."

Capalli's head was slightly raised and he stared at Pisano from the corners of his eyes. The silence cut through the Lieutenant's gut like the slash of a razor, and he wanted to slither down and out of the chair. Finally, The General spoke.

"Continue, Lieutenant."

"Detective Mitchell has put the make, model, and license plate number over the wires. If they spot him, Mitchell will be the first to know."

"And what about the time, Lieutenant?"

"General, we've made up some of the gap; we're about two and a half hours behind him."

Capalli locked onto Pisano's brown eyes.

"Two and half hours, Lieutenant, is enough time to cover most of England in any direction."

"Yes sir."

"A Hummer shouldn't be very hard to find in England, Lt. Pisano; you've got the license plate—find him!"

"Yes sir."

The General pushed his chair back and stood up. He took two steps and faced the window and looked down to the Piazza. It was packed with Italians shuffling through the open square on their way to work. It was like a breath of fresh air for Capalli, that's why he liked the view so much. It cleared his head and helped him think straight. None of his staff knew what it meant when he made his frequent trips to the window; but they all knew to keep their mouths shut.

The General rolled his eyes to the church across the piazza.

"What about Capt. Penso?" Capalli asked still facing the glass.

Pisano looked at his watch.

"Sir, Capt. Penso, with the time change, lands 8:00 pm Rome time."

"Find Brosconni," Capalli said as he turned to Pisano, "you lost him, you find him, now, get out!"

CHAPTER 39

Two Range Rovers approached Twickenham Cemetery from opposite ends. One entered from the north side, one from the south. Two way radios buzzed back and forth as the black Range Rovers, with midnight black windows, eased their way toward the roundabout. The Range Rover which entered from the south side reached the first circle and proceeded to the right even though traffic flowed to the left. The SUV from the north completed the second roundabout and reached the road which separated the two circles. Within seconds, the message blurted out of the speaker of the radios inside the trucks—move in! The Rovers converged on the Hummer parked under the English Elm trees, one in front of the Hummer, one to the rear. They both skidded to a stop.

The doors flew open, and three men from each vehicle stormed out and took positions around the truck. Dressed in fatigues, they stood with their Glocks cocked, raised in the air, aimed through the windows in all directions. One man signaled with his right hand and four of the six men slid to a door and braced their hand just under the handle. The other two men each took a new position—one in the front, one in the rear. Again a hand signal, and the doors flew open and the Glocks were ready to fire. The man at the rear reached for the latch and opened the back hatch. The man in the front scanned the cemetery with his gun still trained on the Hummer's windshield. The entire operation took less than forty five seconds, and the Range Rovers screeched off in opposite directions and barreled onto Hospital Bridge Road.

Forty five minutes later, three vehicles approached the Twickenham Cemetery. One Vauxhal Vectra headed to the south entrance, one to the center, one to the north. The sirens were blaring typical English ee ah ee ah as they flew past the gates of the cemetery. They came to a screeching halt at the Hummer, parked like an awaiting limousine ready to accept its fare. All four doors and the back hatch were opened as the Hummer sat deserted underneath the shade of the Elm trees. With two Vectra's parked in the front and one in the rear, blocking in the black SUV, two officers jumped out from each car. Within seconds the Hummer was surrounded, and one of the officers was talking into the collar of his lapel.

"Put me through to Inspector Mitchell." He said.

The officers stepped back and away from the Hummer careful not to contaminate the scene. In a six foot circle of the SUV, two men arched their necks to look inside. Two other officers had stepped back to their Vectra's and were taking notes on a computer. The sixth man, with the radio, listened as Inspector Mitchell identified himself. The officer on the scene responded.

"Inspector, we found Brosconni's vehicle abandoned in Twickenham Cemetery. All the doors and back hatch were opened and the keys are still in the ignition……..Yes, inspector, the plate matches."

As the officer spoke, two of the men around the Hummer started to span out and search the grounds. A grounds keeper had called in the report, when he found the vehicle empty. He had come in late from a doctor's appointment and had found the Hummer as it now stood. One of the officers taking notes started his Vectra and drove down to the service shed to question the grounds keeper about what he'd seen, but he had not observed any activity. By the time he arrived, whatever happened was over.

"Yes inspector, I'll secure the scene until the forensics unit arrives…….No, there is no sign of Brosconni, but we're searching the grounds as we speak….over!"

When forensics arrived twenty minutes later, the officers had found no sign of Brosconni. A team of four CSI experts jumped out of a van and dusted the Hummer for prints. They checked the surrounding area for footprints but found nothing of value on the asphalt or the grass. There were no signs of a struggle, no traces of blood, or evidence Brosconni resisted. And the fact that the Hummer was left deserted, with all of its exits opened, and the key still inserted inside, indicated to the commander the shipping tycoon was abducted by surprise. But what seemed at odds with the commander's theory, and perplexed Mitchell when he arrived, was what they found in the back of the Hummer in a strewn out chaotic mess—a pile of Brosconni's disheveled clothes.

CHAPTER 40

Christina Sheppard stared at the label on the Chianti bottle as Hancock talked. The sounds were audible to her, but the content was not. Behind a subtle buzz, she was zoned into the quarter of a bottle of red liquid remaining behind the glass. After a couple of glasses of the wine, her feelings had begun to surface, and she despised the sensation of losing her grip. And Hancock, who looked similar too, and had mannerisms much like that of her deceased husband, Ray, taunted her eidetic recall to look back and reminisce. She rubbed her eyes and tried to focus.

"Christina, did you hear what I said?"

"No, sorry."

"Are you alright? You look distraught."

"I'm fine."

"Are you sure?"

"Yes, I'm fine." She said with a deep breath and turned toward the beach with the colorful boats. "I need to go, Hancock."

"Alright, I'll call you in a day or two and tell you where we'll meet."

"No, Hancock, I mean, I'm going back to New York."

Christina still faced the water, unaware of Hancock's reaction. Not that she cared. She needed the safety of her showroom and the control she felt in filling her life with her work. She'd been in Italy too long. Being idle produced too much time to think. And the Italian landscape had tugged at her concrete encased romantic side which hadn't made a peep in six years. Hard to believe, but Christina Sheppard, when she met her husband Ray, yearned for the affections of the heart. She loved candle light dinners, lying by the fireplace, breakfast in bed on Sunday mornings with the warmth of her husband's naked body next to hers. But when the plane went down, the lights went out, and she pulled the breaker just to be sure. And right now, she felt scared to death of letting her emotions back in.

Hancock took a slug of the wine. He looked at the back of her head, the blonde hair flowing down to her blouse and as he spoke, the shortened breath in his words gave his desperation away.

"Christina, you can't, I need your help; I can't get to the desk without you!"

"What makes you think they'll find the desk, Hancock? It's been over a week and a half since I laid eyes on the piece." She turned and looked into his eyes. "I'm going home to Manhattan and getting back to my work."

Hancock jumped up from his chair and scooted over to the rail. He grabbed the wrought iron with both hands and leaned toward the water as if looking for the right thing to say. He turned.

"Christina, listen, this is not just about me, my wife, my God, if something happened to my wife, I couldn't bear it. I have to get to that sealed correspondence, Christina, don't you understand."

Her stare went blank. Christina's blue eyes went watery, and she sat in her chair as if frozen by Hancock's words. Hancock watched as she retreated deeper into herself, and he could feel her presence as it drifted away—like an apparition fading into the darkness of the night. He had to bring her back. He wasn't going to tell this part of his story, but he had no choice. Sheppard had already boarded the British Airways 747 and was somewhere over the Atlantic headed for JFK. He read it in her eyes, and he felt it in her heart. And he couldn't afford to lose her now.

"Christina, there's something I need to tell you, and I hope it will change your mind."

Sheppard looked up from her haze, and Hancock spotted the life seep back into the blue of her eyes.

"I'm dying, Christina, I have maybe six months to live. I've spent most of my life savings researching and writing this novel. What I didn't spend, I lost in the market crash of 08. My wife doesn't know about our finances, only about my health. I need this book, Christina. I need it for my wife: it's a life insurance policy for her after I'm gone. Without it, she's broke."

Christina looked into Randolph's eyes. The brown pupils had glazed over. He looked away.

They jumped at the ring of Sheppard's cell phone coming from the side pocket of her blazer. Hancock looked back.

"Excuse me," he said, "I'll be a minute." He needed to collect himself.

Hancock stood up, and walked into the restaurant, and entered the bi-gender bathroom. Sheppard pulled out her phone and looked at the caller ID—unknown. She answered the call.

Hancock stood at the water closet relieving himself as his head went back, and he thought about what he had just done. There was too much at stake to not use the story to persuade Sheppard to stay on the Italian peninsula. He had come too far, and he was too close to not pull out all the stops. He stared at the blue and green hand painted fish on the bathroom ceiling, and he knew he had done the right thing. He saw it in her eyes before the phone rang. Hancock gazed down as the stream slowed to a drizzle and decided to let his instincts lead the way. But he had to be careful. Her infallible memory was a danger, and it could definitely trip him up.

He stood at the mirror for a couple of minutes and attempted to relax. He splashed some water on his face, dried off with a paper towel, crumbled it up and tossed it in the wicker basket. He looked in the mirror and took a couple of deep breaths. *You don't look so bad for a man with six months to live, Hancock.* He exhaled and exited the bathroom.

Sheppard's cell phone sat on the table next to her wine glass as she looked out toward the water. Hancock arrived back at his chair and sat down. She turned to Hancock but didn't say a word.

"What is it, Christina, the phone call?"

Sheppard had a puzzled look on her face, and her eyes looked to be searching for an answer.

"Christina?"

"I guess I'll be staying after all, Hancock."

Hancock felt his shoulders relax.

"I just received the strangest phone call," she said, "and I'm not sure what to make of it."

"Who was it?"

"I don't know."

"You don't know?"

"No."

"Would you like some more wine?" Hancock asked as he lifted the bottle.

"No!"

"Do you mind if I finish it?"

"No."

Hancock poured the remainder in his glass. He placed the bottle on the table and looked across to Sheppard.

"So, the phone call?"

"We're going to London."

"What?"

"London, England, that's where the desk is and apparently Brosconni too."

"Back up, Christina, who said that?"

"A man who wouldn't identify himself: he said, if I travel to London I will receive instructions on where to find Brosconni and the Hepplewhite. He also said if I contact anyone, particularly the police, I can forget about finding either one."

"And you believe him?"

"How else would he have my cell phone number? He said he got it from Brosconni's Smartphone. Do you think we should call the police?"

"No!"

CHAPTER 41

"They found the Hummer?" He asked.

"Yes General," Capt. Penso said as he stood just beyond the closed office door. "In a cemetery southwest of London, in a town called Twickenham, the Hummer was abandoned."

The General stood up and stepped to the window.

"At ease, have a seat Capt," he said facing the glass. "What else?"

Capt. Penso sat in the left winged back chair.

"Nothing, no sign of a struggle, all they found was his piled up clothes in the back."

"His clothes," Capalli asked as his hand lifted to his chin.

"Yes, General, even his silk jockey shorts and pants."

"What else?"

There's no trace of Brosconni. They've searched the cemetery and surrounding streets—nothing."

"Southwest of London, you said?"

"Yes General."

Capalli turned from the window and looked to Capt. Penso.

"So Brosconni's headed west. Someone must have met him in the cemetery, Capt. and made him strip to be sure he was clean. Whoever it was, is careful, smart, and knows Brosconni doesn't do what he's told."

"Yes, General"

Capalli sat and leaned back in his high back chair.

"What is Scotland Yard's reaction?"

"Inspector Mitchell has sent a picture of Brosconni across the wires to all precincts with a description of his approximate weight and height. He has instructed the highway patrol to be on the lookout for him, but if they find him not to engage. Inspector Mitchell specified he wants him followed until he reaches his destination."

Capalli connected with Penso's eyes.

"We don't know what type of car he's in, what he's wearing or even if he's continuing heading west." He said. "Maybe Brosconni wasn't met by anyone, Capt., perhaps he planned the whole charade. He changed cars, clothes, and direction. Contact Inspector Mitchell and advise him of that!"

Two hours earlier, at Twickenham Cemetery:

Brosconni followed his hand with his eyes and pulled out his Smartphone from his pocket. He opened up the text.

*Strike two, Brosconni, one more and the ballgames over!

Brosconni stared at the text and continued to read the message.

*You think I'm capable of hacking your hacker and not detecting a satellite tracer? Keep your hands in the open and the tracer in your pocket! If you fail to follow these next instructions exactly as I say the silence will be deafening. Don't doubt my resolve, Brosconni; I can see your every move.

Brosconni scanned the cemetery a second time. The place was deserted except for rows of headstones dotting the flat landscape in perfectly symmetrical lines. Mature Ash and English Elms shaded the graves and the roads that circumvented the organized plots of occupied earth. *Either the son of a bitch is around here, or he has a live video feed.* Brosconni turned to the green car an examined the rear. The trunk was partially opened. *Son of a bitch!* His eyes turned down to the remaining unread text.

He stood frozen behind the Hummer as his opaque brown pupils stared at the words, and he took in the list of instructions. His lips twisted into a tight configuration, and the brows above his eyes inched upward. He raised his head and looked to the Taurus with his hand still in the air, and the Smartphone positioned in its palm. *You fucking piece of shit, I'll have your fucking eyes ripped out!* Brosconni slid the phone back into his pocket and stared up at the green Ford Taurus. *No fucking way you son of a bitch.*

Brosconni's body fell back against the Hummer and didn't move. He raised his hand to his mouth and wrapped his finger around his lips. He knew he had no choice. It was the moment of truth, either follow the instruction or say goodbye to the Hepplewhite. There was no question in Brosconni's mind the son of a bitch meant everything he texted and would follow through with his threat. He took one last search of the cemetery, and stopped as he faced the back hatch of the Hummer, reached to the lever above the license plate, and pulled open the back. Then he slid out of his blue Armani blazer and placed it inside the open truck.

He hesitated a moment. Without the blazer on, the custom made Egyptian cotton button down revealed a thin framed small chested man. He didn't look so big or so powerful with just the shirt and red Hermes tie on, which streamed down the pressed white shirt and stopped just short of the buckled brown leather belt. He turned his head and gazed over his shoulder at the green Taurus and then back to the cavernous hole in the open back of the parked black Hummer.

Brosconni's hands reach up to the Winsor knot snuggled into the collar around his skinny neck, grabbed the loop with his first finger, pulled it forward and down, and with his other hand slid the fat piece of the tie upward and out of the knot. He slipped it out from underneath the collar and tossed it into the back of the truck. Then he turned around and leaned his butt against the bumper, and his head dropped slightly toward his chest.

Next the shirt came off, which exposed a thick black hairy upper torso. It was tight curly hair, much like the coarse hairs of his head. He slipped off his Ferragamo loafers and Hermes socks and shoved them in the back. Then his pants, his tight black silk jockey shorts, which exposed legs as covered with hair as his sunken chest. Naked as the day he was born, Brosconni turned, lifted his arms in the air, and pulled down the hatch of the Hummer and slammed it shut. All of this, he accomplished within a matter of seconds, and then he raised his hands in the air again, took two steps, did a three sixty pirouette, and darted his naked body to the trunk of the Ford Taurus.

In the shadow of the massive Hummer, the Ford Taurus looked mighty small, and compared to the two vehicles, without a stitch of clothes on, Brosconni looked like an emaciated pigmy. Hard to believe, but he looked like a scared little rat. He lifted the lid of the trunk, and as the instructions indicated, he spotted a one piece jump suit which he reached for and quickly pulled out. Brosconni stumbled as he stepped into the right leg, and then again as he stepped into the left. He pulled the upper body up to his arms and slipped them into each sleeve, grabbed the two sides at the chest, brought them together at the neck, reached down, picked up the zipper between his thumb and first finger, and zipped it up to his chin.

Now dressed in the gray overalls, Brosconni slammed the trunk lid shut, searched to see if anyone caught a glimpse of the tiny endowment between his legs, and slid around the side of the Taurus. The driver side door was unlocked as the text message indicated, so he opened the door and slipped inside. Brosconni pulled the sun visor down, and the keys landed in his lap. He stuck the key in the ignition, put it in drive, and proceeded to complete the circle of the roundabout he had started ten minutes before. The green Taurus crawled down the main entrance toward Hospital Bridge Road. When the Taurus pulled under the wrought iron pillared gate, which connected the name Twickenham Cemetery on top, Brosconni eased of the gas pedal and turned left onto Bridge Road heading south.

At the roundabout, Brosconni turned right on 316 and headed southwest at his aggravating, below speed limit pace. He realized, by what just happened, he was on his own. Every piece of Enrico Brosconni, with the exception of his frail hairy body, sat back in that Hummer under two English Elms in the graveyard of Twickenham cemetery. And, as he passed a warehouse on his right, the texter's intent hit Brosconni like a piece of hot lead between his dark sullen eyes: Brosconni, in one of the rare moments of his life, had been neutralized.

About five and a half kilometers down 316, the sound of a cell phone went off. Brosconni jumped and jerked the wheel. He pulled to the side of the road and tracked the ring to the arm rest consul to his right. He lifted the latched top, pulled out the phone, and flipped it open and put it to his ear. He waited.

"Brosconni," a calm, low voice said, "you are halfway to your Hepplewhite. Follow the instructions, and you will soon be sitting at your desk."

"So you have a voice," Brosconni said, "do you have a name?"

"No questions, Brosconni," the voice said, "that's not important. Listen carefully, because I understand your repugnance to rules, and your uncontrollable obsession to break them. Here's how the game's played. The car has a satellite tracer on it: I will know where you are at all times. And, I can see and hear everything you do. If you stop at any place, at any time, other than where I designate, strike three. Don't bother trying to call out on the phone—you can't. Continue on M3 until it connects with M25. Take M25 east. You will receive instructions at intervals appropriate to your travel. One wrong turn, one stop, one brainless attempt to contact anyone—strike three!"

The phone went dead as Brosconni headed in the opposite direction as the Hummer, in the cemetery, with the live U2 tracer in his silk blazer pocket.

CHAPTER 42

The green stolen Taurus, with borrowed license plates from an unknowing couple who spent four months a year in the states, crawled down A25 toward Leatherhead. Behind the wheel, in gray overalls, a cell phone in the top breast pocket, and a bare foot on the gas pedal, was Enrico Brosconni. He had been in the far left lane for the last 20 miles with his jaw clenched as tight as his grip on the wheel. Out of his element, his clothes, and his monetary cocoon, he drove along the country side with a blank agenda in his conniving mind. Brosconni was out of ideas.

About a mile outside of Merstham, the phone rang. Brosconni removed the flip phone from his breast pocket and opened it up.

"Yes?"

"Bravo, Brosconni, you've managed to follow instructions for a whole half an hour. You must be exhausted."

"Just give me the fucking instructions, you son of a bitch."

"I'm going to let that one go, Brosconni; I'll attribute it to driving fatigue. However, one more and your phone will go dead! Half mile on your left will be the entrance to A23 south. Proceed onto A23 until you receive further instructions."

The call ended. Brosconni closed the phone and placed it back into his pocket. As he approached the entrance ramp to A23 south, he slowed and the line of traffic behind him laid on their horns. Oblivious to the noise, he kept his eyes glued to the turn. He veered off A25 onto the entrance ramp and crept around the long sweeping roadway until it merged with A23.

The road cut through the pastures divided by hedgerow as the landscape changed to open farm land dotted with a few country homes. As the Taurus puttered along the highway, Brosconni's scheming brain perked up. He had to come up with a plan, some way to get an edge, so he looked out the driver side window and examined what options were left. His covert ops guys had chased the empty Hummer and were probably on their way home. He had no phone, nor the ability to stop, and all his resources had been cut off. Disgusted, Brosconni looked back to the road. *God damn cow farmers*, he said as he continued on toward Smallfield.

As he passed through Surrey, he thought back to the Duomo di San Gennaro and felt the saliva form in his mouth. *How did he know of the church?* He remembered how the son of a bitch duped him back in Naples. He had sent him to the cathedral to seek instruction and instead made him violently ill. Brosconni tried to suppress the memories that had now begun to swirl inside his head. The muscles in his stomach twisted at the walls, and the water in his mouth had begun to gush. In childhood, Brosconni had been controlled by the sick sexual desires of a catholic pervert, and when he finally escaped, he vowed never to be controlled again. And now, for the first time since his youth, he felt succumbed by the conniving manipulation of another human being. He puckered his lips and spit the excessive amount of liquid gathered in his mouth toward the passenger side floor, and he studied the sign which read Shipley Bridge.

As he passed the sign indicating A264 up ahead, the phone rang. Brosconni took it out and opened it up. Brosconni said nothing this time.

"Take a left onto A264 toward Copthorne and continue until instructed."

The caller hung up.

Brosconni looked at his watch, 2:15 pm. He had driven more since the City Airport than he had in the last ten years combined. His neck was stiff and his shoulders hurt. The strength of his grip on the wheel had tensed his entire upper torso; he needed a break. But he couldn't stop unless instructed, and Brosconni realized that would only happen when he arrived at his instructed destination. He released the wheel with his right hand and rubbed his neck as East Grinstead passed on his right.

Also, being trapped in the car alone for so long had deprived Brosconni of the human contact he depended upon to keep his brain from shorting out.

Introspection, to Brosconni, was a practice vacated in youth. The closest thing he had to self revelation was admiring some new acquisition in a self induced narcissistic trance. And beyond that, if he wasn't scheming, he was implementing some horrific nightmare he unleashed unto some unsuspecting soul. Alone time for Brosconni meant time down, literally, near depression down. The inside of the tycoon's head was like a horror movie gone bad, and plucked from his world of excess, trapped in the car alone, dreadful things had begun to appear on the screen. So he changed the reel as he drove down 264 and focused on Alberto Giuseppe Capalli.

Brosconni pictured the enjoyment he would get as he watched The General take his fall. Capalli happened to be in the wrong place at the wrong time, and the deeper Brosconni got pulled into some other man's hell, the more crazed Brosconni would become. Remember the part about introspection; it didn't exist in his psychopathic world. So if something happened to Brosconni, someone else would pay exponentially more. The tycoon called it instincts.

He once pretended at the top platform of a series of concrete steps that he stumbled and sent a man flailing down fifteen solid treads. He called that retribution. Twenty minutes early, at the early morning street market, Brosconni had been caught stealing two pieces of fruit. After being humiliated by the vendor, in front of the street crowd, Brosconni's twisted instincts kicked in. He didn't know the man, and that didn't matter, because when they put the man on a stretcher and carted him away in a red and white, the pain he had inflicted on an innocent man nursed his wounded ego back to health.

Now, as he passed through Hammerwood, his sadistic motivation to inflict the utmost of pain had reached a lucid crescendo, and the plan emerged before his very eyes as naturally as taking a breath. When Capalli was down, he'd stick a fork in his heart, and he'd use his wife as the means to do it.

Brosconni's misguided and unethical publicists would arrange the details, but the premise was simple and direct. Capalli's wife, Carlota, involved with one of the General's trusted Captains, was caught in the back of their Alfa Romeo going down on the uniformed man. A witness just happened by. It didn't matter to Brosconni if it was believable or borderline absurd, the moment it was released the damage was done, and coupled with Capalli's breaking scandal, it would carry quite the punch. Pleased with himself, he placed his right hand back on the wheel, and for the first time since the Gulfstream, the crooked smile came back to life on his face.

As he read the sign to Langton Green, his Breast pocket rang again, and he reached in and re-did the drill.

"At A21 turn left onto the entrance ramp and continue toward Kippings Cross."

The caller hung up.

Brosconni drove another few miles and the phone rang again.

"Half a mile ahead, turn left onto Lamberhurst Road."

Again silence.

Brosconni's neck muscles ached and his shoulders felt the strain from the death grip on the wheel. His lower back had stiffened, and his bare foot, pushing the gas pedal and applying the brake, had rubbed sore. Besides the physical ailments, the emotional boiler was about to blow. The turn for Lamberhurst approached on the left, and he swung the Taurus wide and entered the desolate country road. It was cut through a wilderness of farm land with the occasional isolated home.

The road continued deep into the Horsmonden countryside with thousands of cordoned off pastures, some planted and green, some plowed over and brown. As he crawled along, he scanned the landscape, and realized he'd just reached the outer limits of civilized hell. All that was visible, as far as the eye could see, were stone walls, hedgerow, crops in symmetrical patterns, and the blue sky. It seemed to go on forever.

Then his eyes rolled down to his breast pocket.

"Ok, Brosconni, I'll bring you in from here. One wrong move, one ignored instruction, and you use your last strike! Up ahead, is a dirt road on your right—take it."

Brosconni slowed to almost a stop and eased onto the pot holed road. It looked like a bombed out war zone. The Taurus bounced and kicked up a trail of dust behind it as the cell phone remained stuck to his ear. His eyes moved side to side as he saw no signs of life. The fields were overgrown, abandoned for a least a couple of seasons he figured, as he tried to find the end. At a small ridge in the road the voice came back to life.

"Up over the incline, off in the distance, you will see your destination."

Brosconni reached the top, and as the Taurus came down the other side, he spotted a small farmhouse about five hundred yards away. When he reached half the distance to the gabled dwelling the voice said, "stop!"

"Turn the car off, Brosconni, and leave the key in the ignition. Open your door, bring the phone with you, and get out."

Brosconni took a deep breath. He pulled the handle, pushed opened the door, and climbed out.

"Now," the voice said, "walk down the middle of the road, up to the front walk of the house, and don't stop until you reach the front door—now Brosconni!"

CHAPTER 43

"Go ahead, Capt. Tinelli, I'm listening."

Capalli stood at the window with his handset on speaker phone.

"General, Detective Stanno and I have been running a search on Collet using the department's data bases, the internet, and files from the FBI. We came up with something interesting."

"Yes," Capalli said. His eyes rolled down to the early morning crowds passing through the piazza, and then rose, as a business man in a black suit disturbed a group of pigeons which went airborne. "And?"

"General," Tinelli's voice said from the tinny tone of the speaker, "we plugged in Arthur Collet's name, and it brought back one hit on a newspaper article in The Washington Times back in 2001."

Capalli's head turned partially toward his desk as if moving his ear in a direct line to the sound of Tinelli's voice.

"In 2001, on "M" street in Georgetown, an antique dealer named William Monroe was found murdered in his showroom. The article claims, Monroe had purchased a desk attributed to Boston cabinetmakers, John Seymour & Son, and the desk had belonged to Alexander Hamilton. It was big news that year. When they found Monroe, General, he had a forty five punched through his forehead—sound familiar—and the desk had disappeared. The case was never solved."

"And the connection to Collet?"

"General, the article produced a hit because Arthur Collet's name was mentioned as one of the two dealers Monroe had called about the piece."

"You've lost me, Capt." Capalli said as his head turned back to the glass, and his eyes rolled down to the piazza. "Connect the dots!"

"Sir," Tinelli said struggling with his words, "Alexander Hamilton was, like Washington, one of the founding fathers, and, the first secretary of the treasury."

Capalli rubbed his forehead with the tips of his fingers. And then his hand stopped and dropped to his chin.

"What the hell are you inferring, Capt., every important person of the United States, whose desk materializes, will prove a death sentence to the dealer who owns it?"

"Sir, I know this is out there, but, it's a carbon copy of the Hepplewhite. And, this Masonic connection can't be ignored. There is no proof Alexander Hamilton was a freemason, but many believe he was. I'm not alone on this, General; Detective Stanno is convinced Collet is involved in both homicides. How do you want me to proceed?"

"Stay in New York, Capt., but you better come up with something concrete—and fast!"

Capalli hung up the phone and turned to the window.

"General?"

"What is it Caprina?"

"Sir, Capt. Penso's on hold."

Capalli picked up the hand set and pushed the button on the blinking line.

"Yes, Captain?"

"General, I think we caught a break," the voice said as Capalli leaned back in his chair and listened. The Twickenham police have received a report of a stolen, green, 2010 Ford Taurus. The owner of the car had just arrived home from a business trip three hours after they found the Hummer in the cemetery. He reported his house broken into and the Taurus gone. Inspector Mitchell has run the plate across Interpol along with the make and model of the vehicle."

Capalli leaned forward, put the handset down so the phone was on speaker, and rested his elbows on the desk. He clasped both hands near his mouth as he spoke toward the phone.

"And they think this is connected to Brosconni?" He asked.

"Mitchell doesn't know yet, but it was reported missing around the same time as Brosconni disappeared from the cemetery, and he had to have some means to travel."

"Is that Mitchell's take?"

"Yes sir!"

"How far from the cemetery was the location of the stolen Taurus?"

"Actually not more than two blocks on Ryecroft Avenue. The entire circumference of the cemetery is residential, town houses sir."

Capalli clicked on the icon of the map of Twickenham and changed to satellite view and zoomed in on Ryecroft Avenue. It wasn't more than two hundred yards from the cemetery. Staring at the flat screen he asked, "assuming Brosconni's driving the Taurus, how many hours head start does he have?"

"We don't know, general. Mitchell calculated the driving time from City Airport to Twickenham Cemetery after Brosconni rented the Hummer. The inspector figured Brosconni arrived somewhere between 12:30 to 1:00 pm depending on traffic. The Hummer was first discovered deserted over two hours later. That makes it 3:00 pm London time. The Taurus wasn't reported missing until six, so Mitchell estimates Brosconni has a four to five hour lead."

Capalli's eyes rolled up toward the florescent lights and then back down to his desk.

"So that could put him anywhere on the English continent, is that correct Capt. Penso?"

"That's correct, General."

"Or perhaps, Brosconni could have taken the Dover ferry to France and is on his way to Paris?"

"Yes, sir."

"And it's possible a few miles from Twickenham, Brosconni could have rented another vehicle, and you have no idea what he's driving now?"

"That's a possibility sir."

"So how is it, Capt. Penso, you've caught a break?"

Capalli placed his hands on the top of the desk and folded them together. Staring at him on the flat screen of his Dell computer was the picture of the big black Hummer, in the cemetery, with all of its extremities open full wide.

"Captain?"

CHAPTER 44

Sheppard stepped from the Jet way and entered gate 32. She looked at her watch, 5:02 pm. Hancock would arrive the next morning on a 10:25 flight. He insisted they travel separately. He had given her a flash stick at the restaurant in Furore and explained it contained his research, his manuscript, and documents pertaining to the authenticity of his work.

"It would be foolish to risk being on the same flight," he said. "If they get to me," he continued," at least you have the evidence, research, and manuscript. But," he finished, "no matter what, you must get to the sealed correspondence, Christina, and use that evidence to prove the legitimacy of my work."

As she passed the check in counter rolling her travel bag, she slipped her left hand into the side pocket of her red silk blazer with the black labels. She grasped the stick in the palm of her hand and squeezed her fingers shut. She would guard it with her life. She had made that commitment to Hancock, and she intended on keeping her word at any cost.

It had taken a while for Sheppard to accept Hancock's premise, and her skeptical sarcasm, at first, simply provided a safe distance between her and the famed historian. But Christina was now convinced that Randolph's theory, and his claims of a covert Masonic cover up, were based on legitimate facts. She just hoped now Hancock would arrive safely, and they had the chance to recover Brosconni's desk.

Prior to their separation, Christina again asked what the correspondence contained. But before she received the answer, Hancock dismissed himself and drove up the Amalfi Coast. He had said, "if we both arrive in London and meet as agreed, I will disclose to you the significance of the two sealed documents, and why two dealers lost their lives over it. But right now I must go. I'll see you on the English Continent," he concluded, "have a pleasant flight."

She cleared customs and headed toward the Enterprise rental counter, and as she walked she thought of Hancock's final words. She let go of the memory stick in her pocket and hoped what he said was true. She didn't want to go it alone, not now. The whole Italian experience had been therapeutic for her, whether she wanted to admit it or not. Rest assured, she felt nothing romantic for Hancock, but after her brief bout of "run back to America" had passed, Sheppard felt invigorated. And even though it meant boarding an airplane and leaving solid ground, the prospect of going to England had excited her, but, now there, the two and a half hours inside the 747 had choked her enthusiasm to a drizzle.

She let go the extended handle of her suitcase and took a breath as the woman in green suit turned around.

"May I help you?" She asked.

Sheppard exhaled.

"I'd like to rent an SUV," she said.

"Small, large, or executive?" The lady asked.

Christina looked away and scanned the arrival board and then turned back.

"Large," she said.

Still shaken from her flight from Rome to Heathrow, Sheppard tried to gather her composure and focus. The plane ride had been another conscious nightmare as vivid images flashed in her mind of chard fuselage, smoldering heaps of twisted metal, and the covered burned bodies of her deceased family—two and a half hours of visual hell. And the worst part was the hallucinogenic hangover which lasted for days. Flashbacks, they happened with the same intensity as they did in the air over France, and the English Channel, and occurred at unannounced random intervals throughout her day. Sheppard had been told by a therapist the visions were normal and would slowly go away. But after six years, they had not, and she often felt her photographic memory was a sadistic curse. She wished she had amnesia instead.

The voice of the lady rang in her ear as incomprehensible noise, and she eyed the papers being slid across the counter as she accepted the pen and rolled her eyes down to the solid black line.

"Christina Sheppard?" The voice said as she signed the rental agreement for the Chevy Tahoe. Startled, she looked to her right. With the pen still on the paper, and the blood drained from her face, she felt her heart race inside her chest.

"Ms. Sheppard, are you alright?" The Enterprise lady asked.

Christina froze as she stared at the man, who was rather tall, dressed in a button down oxford and blue cashmere sweater. He stood just off her right shoulder, and a satchel hung from his left. His blondish brown hair was straight and hung partially over his ears. The Cole Hahn black penny loafers looked perfectly shinned against the sharp crease of his dry cleaned khaki's. Sheppard's eyes rose up his body to his face and locked into the deep blue of his eyes.

"Jermaine?" she said.

"Christina, how are you?"

"Jermaine, I....I..."

Sheppard last saw Arket nearly a year ago at a small restaurant on 82nd Street in Manhattan. After dinner they strolled up past the Met toward the park and stopped at the entrance on 79th Street. Arket had known Sheppard almost four years by then, and romantically, he had never made an advance, partially out of respect but particularly out of the fear it would end their relationship. But the frustration Arket felt, at Sheppard's refusal to move on, had built to a head that night.

After a couple of glasses of Bordeaux, the smell of her perfume, and the stare of her deep blue eyes teasing him from across the table, he felt his lust for Christina explode. When they arrived at the entrance to Central Park, Arket turned to Christina, took both of her arms in his hands and approached her lips with his. Within inches, Sheppard pushed Arket away, stormed off, and hailed a cab. That was the last time she saw Arket face to face.

He called, but she wouldn't return the messages. After two months, Arket gave up. Now, standing in Heathrow Airport, after endless conversations between her brain and her heart, she was torn once again by the two. And as he stood only inches away, her words stumbled from her lips as confused as the thoughts in her head.

"Jermaine, I...."

"Christina," he said and pointed, "finish your paper work."

Christina unlocked her eyes from his and turned her head back toward the counter. Her mouth still partially open, the lady sensed her confusion and smiled. Sheppard looked back to Arket and then back down to the counter and focused on the pen which rested in the crotch of her thumb.

She scribbled her signature onto the various pages and pushed the papers back across the counter. The lady expedited the packaging of the necessary papers and cut the wording of the pre-rehearsed instructions to the absolute minimum allowed by law. As she folded the last of the agreements and put them into the envelope, Christina half twitched and half turned her head toward Arket and released a tight nervous smile. The lady's voice echoed in her ear, and her head snapped back.

"Thank you for choosing Enterprise, Ms. Sheppard, if you take the documents to the rental garage, the attendant will bring you the Tahoe."

Christina scooped up the envelope and turned to Arket.

"What.....I mean, what are you doing here?"

"I live in London, Christina, remember?"

She didn't respond. Sheppard stood with the envelope in her hand, her overnight bag with the handle in the air in between her and Arket, and locked onto his eyes. They were gentle and compassionate and showed no signs of resentment or anger. She watched them as they turned to the left and then back to hers.

"Christina," he said, "why don't you move away from the counter. There are people behind you waiting."

Sheppard reached for the handle to her suitcase. She stuffed the paper work into the side pocket of her blazer and rolled the bag next to Arket as they walked over toward the exit. The silence was awkward as they stepped through the automatic door and onto the sidewalk. She couldn't stand it, so she blurted out the first thing that popped into her head.

"What are you doing in the airport?" She asked.

"I had business in Paris today." He replied and put his hand on her forearm elevated from her grip on the suitcase handle.

"Christina," he said, "I have no animosity toward you. I understand how difficult it's been."

Arket spotted moisture begin to form around the blue of her eyes. It was the first time he detected emotions other than anger or fear in Sheppard, and it surprised him.

"I have to go," she said.

"Of course," said Arket seemingly sarcastic and then, "take care, Christina," and he turned to the curb, stepped onto the crosswalk, and moved in the direction of short term parking. With Arket halfway across the street a voice screamed inside Sheppard's head, but it made no attempt to stop Arket. Jermaine, it echoed like a desperate voice in a hollow hall, wait, comeback!

CHAPTER 45

"Son of a bitch," he murmured, "I was right!"

Capalli studied the transcripts on his flat screen, sent by Scotland Yard. Inspector Mitchell's team had torn apart the memory of Brosconni's Smartphone, which they found in the back of the Hummer in his clothes at Twickenham Cemetery, and chronologically detailed the correspondence he had received from the mysterious texter. Even though Brosconni had erased each message, the team was able to recoup the data off of the sim card and recreate the instructions, and consequently his movements for the past week. It started with the church in Amalfi, and unfortunately ended when Brosconni tossed his blazer into the back of the truck.

Capalli continued to scroll down the text. A little glimmer of a smile cracked his lips as he read the message sent to Brosconni instructing him to strip, walk to the car naked, and put on the overalls. But as he went back, and re-read the transcript from the beginning, his expression changed. The look of amusement was gone and replaced with squinted eyes and investigative intensity. This texter was smart and technologically on the edge of genius, and he had been out front of Brosconni the entire way. He read on.

The General was impressed not only in the texter's ability to remain undetected but particularly with the brilliance of his well orchestrated plan. He methodically outsmarted the most devious and cunningly perverse man Capalli had ever met— Enrico Brosconni. And, he used Brosconni's deranged ego and irrational obsession to accomplish the task. He had strung the tycoon along until he was certain Brosconni got the message of who was in charge. But beyond the obvious learning curve he threw at Brosconni, The General recognized something else. He was playing cat and mouse with Brosconni—trying to get some ulterior message across. Capalli sensed it. Why else would he send Brosconni into three separate churches culminating in the holiest of holy, St. Peter's Basilica? He rubbed the top of his head, pushed away from his desk, and swiveled toward the glass.

Something else bothered Capalli. His eyes rolled side to side as he contemplated the thought. *Why drag Brosconni on the chase? The inherent danger was far greater stringing the tycoon along. If it was about a ransom, why not just collect the money and tell Brosconni where to find the desk?* He thought back to Collet. *Was he the*

271

mastermind behind this well orchestrated plan? The General stood up, faced the glass and rubbed his chin with his hand. Why not a simple exchange? Are they bringing Brosconni in for a reason? He turned half circle toward his desk and pressed the button on his phone.

"Caprina!"

"Yes General?"

"What time is it in New York?"

"It's 2:00 pm, general."

"Get Capt. Tinelli on the phone."

"Yes General."

"Capt. Penso as well and put them through on conference call.

"Right away sir."

Capalli dropped to his seat and went back through the transcripts. He scrolled to the end and read the last set of instructions given Brosconni.

*Head southwest on 316.

Capalli opened up his browser and pulled up the map of England. He typed in Twickenham Cemetery, zoomed in, and followed 316 southwest. It meant nothing. It was just a starting point from which his direction could have changed on the next set of commands. Brosconni must have received instructions from there. There was no way to tell which direction Brosconni drove after that. He left in a car, though, and The General considered that, although weak, at least something to build on. And, the green stolen Taurus, although equally frail, was a long shot he couldn't ignore. Capalli leaned back in his chair and let his head fall into the soft black leather.

"General?"

"Yes?"

"General, I have Captain's Penso and Tinelli on conference call."

"Put them through."

Capalli pressed the button for speaker phone and addressed Penso in England and Tinelli in New York.

"Captains, bring me up to date." He said.

"General, this is Capt. Penso."

"Yes?"

"General, we've located the green Taurus on a farm southeast of London. The local police recognized it from the dispatch and called Scotland Yard."

"Go ahead captain."

"Sir, the plates don't match, but they're stolen too. They belong to a blue ford focus about a block from where the Taurus was taken. The VIN on the Ford Taurus matches the stolen vehicle, it's the car."

Capalli pushed himself up on the wood arms of the chair and stood in front of the desk. He turned and shuffled to the window and put his back to the phone, massaging his forehead with his fingers. The tension in his temples released, and he let out a silent exhale. The pressure he placed on himself to solve the case had mounted to an unbearable push. It was Capalli's way of putting Brosconni's threat out of his mind and tucked away in a place that allowed him to focus. It worked for him, but for Carlota, his wife, she had grown more distraught each day. She had trouble sleeping, and the black circles under her eyes, and the

273

constant stress on her face, was more of a strain on Capalli than his impending fate. He raised his head.

"I'm listening," he said.

"General the farm is located outside a town called Horsmonden. The house is vacant and the property is up for sale. We found the Taurus about three hundred yards from the residence. We searched the farm house and found no signs of Brosconni."

"Anything in the vehicle?" Capalli asked.

"No sir, but some of the trim next to the door has been removed. We think someone had a wire hidden behind the trim, surveillance perhaps to observe Brosconni. Forensics is dusting the car for prints as we speak."

"What else, Captain?"

"We believe there was a second vehicle. There are tracks leading from the barn to the right of the house. They are recent and forensics is making a cast of the tire imprints……. And General?"

"Yes Captain?"

"General, there's something else."

Capalli turned his head toward the desk.

"Yes?"

"Sir, we found blood by the front door, and we think it may be Brosconni's. Forensics is taking a swab for DNA testing, and Inspector Mitchell said he can fast track the results."

"How bad does it look?"

"The bleed out was fairly minor, General, it doesn't appear catastrophic."

Capalli turned his head back to the window. His eyes rolled down to the piazza as he spoke.

"What's the time frame captain?"

"From the condition of the smeared blood, they believe two to three hours, no more."

Two hours earlier at the Horsmonden farm house:

Brosconni moved away from the green Taurus and stared at the stucco building with the steep gabled wood roof in the distance. The two story farm house, with three dormers cut into the roof, appeared empty. The main body of the structure was rectangular, more than likely the original section of the farm house, off of which the later extensions were constructed. Two outcroppings on the left, one taller than the other, probably serviced an expanding family's need for a larger kitchen and more bedroom space. The right side, with its angled deviation from the main structure, was a larger single room. Its single story steeped roof, with white stucco beneath, had a tall stone chimney at the gable end. Brosconni scanned the endless horizon of pastures, stonewalls, and hedgerow, and took his first step toward the house.

He looked for signs of life, but there were none. The farm was abandoned. It still had the definitive separation of one planting field to the next, but it was overgrown and clearly had not been farmed in a number of years. He moved ahead slowly, and as he did, the small stones bruised his bare feet, and the oversized coveralls dragged in the dirt. With each step Brosconni took, he searched for the son of a bitch, Mr. X. The thought never entered his head that this complex escapade could be a trap. But that was

Enrico Brosconni. Once he concocted a premise in his head, it didn't matter if it was right or wrong, it became his reality, and he believed it.

His reasoning for his deduction was this: if the Hepplewhite was sold on the open market, it would command a price equivalent to the Goddard-Townsend Chippendale which sold at auction for a whopping twelve million and change, whoever took the desk was well aware of that. It was obvious to Brosconni the motive was to collect a ransom in return for the prized piece. So as he stumbled down the middle of the road, and amused his deranged imagination by trying to calculate the exact sum the thief would demand, he had no fear. He knew he was protected by his staggering fortune and the fact that he never lost. And, no matter the pittance the punk demanded, there wouldn't be a place on this earth where the son of a bitch could hide. Brosconni would see to that.

As he moved closer to the farmhouse, a rush of adrenaline pumped through his veins as the souls of his feet rolled off the hard packed dirt. Stripped of his opulence, Brosconni felt back to his roots—back to Naples, back to his torn clothes, empty stomach, and steel nerves. It was the purest sense of survival that excited him, and he had missed it. Others now took care of the nasty stuff, and it didn't feel the same to Brosconni. He lived for that moment just before the take, when his heart raced and the lump in his throat made it hard to swallow. Even the failures shot electric current through his icy veins and into his stone cold heart. And although he had amassed a fortune from the teachings of his youth, he missed the hands on, face to face encounters, and the high he felt in victory, as he stared at his prey's defeat.

As his fortune grew, his lack of principles had not changed. His methods had grown more refined, but nothing could replace the sensation of the instant his hand reached out and grabbed a piece of fruit or slipped into the pocket of an unsuspecting tourist on the cobble stone streets of Pompeii. Theft on a scale exponentially more complex, in the world of suits, had insulated him from the thrill he had felt in his youth. But now, as he walked barefoot, stripped of his Ferragamo shoes, Hermes tie, and custom made silk blazer and pants, Brosconni experienced the streets of Naples flowing through his veins once again, and he had forgotten just how good it felt.

He looked back to the green Taurus, then forward to the farm house ahead. He had progressed halfway, and he searched the landscape once more. He examined each corner of the house, the dormers, the front windows, and the large English Elm which stood about a hundred feet in front of the structure, nothing. To the right of the residence was a large barn with a gambrel wood roof. Two large wooden doors were half open, slid one to the right, one to the left. The matching doors on the rear of the structure were open as well. The light siphoned through the two entrances and lit the interior dirt floor strewn with piles of hay. Brosconni stared through the door. It was deserted. He scanned back to the house with his hands clutched in a fist in the side pockets of his overalls.

His feet had become sore, but he liked that too. In Naples, Brosconni sometimes removed his shoes and walked the paved streets until his feet were raw and blistered. It was a test. The self inflicted torture raised the ceiling on his tolerance to pain, and it sent a message to the kids on the street. *Nessuno è più duro Enrico Brosconni*, he would say as his skin burned on the bottoms of his feet, *nessuno, si suini senza spina dorsale, nessuno!* And as he moved now toward the farm house, with his head up, expressionless, his gait increased to an extended stride, and he repeated the words again. *No one is tougher than Enrico Brosconni, no one, you spineless pigs, no one!*

He reached the English Elm and stopped under the shade of the tree. He saw no movement anywhere. The road continued another seventy feet, looped in a half circle, then back around the tree and merged like a highway ramp to the road. Brosconni moved forward in a strong steady stride to the brick walk at the peak of the loop. Without hesitation, he stepped onto the walk and approached the solid wood door which had a big black wrought iron knocker. He stopped, reached for the door handle, and his hand froze at the familiar click of a hammer being cocked back by a thumb.

"If you move, you're dead!" The voice said.

"Fuck you, you son of a bitch: you won't shoot me; you haven't gotten what you came here for."

The shot muffled the sound of his lateral cuneiform and first metatarsal being splintered on his foot. He fell against the front door and slipped to the brick and onto the splatter of his own red blood. Holding his leg, Brosconni stared at his foot. His big toe on his left foot had been completely removed. It was a precise shot with an intended message and Brosconni looked up at the forty five.

"You son of a bitch," he said as he got his first glimpse of the man in the hood. The man held a forty five in his hand and had it aimed at Brosconni's head. Brosconni's foot burn as if on fire, but he didn't flinch. He let go with his hand, his leg straightened out, and he stood upright. Although the bone in his left foot had been smashed, he put as much weight on it as he did on his right. He turned and faced the weapon still pointed at his head and looked directly into the man's eyes, visible through the slits in the hood. Neither man blinked.

With his free hand, the man circled with his finger, indicating he wanted Brosconni to turn around. Brosconni eyes rolled down at the sound of a second click. The forty five was now pointed at his other foot. Brosconni half circled and faced the door. The hooded man approached and stuck the pistol in the back of Brosconni's head, and with his other hand, he pushed Brosconni in between the shoulder blades, pinning his chest against the door.

"Put your hands behind your back," he said, "or the next piece of lead will splinter your brain!"

Brosconni cooperated this time. He heard two more clicks as his cheek laid against the coolness of the wood door. It was the sound of the handcuffs as they clasped shut around his wrists.

The white Ford E-series windowless van eased out of the barn adjacent to the old farm house, picked up speed as it curved around the English Elm, kicked up dust as it approached the Taurus, and dipped into the shallow drainage ditch as it passed the stolen car on the right. In the back, blindfolded, his mouth duct taped, cuffed to the side wall behind the driver seat, was Enrico Brosconni, unaware, just a few feet away, wrapped in two moving blankets toward the rear, was his prized Hepplewhite. As the gas pedal hit the floor, Brosconni's head jerked sideways, and the van pulled off the dirt access road, turned left on Lamberhurst, and shot down the paved farm road as the engine shifted into a second gear.

CHAPTER 46

She approached arrivals at a twelve mile an hour crawl, in the white Tahoe, and searched for Hancock in the crowd. Last night, alone in the hotel, she almost picked up her phone and called Arket. But she didn't. She scanned the sidewalk as the Tahoe neared the crosswalk where she had last seen Arket, and the tightness in her gut melted into a hollow rush that rose deep into the recesses of her chest. She had wanted to call out his name, but her voice had abandoned her, and her mouth felt like rigor mortise had set in. And now, as she approached the crosswalk, her recall posted a snap shot of Jermaine Arket like a giant colored billboard in her head, and the image refused to go away.

She scanned the next group of passengers, but if Hancock was amongst them, she missed him in the crowd and drove on by. Had she stuck the final dagger in Arket's heart? Maybe. She couldn't blame him. This time, though, she recognized what she had done, and his final words as she pushed him away replayed over and over in her head. "Of course," he had said, and then after a polite "take care, Christina" he was gone. It had to be sarcastic she contemplated as she began her loop of the airport. *Of course you want to run, Christina, I wouldn't expect anything less of you!* Still, he must feel something otherwise he would have just passed through the airport terminal without saying hello. But her immediate shutdown followed by, "I have to go," was clear to Arket. She was the same old Christina Sheppard, and when the smallest inkling of human emotion welled up inside of her, she'd run.

She eased on the gas pedal and continued around the airport a second time waiting for Hancock to exit the terminal and tried to force the image of Arket from her head. She focused on Hancock as they had sat in the restaurant in Furore and recalled the conversations they had had. Then something caught her attention, something Hancock had said. At the time it touched off the nightmare of her tragic loss which prompted the content to be lost. But now, focused in on his words, the conflict didn't make sense. And as she turned back onto the airport entrance, and shifted into the lane for arrivals, she dialed up an article she had read years ago, and the discrepancy became crystal clear in her head.

Before her husband had passed away, Christina was in their Central Park West apartment and had eyed an article in an antiques magazine which was opened on the breakfast nook table. Her husband Raymond had been reading it. He was researching a Nicholas Brown, circa 1760's, desk and bookcase he had purchased. The cabinetmaker's business resided in Newport, Rhode Island. The article featured and interview with Randolph Hancock, famed historian, and centered on his research about Newport, and how the town emerged in the 1740's as the leading trade center for the colonies. But what Sheppard's photographic memory had brought to the screen was the opening sentence by the interviewer, who expressed his condolences to Hancock and thanked him under the circumstances for doing the interview. Hancock had lost his wife to cancer three months before.

As Sheppard approached the arrivals terminal, her infallible recall focused in on their conversation in Furore. Hancock had insisted they meet in the little village because his hotel room had been ransacked, and they threatened to kill his wife of twenty eight years. According to the article, his wife died in two thousand and four. Focused on her own loss she never put the two together. Instead, she felt the need to do whatever she could to help Hancock, because Sheppard knew all too well what losing a spouse was like. That's how she got sucked in. But now, as she searched the crowd, Hancock's deceit hit her like a brick falling from the sky, and she felt the anger intensify at his intentional lie.

Sheppard was absolutely clear on the facts. She didn't have to verify if she was confused or made a mistake; her ability to recollect never failed. So she pulled up the image of Hancock as he sat at the café table and examined his expressions as he spoke. She observed him as he started, and then stopped—acted all choked up—and then said, "I couldn't go on if they hurt my wife: I wouldn't want to go on." And then Sheppard, through her flawless memory, watched Hancock put the finishing touches on his fabricated charade as his eyes grew moist and clouded with pain.

As she approached the terminal, she spotted Hancock who stood on the curb with one small overnight bag, and the full weight of his lie raced through her veins like the shock from two hundred and twenty searing volts of electricity. She eased the Tahoe to the right, came to a stop at the curb and looked at Hancock's face as he opened the door. She felt betrayed and angry, and she wondered what else the historian had concocted, and she tried to fathom why.

Happy to see Sheppard, he stuck his head inside the truck and said a cheerful Hello. Sheppard looked straight into Hancock's eyes.

"Throw your bag in the back and get in." She said.

Hancock squinted, confused. "What's wrong?" He asked.

"Do as I say, Hancock," and she turned her head away.

Hancock tossed his bag on the back seat and climbed in. Before the door slammed, Sheppard hit the gas.

"What is it?" He asked again.

Christina maneuvered the SUV through the line of traffic sliding in and out from the curb. Hancock studied her face as she did. Sheppard cruised down the exit road, eased left onto the on ramp for M4, and headed east toward London. Hancock had no idea what was wrong, but Sheppard's eyes from the time he climbed into the Tahoe, had stared straight through the windshield and onto the road. She hadn't said a word since she commanded Hancock to obey her instructions, and she didn't look in a hurry to talk. Whatever was on her mind, he'd wait to find out, because he had already tried and asked her twice.

About four kilometers down M4 Sheppard veered left off the highway and onto a small access road which led into the parking lot for Links Golf Club. She found a vacant slot, rolled the Tahoe between the white lines, brought the truck to a halt, and slammed the SUV into park. Then she slid her body around and put her back against the driver side door. The softness in her face was gone, and she cast a cold stare toward Hancock.

"We have a problem, Hancock, and the moment I find a discrepancy in anything you say, your trek to confirm your research is over. And let me remind you, it is impossible for me to forget one word, of one sentence, of any conversation we've had. So, let's start with this conspiracy theory crap, the premise of the revolution, this new world order, Langdon, Hancock, Washington, The Sublime Prince of the Royal Secret, and the Prince of Mercy. How much of what you've told me is true?"

Hancock's eyebrows were scrunched so far they almost met the sockets under his eyes. He was dazed by the question. It had gone against his very nature to disclose to Sheppard the information he had. Everything he had said was based in fact, and aside from the aforementioned individuals, and those along the historic trail in the Masonic craft, Sheppard had become perhaps the only human being outside the top echelon of the Freemason faith to have authenticated knowledge of the sacred secrets of a wealthy few. And as he sat there and pondered what had changed, why she would suddenly question him with such vigor, he was totally perplexed at what had happened to illicit such a dramatic change.

"I've shared with you," he said, "the absolute truth based on historical fact. I have entrusted information to you, which I have entrusted to no one. There is no reason for me to fabricate or embellish research, which, if public, could well end my credible career. Quite frankly, Christina, I am miffed by your sudden inference."

Sheppard looked directly into Hancock's eyes, locked them in a stare, and shot out her question.

"How is it, Hancock, your wife is in mortal danger, hiding at her sister's in California, when she died in 02 of cancer?"

His expression had not changed; his eyes hadn't flinched. On the exterior, Hancock proved the metal of a profound intellectual, capable of camouflaging chaos inside. On the interior, he scrambled for an explanation for his deceit. He knew if he compounded the lie, she would see right through it, and he couldn't take the chance, not now, not so close to the Hepplewhite. He dropped his head in a gesture of guilt, and he held the pose to enunciate the drama, and then, like a middle school child sent to the principal, he looked up with solemn remorse.

"Let me explain," he said.

"It better be good, Hancock, or I'm going after Brosconni and the Hepplewhite alone, and I mean alone."

CHAPTER 47

The van continued down Lamberhurst until it met 21 and turned left heading southeast. Brosconni's wounded foot was draped over his good leg to cushion the movements of the speeding truck. The bleeding had stopped, but the pain pulsated like a hammer was pounding on his mangled foot. But that didn't bother Brosconni as he sat there in the darkness behind the cotton cloth tied at the back of his head, because his thoughts were on Rocco Ricchiettore. Rocco, who never made it to his sixteenth year, took the twelve year old Brosconni under his wing and taught him how to deal with a punk like Nico Sparanzo after Sparanzo had shaken him down.

"How far are you willing to go," Ricchiettore asked Brosconni, "and how much are you willing to lose?" When you can instill fear in the devil himself, and you are willing to die to do so, defeat will no longer exist. Harness the energy of your pain,"

Ricchiettore told the young Brosconni, "and unleash the wrath of hell upon your victim."

And as Brosconni crushed the bones of Sparanzo's legs, and saw the look on Sparanzo's face as he hit the ground, the young boy from Naples felt the full power of Ricchiettore's teachings and he marveled at its potential employment to manipulate the world for his personal use.

So, once again, the wounded tycoon pushed his twisted mind into a psychotic trance and became oblivious to the moving truck, his mouth taped shut, his hands cuffed at the wrists, or the blindfold over his eyes. He focused only on the throbbing in his foot, and he let it overtake his body and his mind. And when the intensity of the pain pushed his psyche into the darkness of that twelve year old boy, he planned his retribution with such a vengeance it would descend the hooded man straight into the depths of hell.

As Brosconni obsessed, the Ford e-series sped down the paved country road. Two miles ahead on 21 the van turned left onto Lady Oak Lane. Another short distance it took a right onto a dirt road surrounded by pastures, but these divided plots of land were not for planting but for feeding instead. It was a livestock farm, and like most of Kent's flat sprawling land, it was separated into parcels of pasture.

The white truck continued down the long dirt access road, and the driver made no adjustments for the pot holes and the bumps. The high speed kicked up a trail of dust that rose into the air and hung effortlessly before it floated back to the earth. But as the van progressed further into the wilderness of the farm, no livestock appeared in the pastures, or on the road, or off in the distance. The land, like the previous farm, was abandoned.

Another five minutes, the Ford approached a farm house with three livestock barns behind it. The main house and additions were small in comparison to the acreage of the estate. The residence was one story with a steeped pitched roof, two additions, one on each side, and a detached two car garage. The outside was stucco with white paint, and the road led up to a walkway which led to a dark wooden door. Past the walk, on the left, was a parking spur. The van pulled up to the front walk and stopped, and Brosconni heard the driver side door open. Then it closed.

Brosconni turned his head to listen. A latch released, and he heard the sliding of the door, then a click, and it stopped. The back doors unlatched and opened, and the hooded man stepped in. Brosconni twisted his head again toward the noise and thought he heard the sound of rope being untied. Then something slid on the floor of the van, then nothing. Brosconni sat in the dark silence and waited for the first opportunity to unleash his attack.

He lifted his head at the sound of shoes landing on masonry which grew louder with each step. He could tell by the impact there was only one person and when it stopped, a foot landed on the running board, and a voice spoke.

"Ok, Brosconni, you get to see your prized Hepplewhite."

Brosconni felt the cold metal barrel against his left temple as the man put a second set of cuffs on Brosconni's wrists. This set, though, was not thread through the restraint bar. The man unlocked one cuff from the first set and Brosconni heard the metal restraint bang the metal inside of the van as it was removed from behind the bar. Brosconni was pulled by his forearm toward the open door, slid to the edge with a cuff dangling loose from his wrist, and then the man spoke again.

"Stand up!" He said.

Brosconni searched with his good foot until it found the ground, and the man pulled him up and out. His arm was tugged forward, and he felt the uneven surface of the walk as it scraped his wound, and he tried to put the weight on the heel not the ball of his injured foot. He walked as if he felt no pain as the aggressive lead on his arm pulled him toward the front door. The door open. Then he sensed the cool touch of a smooth surface on his bare feet, which he guessed was solid hardwood, and he was led through one room and into another. Brosconni was pushed to the floor, and he sat with his back to a wall. The loose cuff was slipped through a metal bar and reattached to his wrist. Then the man walked away.

Brosconni slid his head back against the wall and took a deep breath. He knew there was dirt in his wound, and without treatment it would soon become infected. He lifted his bad foot and placed it over his right leg, in an attempt to elevate it. He took another breath and from behind the darkness of the cotton cover, and then Brosconni attempted to evaluate his situation so far.

The room was empty. The man's shoes as they hit the wood floor made a slight hollow echo as the sound bounce off the plaster walls with no furniture to absorb it. *The house was abandoned,* he figured; *why else would he have chosen the location? He hadn't traveled far from the other farm house; the van ride took less than fifteen minutes. And it was obvious the man had professional training. He put a second pair of cuffs on before he detached the first. The man had experience dealing with prisoners either in combat or out in the field on a local police force. He knew how to take down a suspect without giving up his edge, and he hadn't made one mistake thus far.*

Brosconni eased his head from the wall as drew a strategic deduction from the information he had. If and when he had the opportunity, he'd better make it precise and quick. There would be no second chance. And as he heard the sound of the van's engine seep into the house, he decided he'd jump the son of a bitch the first chance he got, and with such ferocity he'd either be killed or take control. And when he gained the advantage, and the weapon was his, he'd shoot the son of a bitch himself—one bullet at a time until the clip was empty.

Brosconni turned his ear toward the sound of the man re-entering the house. He listened as the echo of his footsteps approached, entered the room, and then stopped. Brosconni looked up even though he was blinded by the cotton cloth.

"So this is the great Brosconni?" The voice said and then laughed. "You look more like a homeless street bum than a ruthless, conniving suit."

The man's feet shuffled on the floor as if he started to walk away, and then stopped.

"What's that, Brosconni, you have nothing to say?—no tricks, no games, no threatening remarks? I think you make more sense with your mouth tapped shut."

Brosconni heard the shoes pace back and forth. Periodically the sound stopped and then picked up again. It seemed the voice searched for the next remark. The pounding of the shoes went silent.

"Get comfortable, Brosconni, this will be your home for the next few days. You and I have some business to conduct, and when we are through if you have fulfilled your obligation, I will leave you alone with your desk. But be forewarned, act on the thoughts that now occupy your sick, demented skull, and you won't leave here alive."

The footsteps moved away from Brosconni. Not far, six or seven strides Brosconni calculated in the darkness behind the blindfold. They stopped, and Brosconni turned his head to listen. Then he heard knocking, like the hooded man banged his knuckles on wood.

"Do you hear that, Brosconni? What does that sound like to you? Is it the tone of something very rare, very special, like the music that flows from a Stradivarius or a Guarneri and confounds intrinsic pleasure from its harmonic pitch, or, is it just the noise of a man's knuckle on a hard piece of wood? You see, one is an appreciation for the harmonic tones of beauty, and the second is just the pounding of a hand on a piece of wood. You, Brosconni, cannot fathom the first. You live in the darkness, where life's meaning is interpreted by that which you can possess. The only value this desk has in your world is as an object you can add to your hoard—another expensive hunk of wood owned exclusively for you."

Brosconni twisted his head and tried to stretch the tension in his neck. He listened to the man pace again, back and forth across the room. Then the footsteps stopped, and he heard two heavy blankets hit the floor. The man walked toward Brosconni.

"It was easy to get you here, Brosconni. All I had to do was waive in front of you that which you no longer had—the Hepplewhite—and your obsession would defy your own safety, your own microcosm of a pathetically protected world. Well, Brosconni, obsess," he said, as he ripped off the blindfold and the light sent daggers into Brosconni's eyes. "I'll leave you, and your pathetic meaning of a life, alone together."

CHAPTER 48

Capalli continued with the conference call.

"Capt. Penso" he said, "how does Scotland Yard intend to proceed?"

"General, Detective Mitchell and will begin conducting a door to door search of the surrounding farms to see if anyone had seen or heard anything. Kent has a number of vacant farms for sale; we plan on searching those as we run across them. If Brosconni's in the area, we'll find him General."

Capalli looked up from the piazza and rolled his eyes toward the clouded sky. Like before, Brosconni had a two to three hour lead. He could be just about anywhere in England. And now, with Brosconni wounded, probably taken hostage in a new vehicle and needing medical attention, time was running short. And in the back of Capalli's mind, although he wasn't proud of it, was the thought that Brosconni could be dead. Or if not dead, with an individual who didn't think twice about using his weapon on the tycoon, and Brosconni, with his defiance, arrogance, and big mouth, could certainly end up dead—soon.

If that was the case, Brosconni's attempted ploy to destroy Capalli's career would have ended with his life. The prospect, although a simple flash across Capalli's brain, gave him pause, and the thought that he could order Capt. Penso back to Rome, and no one would question his command, surfaced as a result. Capalli lowered his gaze to the street.

"Captain!"

"Yes General."

" I want Brosconni found, do you understand me, find him!"

"Yes General."

Capalli turned his head toward his desk.

"Capt. Tinelli?"

"General?"

"What's the status on the Collet investigation?"

"General, Detective Stanno and I have made several trips to the Grand Lodge of New York, on 23rd street—Google it General. Type in Grand Lodge of New York, and at the site go to, "Our grand lodge" and take the virtual tour. The size and the architecture are like nothing I've seen before. This is not some simple organization with a modest meeting hall. It's….."

"What does this have to do with the investigation, Capt. Tinelli?" Capalli asked as he turned, fell into his leather chair and swiveled around to his desk. He pulled his key board out from underneath the drawer, typed in the words Tinelli had given him, and brought up the site. As Tinelli continued, Capalli took the virtual tour. He understood now why the Captain had mentioned it. The complex motifs of each individual room, the size, and the breath of each historical theme, exuded political and personal power on an unprecedented scale. He listened to Tinelli as he examined the Masonic mansion, and he sensed by the photographs something much more elaborate than a group of men practicing a Masonic craft. He couldn't explain it, but it was there.

Each of the twelve rooms, rich in extravagant architectural details, had to have cost a small fortune. Every room had its own pipe organ, and was designed within a specific period of history. The Grand Lodge room, vaulted two stories high, sat over twelve hundred, and had ceilings that would make the Titanic look like a dilapidated slum. It was not what Capalli expected.

"General?"

"I'm listening, Capt. Tinelli."

"Sir, Det. Stanno compiled a list of the thirty two different levels of the hierarchy of the Masonic lodge. Collet, at the top, is called The Prince of the Royal Secret. The lodge is riddled with unusual rituals and ceremonies much of which Collet is unwilling to discuss. Stanno and I decided to interview the individuals who hold positions just under Collet to see what we could learn. Of the ten directly below Collet, we were able to contact all except one, number 26—The Prince of Mercy."

The General's head came up. He pushed his chair back and propped his chin up with his hands clutched together underneath.

"Go ahead, Captain," he said. "what did you learn?"

"General, of the ones we talked to, they're as closed mouthed as Collet. It's like they have some sacred oath and are forbidden to discuss anything about their positions, the ceremonies, or the mysterious history of the lodge. All they would say was the same three things: Masonry does things in the world, does things inside a mason, and masons enjoy each other's company. They all repeated it like a practiced chorus to satisfy the curiosity of the questioning masses."

Capalli swiveled around to the window and made the steeple with his two fingers at his mouth.

"And twenty six?" Capalli said.

"General, when we questioned the others about The Prince of Mercy, and his whereabouts, no one seemed to know. So Stanno did some digging."

"And?"

"Well, sir, he hasn't been seen in his apartment on the east side for well over a week. Stanno questioned some of his neighbors, and they said they couldn't be sure just what day he left, but, they said they were sure it's been weeks not days. He travels often for business, lives alone, and keeps to himself when he's at home."

"How long has he been a member of the lodge?"

"We can't get a straight answer on that, but from what we understand, most of his adult life."

Capalli swiveled back to his desk, reached for the mouse sitting on the pad, and clicked out of the Grand Lodge. He brought up the murder file on Miller and Bennetto and scrolled through to the first homicide—Miller. It had been just over a week and a half, twelve days to be exact, and Capalli made a mental note. He clicked out and pulled up the file on Collet. Miller had made the call to Collet exactly thirteen days earlier. Capalli calculated the sequence of events: *the call came in at 3:00 pm New York time, if "The Prince," caught a flight out that night, he could have committed the crime the next day, tight, but possible.* Capalli looked up.

"What else do you have on this guy?" He asked.

"Well, General, the guy has a respected career. He taught at NYU for a stint, is a published non-fictionist, and when Stanno ran his name, he came up clean. His neighbors said he's friendly, respectful, but keeps to himself."

"What about the Lodge, anyone have anything to say about this Prince of Mercy?"

"It's like I stated before, trying to get information out of anyone is like talking to a Buddhist monk. That place is serious business, and no one is going to divulge a thing."

Capalli jumped up from his seat and turned and faced the window. His eyes circled the piazza as his hand rose to his mouth. The last time he experienced an organization this tough to crack, he failed, one of the few times, but he failed. It was the holy city, the Vatican, and even though the case led to the inside, The General was shut down as if he had been a patrol cop and had no business being inside. There seemed to be a shroud of impenetrable steel around the city, and unless you were God, you couldn't get in. Capalli had the same feeling now. The mob was easier to break than this Masonic mystery, and they, like the Vatican, seemed protected by a holy decree.

"What about Collet?" He asked.

"Collet refuses to talk unless his lawyer's present, in which case, we have a one sided conversation with his attorney. And Stanno has gotten pressure to back off. He was told it's coming down from the commissioner. But, from what Stanno's heard, it's a lot higher than that. His Captain told him either make an arrest or back off. I don't like the smell of it, General, we're being blocked on every side."

Capalli paused. He was wasting his assets with Tinelli in New York. It was a foreign country where he had no control, and he had no clout. The commissioner's word, who personally said the department would cooperate with his investigation, seemed a hollow promise now. *Bring him home, or leave him there?* He thought back to the Vatican, all the resources, all the time, the effort, wasted. He knew it when it happened, but he couldn't make himself pull back. He looked to the church across the street and shook his head side to side. *God damn it!*

"Capt. Tinelli!"

"Yes, General?"

"Take the next flight back to Rome."

"General?"

"Let the Americans finish the investigation, Capt., I want you back in Rome."

Capalli pulled his head back and exhaled. When he opened his eyes, they stared at the sound proof ceiling tiles.

"Capt. Tinelli," Capalli said, "I want a picture of this Prince of Mercy sent to me before you leave."

"Yes sir, I'll send that to you now."

"A name, Capt.?"

"Yes sir, his name, General, is Randolph Hancock."

CHAPTER 49

"Well," she said as they sat in the Tahoe at Links Golf Club parked in front of the practice tee, "I'm waiting." Her back was against the driver side door, and her blue eyes pierced through the fog of his opaque brown pupils.

"I'm not going to ask again!" Sheppard said.

His plan, up until now, had been flawless. He knew from the beginning, after the Hepplewhite was stolen, the only avenue to the desk was through Sheppard. And Hancock had been trained for this moment, groomed by the Masonic craft since the age of six. He attended the summer camps in upstate New York. Handpicked for his name sake, the great x 6 grandson of John Hancock, founding father, brother mason, one of many architects of the new world order. It was his destiny, the Grand Master had said, and it had been drilled into him throughout his youth.

So Sheppard's revelation came as no surprise to Hancock. Her eidetic detective work was just another bump on his way to recovering the Hepplewhite. He was, after all, The Prince of Mercy: sworn to protect, at any cost, the most sacred secret of the Masonic craft. Sheppard was simply the means to the end that would help him carry out that task. And she, like Brosconni, would join Miller and Bennetto when his mission was complete.

Hancock sheepishly looked to Sheppard, and shook his head as if in affirmation of his guilt.

"Alright, Christina, I'll explain," Hancock said, "but don't judge me until you hear the reason why." And then he paused for effect.

Hancock, like all the hierarchy of the New York City Grand Lodge, was the legacy by which the new world order was governed. Handed down generation to generation, only the elite few commanded the covert policies which governed the original thirteen colonies and had now expanded to fifty individual states. In literally all walks of life, the Masonic brothers implemented the directives of the chosen few. Supreme Court justices, presidents, vice presidents, generals, virtually every structured organization in America had been under the directive of the Masonic craft since the American Revolution. All of what Hancock had said was true, used to lure Sheppard in, but she'd never live to tell a single word of it—never!

The lie, Hancock had calculated, was to bring her on board emotionally. His research team in Manhattan had done their homework on Sheppard. He had been trained in the psychological preparation of a nosam: the term used by the craft which signified an outside individual being used unknowingly with a particular purpose and outcome at stake, one which would benefit the secret order of the Masonic lodge. Richard Nixon was a blundering example of a nosam. His useful life as a political asset was marred by his love of scotch and his crazed paranoia of those around him. The Grand Master had little time to cultivate a replacement as the American public had grown restless, and his excesses became more extreme. So they replaced the Vice-President, Spiro Agnew, instead with brother mason, Gerald Ford, who had been an important member of the Warren commission investigating JFK's death. Thus Ford became the first, and only, non-elected President of the United States after Nixon resigned.

Although Sheppard was not a world figure, with great political power and influence, she held the key to the most incriminating piece of evidence in Masonic history. The two pieces of sealed correspondence hidden behind the back panel of the mahogany veneer, if discovered, and made public, had the potential to incite a modern day revolution. So Sheppard became the ideal nosam, primed by the knowledge Hancock had received from the lodge. The research team left him with one caveat, though, and stressed the importance of its use. Her photographic memory, supplied with non-verbal subliminal images could be referenced by her at a later date, particularly, when she questioned his intentions or the accuracy of what he said.

Hancock had carefully orchestrated and monitored his facial expressions and posture in

Sheppard's presence. And he used the timing of the introduction of specific subjects, in coordination with the aforementioned strategy as a means to enunciate its importance in her recall. Every aspect of his relationship with Sheppard had been methodically planned and rehearsed. Two hundred and twenty four years earlier, when Washington's desk mysteriously disappeared, Hancock's position, The Prince of Mercy, was assigned one specific task: ride through the generations prepared to recover the undelivered documents hidden in the back of the desk. And Hancock was determined to succeed.

It was crucial Hancock use the tragic death of her family to his advantage. And he left no stone unturned. Hancock had studied photographs and video tapes taken from Sheppard's apartment to recreate the actions and images of her late husband, Ray. It was not only important to look like him, both in appearance and dress, but in mannerisms too. Hancock had practiced his walk, expressions, hand actions, and how he sat in a chair. And he drilled Ray's physical persona into her infallible memory as he spoke. It was a critical tool in his psychological arsenal.

And, he believed he had used the potential loss of his wife, and intrusting his life's work in Sheppard's hands as a brilliant tool in her grooming. Even though the unexpected recall of an article, eight years before, came as a snag, Hancock was not rattled in the least. In fact, Hancock performed best when he had to improvise. So as Sheppard had thrown out the curve ball, Hancock's instincts were ready to hit it out of the park. He dropped his eyes toward the floor, hesitated, and then spoke.

"My wife died eight years ago, after a two year battle with ovarian cancer which ate out her insides and finally took her life. I'm sorry," he said as he covered his eyes with the palm of his hand, a movement he mimicked from her husband which he had learned on one of the tapes. "It's been eight years," he said, and again paused, took a deep and painful breath, "but it still feels like yesterday." He removed his hand, lifted his head, and looked at Sheppard.

He saw her face begin to soften. Her hand dropped from the steering wheel to her lap, and her eyes rolled down toward the leather seat.

"I know I need help, Christina. When I'm alone at night, I want to join her; I've thought about it. The only thing that has stopped me was the promise she made me make the night she died. She made me give an oath to finish my work. No matter what, she said, do it for me, and the love that we shared together. The only way I've been able to continue my research is to pretend she's alive, and I make believe she's there looking over my shoulder when I work. And when I'm alone, having dinner, I talk to her at the table, and I swear I see her sitting there across from me with her innocent little girl smile. When I told you I had only six months to live, I meant it. But not like you think. I made my own pack, and when I have completed my work as I promised, I will join her. My time here on earth will be done. I don't expect you to understand, Christina, but it's true, and I've never told anyone about this except you."

Hancock stopped. He let the full effect fill the space inside the Tahoe. Although he couldn't see, her eyes had become moist, and she had retreated into her own living hell. He waited a moment more and then finished her off.

"You can take me back to the airport, Christina, if that's what you wish to do. I won't bother you anymore."

Sheppard looked up and over to Hancock. He now saw her glazed over blue eyes, and her face was drawn and lifeless.

"I understand more than you know," she said, "I'm sorry."

Sheppard started the truck, put the Tahoe in reverse, and backed out of the space. Hancock left her in the silence to reminisce in her own personal horror, ignited by his words and his actions. She exited the parking lot and headed toward M4 like a zombie staring through the darkness of the night. For over two centuries, generations had waited for the Hepplewhite to surface, trained and prepared for the event, and Hancock now felt the weight of his unfulfilled predecessors as Sheppard helped him carry out his mission. And it was a fate unknowing to Sheppard that would ultimately lead to her death.

CHAPTER 50

Brosconni peered out the slits of his eyelids as his pupils adjusted to the light. At first, the room appeared as a bright flash as he sat cuffed on the floor. But in the passing moments Brosconni's eyes opened wider and what first appeared as a dark blur ten feet away, slowly came into focus. He devoured the rich color of the golden brown patina for the first time since the night at Villa Marcella, and he yanked on the cuffs as if to break loose so he could stand and race over to his prized Hepplewhite.

But feeling the pulsating pain, Brosconni broke his stare and glanced down to his foot. It was covered in dried brown blood and had loose skin hanging where his toe had been. And it was swollen and grossly distorted.

He rolled his eyes up and scanned the room. It was empty except for the desk which sat in front of a large open hearth fireplace built with local stone. The chimney rose up to the ridge of the cathedral ceiling and the walls were tied together by two round trunks of tree. The plastered walls were covered in white paint, interrupted by a window on each side, and the floor was wide wooden planks. He locked his stare back onto the desk, blinked to clear his vision, and as he did the sound of a voice startled him from the right. His instinct to attack made him lunge toward the figure, but the metal bar the cuffs threaded through stopped his assault, and the hooded man let out a sarcastic laugh and spoke.

"I thought you'd like to see the farm house where the Hepplewhite was discovered." He said.

Brosconni studied the figure in the ski mask as he entered the room through the wide cased opening to the right.

"You having such a nostalgic appreciation for historic fact, Brosconni, it seemed the appropriate place for a disingenuous reunion."

Brosconni followed him with his eyes as the man approached. His frame was not stocky or thin, it was solid beneath his black, long sleeved, collarless shirt tucked into his faded blue jeans. In the waist of the pants, just above the zipper, was the forty five. It was holstered behind his thick black belt. His head was covered in a cotton mask, with slits at the eyes, and his hands were covered with latex gloves. The boots, Forze Armate dello Stato issue (Italian military) made a heavy sound as they pounded the wooden floor. Although the soles showed wear from the years in Special Forces, the leather was shined to look like new. The black boots stopped as they reached Brosconni.

The arrogant tycoon's first reaction was to tell the son of a bitch he was dead, but the tape froze his lips as he tried. So he spoke with his eyes as he breached the slits of the hood, and spit the words with his stare. *Blink, you son of a bitch, and I'll crack you in half so quick you won't know what hit you!*

The man in the hood stared back. The intensity of Brosconni's visual attack lasted only a moment, and then the man turned and chuckled.

"You don't know when you're beat, Brosconni, any other man would have their head hanging and their mouth shut. You just keep asking for more. Well, you can marinate until you're ready to cooperate!" He said as he moved through the cased opening and disappeared.

Brosconni's head leaned back against the wall. The sun had begun to set, and the room was shaded in partial darkness. With it came a chill, which Brosconni first felt on his feet and rose to his butt on the cold wooden floor. But Hunger and cold was not new to Brosconni. As a child, the two were intertwined, and at night as he lay in bed with only a thin sheet, no heat, and an empty belly, he learned how to shut down his mind and disregard his body. And in the darkness, in the moments just before sleep, he reveled in the fact he could take more pain, and abuse, than any other human being alive. It's what set Enrico Brosconni apart from the rest, and he thought of that as he looked at his desk and then closed his eyes. Within moments, Brosconni was asleep.

Somewhere in the night, the man walked in and kicked Brosconni's leg. Brosconni shook his head and opened his eyes. The room was filled with the black of night except for the flashlight in the man's hand, which he shined into Brosconni's eyes.

"Having a good rest are you, Brosconni, good. You and I have some business to attend to tomorrow, and if I see that look in your eyes again, I'll blow off your toes one by one."

Brosconni followed the light as it lit a trail across the room, moved out the cased opening, and shut off when it turned the corner. His left arm had fallen asleep, and he moved forward away from the wall and flexed his hand in and out. The feeling started to come back. His butt was sore from the hardwood floor, so he leaned right as far as the cuffs would allow and rested on the edge of his right hip. The musty smell of a closed up house permeated the air and started to wreak havoc on his sinuses. He dosed in an out for the next hour or two, and when he awoke, he sneezed, and the mucus shot out of his nose, and he tried to wipe his face on his shoulder but he couldn't reach, so he started blowing out his nose to clear it. His airway was partially blocked by the mucus, and it became harder and harder to breath. By the time the first light appeared, Brosconni was tired, cramped, and had to take a leak.

Brosconni examined the back of the desk which was all that was visible from his position on the floor. He thought back to Villa Marcella, to the escape tunnel, and wondered how the son of a bitch knew it was there. Someone on the inside told him, Brosconni surmised, there was no other way. Not only did he learn of the secret passage, but also that the Hepplewhite was in the room. That was not a coincidence; that was a planned operation waiting for the right payoff, and the Hepplewhite fit the bill. And as Brosconni stared at its silhouette in the breaking dawn, he was determined to find out who had betrayed him, and when he did, the escape tunnel at Villa Marcella would become his grave.

As the sun turned darkness into full light, the smell of coffee floated in the air. Brosconni's stomach hurt from hunger, and the aroma of the fresh brew made his mouth salivate behind the duct tape stuck to his face. As he looked down to his foot, he figured the burning and pain indicated an infection had set in, and the redness confirmed what he felt. But Brosconni wasn't bothered by that; he figured he would soon be free and have his Hepplewhite and take his revenge. The hooded man had to undo the cuffs so Brosconni could take a leak, and the minute he did, Brosconni would unleash his hell.

Brosconni calculated the sun had been up almost an hour when the hooded man came back to the room. He checked the man's waist and saw the forty five still behind his belt. The man approached him and stopped.

"I'm going to free up your mouth, Brosconni, keep it closed." He said as he reached down, grabbed a corner of the tape, and ripped it off in one instantaneous jerk of his hand.

Brosconni didn't flinch even though his skin and lips felt like they had been ripped off with the tape. He stared up at the hood as if nothing had happened, and in his arrogance even cracked a grin. When the hooded man turned to walk toward the desk, Brosconni opened his mouth and stretched his jaw and moved it side to side. When the man turned back, Brosconni's face froze, and his eyes pierced the space between them, and he shot a defiant glare into the slits of the mask.

"Look at you Brosconni: you have mansions, limousines, private jets, enough money to fill this room tenfold, and here you are chained to a wall, missing a toe, and about to piss in your pants, and for what, a dead piece of wood?"

"Fuck you!" Brosconni screamed.

"You're a fool, Brosconni. You've committed acts which violate every fiber of your being: entered the house of the lord, repeated ten hail Mary's', run from place to place under my command, even stripped down naked in the deceased place of rest, just so you could get back what you thought was yours. And you sit there, you little maggot, and look me in the eyes like you have the power of the devil himself, and you can destroy me with your evil will. Well you're nothing but a little Italian fuck, you're no different from the rest of the garbage on the street, and the next time you try to stare me down like you have some mystical power to turn me into a pancake, I'll cut your eyes right out of their sockets and stick them in the pocket of your overalls."

The hooded man turned and started to walk out of the room.

"Hey," Brosconni yelled, "uncuff me so I can piss."

Without breaking his stride, he continued toward the cased opening.

"You son of a bitch, take these off now," he screamed.

CHAPTER 51

Capalli sat at his desk with black circles under his bloodshot eyes. He had spent most of the night in the emergency waiting room, while his wife, Carlota, was being administered a battery of tests. Alberto sat alone as doctors consulted on the results of the lumbar puncture, CT scan, and MRI to determine the severity and current conditions of the hemorrhagic stroke Carlota had suffered earlier in evening. It was fallout from the pending situation, and Capalli knew it. The prospect of a national scandal with the Italian press had taken its toll. In the past, Alberto had kept Carlota insulated from hardship and stress, and with the exception of one other major trauma in their lives—the loss of a child—he had shouldered the burdens quite well. But now, alone in Carabinieri headquarters, remembering the death of their son, Capalli was faced with the gut wrenching reality he had failed both his marriage and his career.

Two years into their marriage, Carlota became pregnant, and from the beginning, she experienced difficulties after conception. As her term progressed, her doctor feared for the health of both the mother and the child. Finally with two months of her term left, Carlota was confined to her bed. Alberto was a major in the Carabinieri stationed at main headquarters in Rome. Focused on his career, and soon to be promotion to Lt. Colonel, Capalli worked long hours and traveled much of the time. In the last month of her pregnancy, Capalli was assigned a case involving the infamous theft of Caravaggio's "The Sacrifice of Isaac," from the Uffizi Gallery in Florence. The stolen masterpiece was believed to have been smuggled out of the country and into France. Capalli was in Paris when he received the news that his wife had been rushed to the Policlinico Umberto hospital in Rome. He flew out of Paris that night.

By the time the Colonel had arrived, Carlota had experienced a miscarriage, had bled profusely, and was in intensive care. Capalli had lost his unborn son and almost lost his wife. Carlota was angry by his absence and devastated by the loss of their child. She spent two weeks in the hospital recovering, and after the first week, Capalli went back to France. Carlota rode in and out of depression for the next year, and although Alberto longed to have a son, she refused to conceive again. Capalli recognized he'd never have the heir he'd hoped to have, so he doubled his efforts advancing his career. His service in the Carabinieri flourished, his marriage had not.

Three days earlier, when he told Carlota about the stolen artifacts and the bribe, she had become despondent and depressed. And as usual, Capalli went to work. His obsession to solve the theft at Villa Marcella, before Brosconni broke the news, had pushed her close to a nervous breakdown. Instead, she suffered an intracerebral hemorrhage of the left hemisphere, and although the bleeding had stopped, she was partially paralyzed on her right side and in critical condition. The doctor's had induced a coma until the brain swelling subsided, that was if she survived. Now, alone in his office at his desk, the reality had just begun to sink in. He had ended his career by an unconscionable bribe, and now it may have killed his wife too.

Capalli stared at the wall of plaques, empty, alone, and despondent. He knew he had been a lousy husband. And he also realized he had tried to compensate for his failed marriage by his determined efforts to be the best Carabinieri in the Italian military. But none of that mattered now. His wife was knocking on heaven's door, and the fact remained, no matter how much he tried to rationalize it, he had made a career ending pact with the devil. And as he stumbled through his thoughts, he swiveled his chair and gazed in a remorseful trance to the near empty piazza.

He was shaken to the core by what he now felt. Even at the height of his bout with gambling, he still loved his work, thrived on it. But as he sat staring at the Sant Lgnazio, it seemed the military blood had been siphoned from his veins and left a hollow shell of a uniformed man alone to grapple with the carnage.

Capalli pulled back from the window at the sound of a woman's voice and swiveled his chair around to his desk.

"Yes Caprina?"

"General, Capt. Penso's on the phone from England........."

The General's head fell back against the leather of the high back chair. His eyes rolled toward the ceiling. And then he closed them.

"General, are you ok?" She asked.

Capalli opened his eyes and took a deep breath.

"General, would you like me to tell Capt. Penso you'll call him back?"

Capalli turned toward the phone.

"Put him through."

"Yes sir."

"What is it Captain?" Capalli asked.

Capt. Penso cleared his throat and then spoke in a quiet soft tone.

"General, we're sorry about Carlota, sir."

The General, still in a daze, rubbed his eyes with his hand.

"Yes Capt." he said as he tried to regain the voice of a man in command. "What is it?"

"Sir, Scotland yard ran a check of customs. Randolph Hancock arrived at Heathrow this morning. He went through customs at 10:35 am."

Capalli had his elbow on the wooden arm rest, and his forehead propped up with his hand. He felt like the air had been knocked from his lungs and struggled to take a breath. He massaged his temples with his fingers and tried to compose a response.

"General?"

"Yes Captain, I'm listening."

"Sir, we haven't been able to get a fix on how he left the airport. There were no records of Hancock renting a vehicle. Scotland Yard is checking to see if he entered on the date Miller expired. I received the picture of Hancock from Capt. Tinelli and we're sending it across the wires as we speak. Hold on General...... .Detective Mitchell just confirmed it, General, on the morning Miller was shot, Hancock went through customs at 6:00 am. Sir, I think we've finally got something."

Capalli dropped his hands to his lap and gathered his senses.

"Stay on it Capt." He said. "What's the status on Brosconni?"

"Nothing yet, General, we're still checking the country side of Kent, but we only have two men on it: that's all Scotland Yard can spare."

"Very good, Capt. keep me informed. Capt. Tinelli arrives from New York this morning. I'll have him contact you the moment he arrives. If anything major breaks, contact me on my cell."

"Yes, General."

Capalli hung up and pressed the button for his secretary.

"Caprina!"

"Yes General?"

"Cancel my briefing this morning. In fact," he said as he took a deep breath, "clear my schedule for the day; I will be at the hospital until further notice."

CHAPTER 52

Sheppard drove toward Bromley, as instructed by the caller, where she was to stop at an old tavern inn and wait for further instructions. Rattled by Hancock's performance, she managed to slowly bring herself back. As she passed through Sutton, Sheppard had regained enough of her balance to initiate a conversation with Hancock. She turned and asked him the question she had asked a week ago on the Amalfi coast, one in which she never received the answer. It caught Hancock off guard.

"So what's so earth shattering in the sealed correspondence, Hancock, that it could throw The United States into chaos?"

Hancock looked out his window at the row of housing beyond the park. He had no intention of telling her the truth when he chose her as his ticket to the Hepplewhite, only enough to reel her in. When he learned he could trust her, and she kept their conversations confidential, he toyed with the idea of exposing the truth. After all, Sheppard would never live to tell it. But the oath he had taken, to disclose only that which was needed to complete his work, dictated how much he had said to Sheppard. And, she was already committed to his mission, why tell her now?

Still, he needed to tell her something. He knew Sheppard's personality would demand that he continue until he completed the story, after all, her work depended on a strong curiosity with the goal of discovering all the facts. This was no different to Sheppard than when she examined an historic piece, and Sheppard didn't quit. That's why she stayed on the Italian peninsula, and why she was in England with Hancock now. So Hancock decided to go slow and draw the story out, and perhaps, he'd never get to the end. And if he did, it didn't matter, because the end would be close to the end.

Hancock brought his focus back into the truck and rolled his eyes to the left.

"Well," she said.

"Well," he said, "first, there's one more missing piece of the puzzle—Alexander Hamilton."

Christina removed her eyes from the road and snapped a look to her right. Hancock's brows were raised deep into his forehead, and his lips were clamped shut tight. He had that look one has when a person knows they've just surprised their listener. Sheppard turned her attention back to the highway as she spoke.

"Hamilton?" She asked.

"Hamilton," he said as a definitive tone, "Aide-de-camp to General George Washington during the Revolutionary war, first Secretary of the Treasury under the first president, primary author of Washington's economic policies, and, last but not least, scandalized by an American President, Thomas Jefferson. He resigned in shame as Secretary of the Treasury, and then later was shot and killed by Mr. Jefferson's Vice-President, Aaron Burr—all in the course of shaping a nation."

"What do you mean," she asked as she looked to Hancock with a curious giggle, "all in the course of shaping a nation?'"

Sheppard put her hand out. "Wait," she said as she read the sign which assured her she was on A232 toward Croydon. "Sorry, go ahead."

"The history books tell you Hamilton insulted Burr, Burr had to regain his honor, so he challenged Hamilton to a duel, and, even though dueling had become illegal in New York, and a Vice President of the United States while in office had never killed another human being, they crossed the Hudson to New Jersey. Aaron Burr put a bullet in Hamilton's abdomen above his right hip, piercing his liver and spine. Hamilton, needless to say, died shortly thereafter."

"And your version, Hancock?"

Hancock peered out the passenger window at the passing landscape. The question took him back to his induction as a master mason of the 26th degree. Only a chosen few broke into the last eight degrees of Masonic Craft, and he remembered that night as if it were yesterday.

Until that moment, like ninety nine percent of all freemasons, Hancock knew nothing of what went on at the top, and he recalled entering the Grand Lodge on 23rd Street, being escorted to a room on the first floor, instructed to remove his clothes and replace them with the brown full length robe with a hood. He was then led into the colonial room and subjected to a complex set of rituals and ceremonies which conferred onto him the title of "The Prince of Mercy." The moments that followed consummated Hancock's indoctrination into the inner circles of the Masonic craft. And it gave him access to the actual account of historical events from the original thirteen colonies right up to present day.

Hancock was led to a narrow room with encased glass bookshelves which ran the length on opposite walls. In the center was a conference table and chairs, and at the end of the room, rising over ten feet in the air, was a golden statue of fellow mason, and first President of the United States—George Washington. The Grand Master, The Sublime Prince of the Royal Secret, approached the statue, touched Washington's foot, hand, and Masonic apron, removed a key from his neck, slid it into a small recess on the side of the Presidents shoe, and turned it to the right. The Grand Master then walked to the first set of bookshelves, opened the eight foot glass door, pushed the entire rack of books by the corner and exposed a thick tall metal door. He put in the combination and slid the metal door open toward the inside of the room.

Hancock's education had begun. Inside were over six hundred manuscripts which dated as far back as 1730 when Freemasonry was first introduced into the New York Colony. The text, housed in the temperature controlled, fire proof environment, could only be accessed by one man—the thirty second degree of the Masonic hierarchy—The Sublime Prince of the Royal Secret. Inside, was the story of the Masonic new world order from Benjamin Franklin to George W. Bush, and Hancock spent the next number of years reading a great deal of the contents of that room, and when he finished, he had learned the historical truth of the distorted facts planted over the generations by his predecessors.

Hancock's reputation as a famed historian was a responsibility he incurred upon indoctrination as Prince of Mercy. The results of his efforts were exactly the opposite of what it seemed to the average American citizen. His job, besides the enforcement and protection of the Masonic secrets, was to write history as the Master Mason's intended it to be portrayed, not as it actually occurred. And, as Hancock had learned in that security vault of a library, his profession had been practiced for over two hundred and fifty years. History had been documented by famed historians to instill a cover for the Masonic craft. "Fashion the truth," the instructions read in the secret volumes on 23rd street, "in a manner by which your subject would never be considered suspect or called anything other than indisputable fact."

"My version," he said as he turned to Sheppard and snapped out of his ceremonial recall. "How much time do you have?"

"I'll drive," she said, "you talk!"

Brosconni had dozed, and his head snapped up, as the wall of water slammed him into consciousness.

"You smell like a God damn sewer, Brosconni, pissing in your pants and on the floor."

The hooded man picked up a second bucket and doused the tycoon again.

"You think I'm stupid, Brosconni, let you off the cuff. Get used to it.

He picked up the two empty buckets and exited the room. Brosconni shook his head like a dog after a swim and looked down at the puddle of water—*son of a bitch.* With his eyes squinted, he turned his head toward the window and checked the location of the sun. *Close to noon,* he figured.

"How about something to eat," he screamed as water dripped off his checks. "I, said, how about some fucking food!" he screamed again, nothing. Brosconni's head fell back against the wall, and he let out a shallow exhale.

The hooded man returned and stopped at the desk, lifted his arm, and looked at his watch.

"11:15, Brosconni, that means your Swiss friends have gone to lunch. We'll wait another forty five minutes, until 1:00 pm Swiss time, and then you and I have some business to conduct. You, want your desk; I, want your cash—one million American dollars to be exact. I think that's a fair price for a desk owned by an American President. We're going back to the three strike ballgame, Brosconni, and here's how we play:

You will talk to your friendly banker in Switzerland and transfer the money from one Clariden Lue account to a second already set up. Your personal contact is a man named Clouster Van Templand. I have all your files from your computer and Smartphone, Brosconni. I will know if you give any incorrect information or try to give Templand any reason to think you're not just making a simple transfer of cash. You so much as twitch the wrong way, the price goes up a half a million dollars, twice, a million, three times you're dead."

The man headed toward the cased opening. He stopped as Brosconni spoke.

"You won't live to spend it." Brosconni said.

"One point five, Brosconni, you have two strikes left!"

"Alright, you drive, I'll talk, but I have to warn you, this is a very complicated story."

"I'm listening," Sheppard said.

"First, you need to understand that Thomas Jefferson and Alexander Hamilton were on opposite ends of the political spectrum. They served under Washington: Hamilton as first Secretary of the Treasury, Jefferson as the first Secretary of State."

"What does this have to do with Burr and Hamilton's duel?" Sheppard asked as she passed a car on the right.

"I told you, it's complicated, don't interrupt. Jefferson vigorously opposed Hamilton's proposed concept for the future of the United States. But, in the end, Hamilton had Washington's approval, which changed the landscape of the American economy."

"What was approved?"

"I'll get to that, just drive." Hancock looked up toward the ceiling of the Tahoe, took an obvious breath, and then continued.

"Jefferson had no way of knowing, but the cards had been stacked against him before he even argued the case. Washington, a freemason sworn in as the first President of the United States by the Grand Master of the New York Grand Lodge, was designing the blueprint for the new world order from the ground on up. Alexander Hamilton was what the Master Masons of the last eight degrees call, an invisible brother of the Masonic Craft. His name had been stricken from any written records which could identify him as a member of a Masonic Lodge.

This had been done throughout history to nullify any insistence that the country was controlled by a select few. Only chosen figures, like Washington, were kept on record: one, because they were immensely popular, and two, because historically the masses of the craft needed a fellow brother they could revere as a member of their lodge. The other important individuals that surrounded these figures remained, in the public's eye, as American citizens with no affiliation to the lodge. My point is, Thomas Jefferson, had no idea Washington would have gone with Hamilton's proposal no matter what, which pushed Jefferson, a non mason, further from the ideologies of Washington's policies and into the new democratic-republican party."

"Your swelling my brain, Hancock, in my book less is more, what about Burr?"

Hancock read the sign which said Bromley thirty two kilometers. He calculated they had forty minutes more in the Tahoe. *If her brain was swollen now,* he thought, *it will have exploded by the time we arrive at the Inn.* He turned his head back toward Sheppard.

"Jefferson," he said, "had an intense distrust of Hamilton, and that distrust had become a burr under his saddle, no pun intended. When his buddy, Madison, offered Jefferson information about a salacious affair Mr. Hamilton was involved in Jefferson went straight to work. He managed to arrange for the damaging story to fall into the hands of a muck raking reporter (by the way the same reporter who first broke the story on Jefferson and Hemmings years later). The reporter published pamphlets acknowledging Hamilton and a woman named, Maria Reynolds, were having an affair. Thus began the first political sex scandal of the United States of America and the first member of government to resign because of that affair."

"You haven't told me one thing I can't look up on the internet, Hancock."

"Aaron Burr represented Maria Reynolds in her divorce from her husband: the same Aaron Burr that later became Vice-President under Jefferson, and the same Aaron Burr who shot and killed Hamilton in a duel."

"Go ahead Capt," Capalli said as he sat in the private hospital room with his wife Carlota. Her eyes were shut, she had an intubation tube in, and she lay in an induced coma in the bed. Alberto had arrived a half hour before, and the doctor briefed him on his wife's condition. It was too early to fully understand the extent of the trauma to her brain, Dr. Pietro had said, until we bring her out of the protective coma, tomorrow. We want to be sure the swelling has subsided before we do. Capalli, as it had been a part of his personality from a very young age, looked like steel on the outside—a commander's posture. But now, as he sat next to the bed in a high back chair, Alberto was scared to death his wife might not ever recover.

"General, how is Carlota sir?"

"We don't know anything yet. What is it Capt.?"

"Sir, we confirmed Hancock went through customs at Da Vinci airport on the morning Bennetto was murdered." Penso said.

"What time?"

"10:00 am Rome time."

The General stood up and turned to the window. He gazed down from the fourth story of the hospital Policlinico Umberto I at the traffic maneuvering the street below. He knew in his investigative instincts Hancock murdered Miller and Bennetto, and he believed it had been directed by Collet. And now, Hancock was in England after Brosconni, and if they didn't find this "Prince" before he located his target, the tycoon would certainly end up dead. Again he paused at the prospect, but then quickly erased the idea from his mind.

"What about Hancock," The General asked, "any progress on how he left Heathrow?"

"Well, sir, we tried a long shot and maybe got lucky."

"What is it Capt.?"

"General, we ran Sheppard's name through customs.

"And?"

"And we got a hit. Christina Sheppard cleared customs the afternoon before Hancock arrived."

Capalli turned and looked to his wife lying on the bed unconscious. He felt his insides crumble. Nothing had changed. The General had left his office to be by his wife's side, and here he was standing over her comatose body conducting business as usual. He felt ill.

"Capt., I'll call you back in a moment." He said and hung up.

Capalli dropped his arm to his waist with his iphone in his hand. He scanned the room, looked to his wife, and then walked toward the solid wood door. He opened it, passed through, gazed in both directions down the hall and spotted a sign above a door which confirmed it was the waiting room. He marched down the spotless glazed tile to the room and went inside. It was empty. He moved to the window, lifted his hand, and punched in Penso's number.

"Capt.," The General said, "continue!"

"General, Sheppard rented a white Chevy Tahoe that morning. We've sent the description and plate number over the wires. It's obvious whatever is happening is going down in England. We believe the location is in the Kent country side where Brosconni left the stolen car."

Capalli stared through the glass at the building across the street. Even though Sheppard and Hancock arrived on different flights at different times, The General sensed the connection: he was sure of it. Someone was pulling everyone involved with the Hepplewhite to one central location, *but why? Had Sheppard been involved from the beginning? Have we been careless and missed a clue?*

Capalli thought back to Villa Marcella, and Sheppard's demeaning demonstration of how the thief accessed the room. *Had she known about it the night before? Brosconni had described how she insisted on halting the examination of the desk. She retired to her room and was not seen again until Brosconni discovered the Hepplewhite missing. But they examined the surveillance tapes; Sheppard could not have left the room undetected, or could she?*

"Capt., that Tahoe is headed to Kent. Locate that white Chevy but don't stop it. We need to find out its destination. I believe Hancock is inside that truck, with Sheppard, and where ever its going, Brosconni and the desk will be there too. Do not stop that Tahoe, Captain, understood?"

CHAPTER 53

Sheppard drove the white Tahoe on the left side of the road, which still felt very strange to her. As she listened to Hancock, and stared out to the pavement, she wondered why, why did the English choose the opposite side of the road? It felt unnatural.

"Did you hear what I said?"

"I'm listening, Hancock, but you're still quoting history books verbatim."

She decided she'd look that up, when she arrived back home, whenever that would be. *Did they do the same with a horse drawn carriage before they invented the car?*

"Christina?"

"Yes?"

"In order to comprehend the content of the correspondence, you need to understand the accepted perception of what was transpiring at the time."

"You've already said that before, Hancock, either give me some new material or get to the point."

"Burr was now a United States Senator from New York aspiring to make the next jump to President of the United States. The senator had a reputation of using political campaigns in much the same slanderous way as modern day politicians but, he also had an intense mistrust of the newly formed government. He believed the government was not transparent and that the country was being controlled by a wealthy few. He had no idea how right he was, or, how close he came to exposing the Masonic lodge as the central seat of power.

Burr asserted Hamilton, Secretary of the Treasury, and Washington, President of the United States, had railroaded an economic policy down the American public's throat to line the pockets of a chosen few. When the Hamilton scandal broke, and Maria needed a lawyer, Burr knew from previous clients that individuals in the fires of passion, particularly in illicit affairs that have become public and thus soured, she would likely need a trusting ear to air her injured psyche. He hoped serving as her counsel she would convey unto him the secrets her lover had shared. Of course this information, used in the proper context, could propel an individual with political aspirations to unprecedented heights.

The high counsel of Master masons feared what Burr might have learned. Hamilton swore he had told his lover nothing, but, his behavior in their eyes was reckless, and his political ranting, which cost Adams the election putting Jefferson at the top, was an intolerable breach of the Masonic code. In short, Hamilton, who orchestrated and implemented the most important aspects of the new world order, had become a dangerous liability to the Masonic Craft. He knew far too much, and his inability to control his comments, had become a loaded political gun."

Sheppard checked the rear view mirror as she interrupted Hancock.

"If the high consul of the Master Masons were so afraid of Hamilton, why didn't they just take him out. According to you, they didn't think twice about illicit protocol."

"They thought of that. Some argued for, some against. Hamilton's accomplishments still sat fresh in some of the consul's minds and, even though they felt he had self destructed they didn't believe he would betray the craft. In time, Hamilton had convinced even his most loyal supporters that he must go. And as practiced throughout the history of freemasonry in this country, you don't have to pull the trigger to accomplish the task. All the consul had to do was to make sure the outcome had the desired results."

"Hold on, Hancock, we're on the outskirts of Croydon. The sign says eighteen kilometers to Bromley. I figure we have ten to twelve minutes before we reach the tavern, and I'm starving, so I'm going to have some lunch. I would like to know, by the time I finish eating, the answer to the following two questions: what was it that Hamilton did that was so important, and what was in the unopened letters in Washington's desk. Given your gift for narration, I fear I may not know the answer to either."

Hancock smiled and thought of the cash in his pocket. He carried over three thousand American dollars supplied by The Knight Commander of the Temple. He would pay cash for their lunch as he had in all their meetings, so no paper trail would exist. Credit cards don't just leave imprints of where you've been; they also left real time data, which showed up immediately for those who looked. If they needed to stay the night, he'd pay for the rooms as well. When the job was done, he had Sheppard's Tahoe to take back to Heathrow where he'd hop a plane and fly back to the states. No trail, no data, except his airline ticket, and that proved nothing other than he'd been in country. Hancock had it all figured out.

"Patience, Christina," he said as his head tilted back, and he brushed his hair with his fingers. Sheppard caught the move out of the corner of her eye and did a double take on Hancock. Although Hancock no longer needed to mimic her husband, it had become habit, and besides, he played performances right to the end. He left nothing to chance.

"I'll do my best on your request." He continued. "Recapitulating my comments on Aaron Burr, the consul feared he still had Presidential aspirations, and they wanted him out of the picture. As Hamilton continued to foam at the mouth, Burr received most of the jabs. He was Vice President of the United States, and although Hamilton had lost most of his political clout, Aaron Burr judged Hamilton's comments with his ego and not his brain.

You know the rest except this: historian, William Weir, contends Hamilton secretly set his pistol's trigger to depress and fire at half a pound of pressure instead of the usual ten pounds. Thus Hamilton could fire quicker and have an unfair advantage on Burr. History professors, Andrew Burstein and Nancy Isenberg, concur, stating Hamilton brought the pistols with a secret hair trigger of which Burr was unaware. But it didn't work, and I'll tell you why."

Hancock did the thing with his hair again as he took a breath and looked out his driver side window. He turned back to Sheppard and noticed her grip on the wheel had tightened.

"Are you alright," he asked, "you look tense?"

"I'm fine, just finish the story," she said, we're almost there."

"Alright, Christina,....easy. Weir was partially right—the part about the trigger. The Sublime Prince of the Royal Secret sent the Prince of Mercy to Hamilton's house the night before the duel. Hamilton had dined out with friends and had no idea the trigger had been adjusted to a new setting. The next morning, when Hamilton loaded in a separate boat from Burr to cross the Hudson River, Hamilton's Wogdon wood handled dueling pistols crossed as well. As was customary in a duel, the man challenged picks the first weapon, and, of course, Hamilton picked his favorite one of the pair. It was common knowledge which pistol he preferred; it had a scratch on the handle from when it was dropped by his son after being mortally wounded in a duel years before. And so, the stage was set, and they squared off in a cleared wooded area below the Palisades in New Jersey.

As Hamilton raised his weapon, and lowered it toward his target, he applied the normal pre-firing squeeze on the trigger. With less than the nine and a half pounds of customary pressure needed to fire the pistol, it discharged early, and the musket ball flew above Burr's head hitting a tree. Burr took aim, hit Hamilton square in the abdomen, and the consul's objective was met. Hamilton was dead, Burr was charged with murder, and although the charges were dismissed, Burr's career was over. He became a one term Vice President and scuttled off in disgrace."

Hancock took a break and looked out his window.

"Two kilometers to the tavern," he said.

"I saw the sign." She said as she drove and contemplated what Hancock had said. As she approached the exit, a thought came into her head.

"Why didn't Hamilton appoligize to Burr and forgo a duel?"

"Hamilton had been in duels before, ten to be exact. Besides, he felt he had nothing to apologize for, and he knew he had the edge."

"I don't understand."

"The Masonic consul knew Burr was an egotistical moron and would defend his honor, even though he was reputed to be an atrocious shot. So they set the two of them up."

Sheppard pulled off 232, maneuvered into the parking lot of Journeyman's Tavern, put the gear into park and shut off the engine. She rubbed her forehead with her fingers, and as she pulled the keys out of the ignition, she turned to Hancock.

"Set the two of them up?" She asked.

"They planted counterfeit pamphlets time after time attributing them to Hamilton. Each pamphlet grew exponentially sharper, until Burr could no longer ignore them. The final straw came in a letter from Charles Cooper, which was published in the Albany Register and claimed Hamilton, at a political dinner, expressed a "despicable" opinion of Burr and his candidacy for president. The article prompted the call for an immediate apology from Hamilton, but Hamilton refused, and said he could not imagine what Dr. Cooper alluded to. But the accumulation of slander had taken its toll, and he challenged Hamilton to a duel.

Thus, you don't have to pull the trigger to accomplish the task. This has been the mantra for two hundred and fifty years of the Masonic Craft and is still practiced today. Contour the landscape, it is said in the secret manuscripts at the 23rd Street Lodge, in a manner which maneuvers the individual's character into a particular posture, and, an assured outcome is secured, it concludes, by the very nature of the beast."

CHAPTER 54

Even though his foot hurt, Brosconni tried to stand. The metal bar the cuffs slid through was an inch and a half thick, eighteen inches long, constructed of wrought iron, and screwed with two lag bolts at both the top and bottom into the English Elm beam. If Brosconni could right himself, there was enough height in the bar that the cuffs could be slid up the steel and allow him to stand. He pressed his back hard against the wrought iron, which poked into the hollow of his back, and pushed upward with his legs. The pain in his foot now burned like a hot branding iron had been stuck into the wound. With most of the weight on his good foot, Brosconni inched up the bar until his legs were straight, and his arms were taught from the restraints.

After a short rest, he leaned forward with the chain of the cuffs pressed against the bar and stretched the sockets of his shoulders and the muscles in his arms. It was the first time he'd been upright since he entered the room blindfolded, and he examined the brass gallery on the top of the mahogany superstructure that rose up from the back of the desk. As his eyes scanned down to the thin square legs, he admitted to himself his only chance of recovering the Hepplewhite, and getting out alive, was to cooperate—a reasoned judgment which opposed his nature and would take every ounce of his discipline to carry out.

As he circled his head to loosen the tension in his neck, he thought of the one point five million the hooded man demanded, and he laughed to himself. The Hepplewhite was probably worth twelve to fifteen at least, and the amount he wanted, to Brosconni, was pocket change. The corner of his mouth turned upward into the faint glimmer of a smile. Soon, it would be back where it belonged, in the sprawling seaside mansion, Villa Marcella.

Brosconni pictured it; the Hepplewhite in the corner of his living room—to the right of the massive sculpted fireplace—with the soft light of an exhibit spot flowing over the rich patina of the mahogany veneer. As he sat in his chair and sniffed his Remy Martin Louis XIII., he would revel in the documents hung above the Hepplewhite encased in gilded gold frames by the hands of a museum conservator. Lost relics of an American President, an historian's dream, but it would be viewed by only one man—Enrico Brosconni. That was the true value to the demented tycoon, its content and meaning would be known only to him, while the rest of world longed to learn of its secrets.

Brought back from his villa by a sound outside the room, Brosconni's head turned toward the encased opening. Chained to the wall, his dark beard bristled with a day and a half growth, and Brosconni's eyes shot side to side as he listened. His overalls still stunk of urine, even though the bucket bath had completely drenched him. As he lifted his wounded foot off the floor, the sound of the hooded man's boots shuffled off in the distance. He turned his ear toward the movement, but then it stopped. What Brosconni couldn't see was the hooded man had set up a command center in a room not far off, in the main part of house—on the other side of the living room in the kitchen.

Old wooden cabinets with their paint worn from age hung on the walls, and an island with a wooden top strewn with knife cuts sat in the middle. The appliances had been removed. A double window above the sink looked out toward the grazing fields, to the left was an exterior door, and in the corner of the kitchen, on two exterior walls, was a brick cooking oven with wrought iron swing arms for hanging pots. A man with a hard sculpted face, black hair, two days growth of a dark beard, sat at the island in front of two laptops. An M16 with a high powered scope leaned against the table, and the forty five was tucked in his belt. He scrolled on the touch pad, and checked the surveillance cameras he had mounted on the polls at the end of the 1.2 kilometer dirt road leading to the farm house. All was clear.

The satellite phone that connected to the second laptop filtered through the secure Skype software. The cigarette hanging from his mouth lit up red, as a stream of smoke drifted out from his nose. On his left leg, which was propped up on the rail of the stool, a black wool hood was draped over his thigh. In his late thirties, the hair on his head, some matted and some stuck in the air, was no more than a half inch long and solid black. He pulled the smoke from his mouth, flicked the ash on the ground, and stuck the cigarette back between his lips.

As he reduced the surveillance streaming in from the end of the road, he brought up the website for the Clariden Lue Bank. Then he stood up, lifted the back pack from the floor and took the spent computer battery he just changed out and slid it into the front compartment. Inside were six more charged backups. He dropped the back pack onto the floor and took another hit from his smoke.

Out back, in one of the barns, was the white van he had brought Brosconni in. Inside the van was a sophisticated set up of two way jamming devices to be used in case of detection. Cell phones, like police radios worked as a two way radio, and with the equipment in the van, he had the ability to compromise all communication within two kilometers of his vehicle. When the hooded man's business was complete, and he packed up and left, he would initiate a denial of service attack as an added precaution.

He took one more draw on his cigarette and dropped it into the jar filled with water which would later be sealed and loaded in the truck—spent butts meant DNA. The only thing he touched with his bare hands was his personal equipment; anything else, he used latex gloves. All the ammunition loaded in his weapons was treated with the same respect. He had also mapped out an escape route through the maze of grazing pastures, in case he was signaled an intruder had entered the main access road. Everything was set up in the kitchen to be dismantled, packed in the van, and driven the back way out before a vehicle could travel half the distance to the house. He utilized all the skills he had learned in his twenty years in the 9th Parachute Assault Regiment, one of the elite forces of the Italian military, and he conducted himself as he'd been taught serving his time in Iraq.

He slipped on his hood and adjusted the slits to allow a full radius of sight. He pulled on the latex gloves hanging from his front pant pocket and picked up the throw away cell phone which sat on the table next to the lap top. The prepaid minutes on the disposal phone, paid for in cash, was virtually untraceable. Besides, it would be used for only one call—Switzerland. After that, he would employ the satellite phone, disguised with encrypted software, and run through a series of slave computers. As he exited the kitchen, he drained his mind and his body of everything but his razor sharp, elite tactical instincts and marched through the living room toward Brosconni.

Brosconni heard the clump of the boots and raised his head toward the encased opening. In the man's absence, Brosconni speculated how all this would end. He knew there was only one vehicle, and once the transfer of money had taken place, the hooded man would leave the farmhouse alone. *So how was he to get out? The man didn't intend to leave me here, cuffed, without any means of escape, did he?* The sound grew louder, and he appeared in the room, and he wasted no time with Brosconni.

"Time to do some banking Brosconni, if I detect a quiver in your voice, I'll cut the balls off your body," he said as he reached down, pulled his pant leg up and slid out an Ontario Special Forces fighting knife from its sheath.

"How am I going to get out of here after you get your money?" Brosconni asked.

"You make the transfer," he said, "I'll attend to logistics. I'm putting the phone on speaker, Brosconni. When the main desk answers, you ask for your contact, Templand. You answer the security questions, and you tell him you want to transfer one point five million American dollars into another account within the bank. I will hold up a piece of paper with the numbered account, you read it, you thank him, and I hang up."

Brosconni felt the sharp point of the knife through the overalls as the hooded man pressed it into his crotch.

"One wrong move, Brosconni, and you'll eat your own mountain oysters."

The man looked down at the phone and pushed the number two and held it. He had the bank on speed dial, and the numbers beeped as they came up. When it stopped, and the quick rings sounded, he held the phone up toward Brosconni's face. Brosconni heard a click and then the sound of a woman's voice.

"Clariden Lue Bank," she said "how may I direct your call?"

CHAPTER 55

       Journeyman's Tavern sat off of Farnborough Way and was a two hundred year old Inn used for those traveling to the coast of Dover by carriage or horseback. Now, the Tavern was frequented by locals, at night, as a neighborhood pub. The few rooms upstairs were rarely occupied. Hancock had researched the Tavern when Sheppard disclosed that she'd been told to stop there and wait for further instructions. He had completed a thorough pre-travel strategy and was fully prepared for any event. He realized it was a place where he could be connected to Sheppard on the English continent, which he had avoided up until now. But he had no choice. So he calculated if he kept his back to the patrons and restricted his identification to just one waiter or waitress, he'd have an easier job cleaning up—of course after he disposed of Brosconni and Sheppard.

As preplanned, he pulled out his cell phone and turned to Sheppard and spoke.

"I have a call to make, Christina," he said, "why don't you go in and grab a table."

"Alright."

"Make it as private as you can; I don't want our conversation to be overheard."

Sheppard stepped out of the Tahoe, closed the door, and headed toward the front entrance of the Tavern. Hancock looked down to his cell phone as if to be punching in numbers. It was imperative not to be spotted entering the Inn with Sheppard, so the illusion would give Sheppard a chance to select a table and settle in.

A few moments later, Hancock walked in, shuffled over to the table in the back corner with his hand rubbing his face to conceal his likeness, and sat down across from Sheppard. The pub was semi-dark with a bar at one end, an old brick fireplace across from it, and about ten tables with chairs. With his back to the room, he checked his watch, 11:15 am. He leaned forward.

"What time did he say he'd call?" Hancock asked.

"He didn't." She responded. "What if he doesn't call?"

"He will."

"What makes you so sure?"

"Why else would he have called in the first place, Christina, he needs you."

Sheppard looked perplexed.

"Needs me?"

"That's my guess."

A waitress arrived at the table with lunch menus. Hancock kept his head lowered toward the table and immediately began to read. She asked in a thick south London accent if they cared for a drink. They both ordered ice tea. She said she'd come back with the drinks and take their orders and left. As she walked away, Sheppard leaned in toward Hancock.

"Your guess?" She asked.

"If this guy was smart enough to take the desk from Brosconni's villa, then he must have enough sense to know he can't trust a man like Brosconni. Brosconni doesn't follow orders, he gives them. He must have known his only chance at completing the exchange and getting away safely was to isolate Brosconni, physically take him to an undisclosed location, and have Brosconni somehow make the necessary payment to regain possession of the desk. But what's missing?"

The waitress arrived with the drinks and asked if they were ready to order. Again Hancock's head never turned or looked up. He ordered a mature cheddar and chutney sandwich on white bloomer bread, and Sheppard ordered a prawn and mayonnaise sandwich on the same. The waitress scribbled on a pad and left. Sheppard turned her head slightly and looked out of the corner of her eyes at Hancock. She was surprised by his deductions.

"Are you a detective now Hancock?" She asked.

"An historian is a detective of sorts." He responded. "So, what's missing?"

"If he took Brosconni to an isolated location, after he collected whatever it was he wanted to collect, he would make his getaway. And Brosconni would be left with the Hepplewhite and no ride."

"Yes and no ride."

"So I'm the ride?"

"Your name has been all over the press since the desk was stolen. You had been summoned by Brosconni to examine the piece. Where can you find a more non-threatening, neutral driver than you, Christina, you, Brosconni, and the Hepplewhite back together again."

Hancock lifted his iced tea and looked up at Sheppard's reaction. She was processing what Hancock had said. If he was correct, and he believed he was, then it was only a matter of time before Sheppard's phone rang, and they were on their way to retrieve the Hepplewhite. And Sheppard had no idea she was about to finally reunite, after six long years, with her dead husband Ray. Hancock studied her expression as she reached in her side blazer pocket pulled out her I-phone and placed it on the table just in front of her iced tea. By the sparkle in her eyes he was satisfied, Sheppard hadn't a clue.

The transaction had gone exactly as planned. As the hooded man left the room, Brosconni screamed something about being released with his desk. The further away the hooded man traveled the louder his tirade got.

"I paid you the fucking money, you son of a bitch, uncuff me!"

Brosconni tugged at the cuffs attached to the wrought iron bar. He plunged forward again, but the only damage was to his wrists. He looked toward the encased opening and screamed with such intensity his face turned red. He kept on until he was exhausted and slid down the poll and onto the floor. His head fell back against the bar as he smoldered in silence.

The man walked into the kitchen holding the hood in his left hand and tossed it on the table. He slid out a Marlboro from the pack next to the laptop, flicked a lighter, took a long draw, and exhaled out both nostrils. With the lit butt hanging from his lips, he plunked down onto the stool, swiped his finger across the touch pad, typed in his password, and as the Clariden Lue screen came up, he took a hit off the lit butt and knocked the ash onto the floor. He pounded out the numbers to the account, plugged in another password, and watched as the main page came up. $1,510,000.00 was listed as the current balance. The one point five was Brosconni's contribution: the ten thousand was the minimum to open an account. He took another draw on the smoke.

He closed out the account page and logged off the computer as his eyes turned toward the opening to the living room. Brosconni had re-ignited his verbal assault, and his defiant threats were rattling through the empty farm house. With the butt still hanging from his mouth, the man's eyes rolled back to the laptop, and he closed the cover, picked up the backpack off the floor and slid the computer into the slot behind the row of charged batteries. Then he picked up the stool, carried it out the kitchen door to the small stone patio, and positioned it next to the wooden crate near the window.

Even outside, he could hear Brosconni's ranting, and he turned and shuffled back inside.

"I told you to bring your ass in here, you son of a bitch. If you're going kill me, then do it," Brosconni screamed, "because you're dead! You hear me, you're dead, even if you kill me, you're dead. I gave them orders to tear your arms off, your legs off, cut your eyes out, while you're still breathing, piece by fucking piece."

Brosconni stopped as the man appeared, hooded, at the encased opening with two buckets, one in each hand.

The hooded man approached Brosconni, put one bucket on the wooden floor, and lambasted him with the other. As he picked up the second bucket, and the wall of water cascaded through the air, Brosconni opened his mouth and tried to catch as much of the bucket bath as he could. He hadn't had a drink in a day and a half, and with all the screaming, his mouth felt like a desert on fire. As he savored the few drops he was able to catch, the man retrieved the second bucket and exited the room. And Brosconni, hunched over, sat like a drowned rat tortured by the puddles of water on the floor.

Back in the kitchen the man threw the hood onto the table, grabbed the second laptop, and satellite phone, and carried them to the crate outside. He re-entered the kitchen, grabbed the Marlboro's, lighter, and a plastic bottle of water, slid the M16 with the high power scope over his shoulder by the strap and turned toward the door. When he got back outside, he sat on the stool, leaned the rifle against the house, fired up a smoke, and swiped the touchpad with the first two fingers of his right hand.

He plugged in his password and pulled up the surveillance video cameras at the end of the road—all clear. He had the computer set on alarm. If the cameras detected motion, and he was absent, a siren would scream from the computer's speakers and alert him an intruder was on his way. He reduced the images and pulled up Skype.

It was time to make the phone call. He dragged on the smoke as he pushed the speed dial code, and the screen began to blink the numbers as they came up on the phone pad. He reached out and picked up the hand set to the satellite phone and put it to his ear. It rang once, and she picked up.

Alberto Capalli sat in a chair next to his wife by the bed. His General's cap was on his lap and each of his hands held one of its sides. After the phone call from Capt. Penso, Capalli had gone to the small park behind the hospital and sat on a bench under the shade of the Stone and Aleppo Pines. He had turned his phone off and studied the thick bed of lavender as he thought back to the first time he laid eyes on the young farm girl, Carlota Capaconneri, from Palidoro, North West of Rome. She was nineteen, and Capalli, into his second year as a new recruit with the Italian Carabinieri, was twenty one. She was as taken by the man in the dark blue uniform with the silver braids on the collar and cuffs as he was by her young innocent beauty. It was to be Alberto Giuseppe Capalli's first and only true girlfriend and soon to be his wife.

Carlota was at the Piazza Sant' lgnazio in Rome to attend a best friend's wedding at the magnificent church which adorned the piazza. Outside, after the ceremony, Carlota stood at the center door as Alberto passed by on his way to Carabinieri headquarters. So taken by the Italian farm girl, Alberto stopped and struck up a conversation. The following weekend he went to Palidoro to meet her parents and have dinner at their quaint but modest farmhouse. Carlota's parents were impressed by the young man's sense of values and his desire to have a distinguished military career. Within two months, Alberto traveled to Palidoro and asked her father for Carlota's hand in marriage. Her father was delighted and said yes.

Like all marriages that slowly drift apart, Alberto believed he worked hard for his wife and the family he wished to have. With each promotion came the equivalent distance which separated the two from the long hours of work. It took years, but Alberto's career and the loss of their unborn child wore thin on the love they had felt on the day they were married. And as Capalli sat on the bench stunned by what he had allowed to happen between him and his lovely Carlota, he realized now exactly what he must do.

So he dragged himself back to the chair, next to his comatose wife, and held the General's cap squeezed between his hands and began to speak even though she could not hear.

"I've made a decision, Carlota, and I hope you can somehow comprehend what I have to say.

Tomorrow, I am resigning my commission as commander of the Carabinieri Art Squad. I won't give Brosconni the satisfaction of ending my career. I will hold a news conference at Carabinieri headquarters, and I will tell the Italian people of my choice."

Capalli's head fell toward the floor. His voice, the general's voice, softened to a whisper.

"I'm sorry, Carlota," he said, "I'm sorry I let our love get away: I'm sorry I put my career over our marriage. When you awake, I'll be here, and we will spend what time we have left, together."

Capalli threw his cap on the end of the bed and took Carlota's hand.

"I love you," he said with his head hung down toward her lifeless body as he paused, "I always have."

CHAPTER 56

Her cell, which sat on the table in front of her, rang just as they started lunch. It surprised them both, and their heads jolted toward the ring. She grabbed it before the second obnoxious tone rang out.

Hello," the man's voice said.

"Yes," she said.

"It's done," he said, "the money's in the account—one point five—he couldn't keep his mouth shut."

She looked at the man across the table and tried to suppress a reaction.

"I see," she said.

"Is he there with you now?" He asked.

"Yes."

The plan had been hatched years before. They had met at a party for her cousin, but in truth, he had sought her out. As a trained professional, he learned all aspects of her personality and her life. He didn't take chances, not with his work, not with his life, and not with those he chose as a target. What she thought was a chance meeting, was in reality a well choreographed, meticulously planned priming of a potential asset. Given her mental state, and their mutual interests, it had been easier than he thought. In the end, it became a matter of the right priceless piece, in the right place, when the Hepplewhite showed up. And the years of waiting were rewarded by what he had considered his life's work.

"Does he know anything?" The man asked.

"No," she said.

"Good, it will give you pleasure to learn Brosconni, as I suspected, has become unwrapped."

He used her hurt and her anger as the fertile ground upon which to plant the seed, and, left alone, he believed it would grow. He was right. Within six months she had contacted him and consented to come on board. As time went on her commitment grew stronger, and she ached for the opportunity to carry it out. By the time Washington's desk arrived, she had to contain her excitement and translated that energy into the discipline needed to conceal any outward knowledge of the sophisticated operation about to take place. And that morning, when Brosconni exploded because the Hepplewhite was gone, it took every ounce of her being to act the innocent part, but she did.

The abuse Brosconni handed out that day, even after General Capalli arrived, more than justified, in her eyes, the theft. It seemed restitution for his behavior. The only twinge of guilt came in the afternoon when Brosconni chewed up and spit out

Anthony Grippato (the security guard on duty that night) and Nonti, who was head of security. After he ripped them apart, he fired them both without pay. She felt responsible for their losing their jobs, but also felt, they were both better off unemployed than working for a man like Brosconni. By that evening, she was sickened by what she had witnessed and believed, without reservation, Brosconni was the sickest, most evil man she had ever met. When she went to bed that night, and she closed her eyes, she couldn't erase his face from her mind.

"Do exactly as we discussed," he said, and then he told her something else, and she fought hard not to show any emotion.

"Yes, I understand," she said and pushed the button to end the call.

"Do exactly as we discussed," he said, and then he told her something else, and after she responded, he hung up.

The man brought the equipment back inside the kitchen and packed everything up except the laptop and satellite phone. With the M16 draped over one shoulder and the duffle bag filled with the kitchen contents over the other, the man walked across the dirt path to the barn. He opened the van and placed the rifle in between the driver and passenger seat upright and clipped it into the sleeve. He loaded the duffle bag in the back and climbed in. He knelt on one knee behind the driver seat and checked the jamming equipment to be sure it operated as planned.

Then he closed up the van and walked back to the house.

In the kitchen, he switched the laptop screen to surveillance and checked the access road to the house—all clear. He took the cotton rag, which was folded to the right of the computer, and dusted the buckets off for prints. Before making his way around the rest of the kitchen, he slapped the pack of cigarettes against his finger, lifted the pack toward his mouth, and secured the butt half exposed with his lips. As the smoke exited his nostrils, he worked until he was confident any evidence of his presence had been removed. Then as one last puff of smoke drifted into the air, the butt sizzled in the water of the glass jar, and he screwed the lid shut tight.

On the island table top was the hood, a pair of latex gloves, an extra clip for the forty five, and the keys to Brosconni's cuffs. The man pulled the mask over his head, slipped on the latex gloves, picked up the clip and keys and pushed them into his front pant pocket. He exited the kitchen and marched toward Enrico Brosconni.

Capalli felt the vibration in his inside jacket pocket. He looked at Carlota with her breathing tube and her eyes shut as he pulled his cell phone out of his coat. He had dosed off after his confessional and was jolted back to life by the silent ring of the phone. As his hand brought the cell up to his face, he rubbed his eyes with his other hand and pushed the button to receive the call.

"General Capalli," he said.

"General, Capt. Penso."

"Just a minute, captain." He said, and he raised himself up, exited the room, and went back to the private waiting room away from his wife.

"What is it Captain?"

"Sir, we've located the white Tahoe."

"I'm listening."

"In Bromley, General, outside an old Inn, the name of the place is called Journeyman's Tavern. We believe they're inside having lunch."

"The plates match?"

"Yes sir, it matches, it's the truck Sheppard rented."

"How long ago did you find it?"

"Twenty minutes, General, and they haven't returned to the truck yet."

Capalli glanced at the pile of magazines on the table with a sense of relief on his face.

"Are you on the scene?" He asked.

"Yes, I'm with Inspector Mitchell in an unmarked car, General."

Capalli turned and faced the window and looked across to the buildings on the other side of the street. No one knew of his decision yet, and no one would until he announced it late in the afternoon tomorrow. It would come as a surprise to his staff, and the entire Carabinieri military for that matter, but until then, he was still in charge. And perhaps he could still go out with a bang. It was obvious they were close. Brosconni, Sheppard, and Hancock were all on the English Continent, and perhaps, although not confirmed yet, Hancock was traveling with Sheppard on their way to meet Brosconni.

"Has anyone gone inside to check if Hancock is with Sheppard?"

"No, General, I wanted to speak with you first. The patrolman who spotted the Tahoe waited until we arrived. It took us twenty minutes to get here from headquarters."

"Send in Inspector Mitchell, no one will recognize him."

"Yes General."

"Captain, no contact, have Mitchell verify Hancock is with Sheppard and then leave, understood!"

"Yes sir."

"Call me when Mitchell reports."

Capalli hung up the phone and sat down next to a table with the magazines. He had been thinking of his speech before he fell asleep next to his wife. When he called Caprina, and instructed her to schedule a press conference at 5pm tomorrow, he told her to brief the media that he had news on the Hepplewhite. He wished he had. It would make what he had to do a lot easier: he could leave on a high note. By tomorrow night it would be all over. He would be an ordinary citizen after all these years, and he would take his Carlota, when she was able to travel, to their second home in Tuscany, in the wine country, away from the Carabinieri and the congestion of Rome.

Capalli's head turned toward the phone in his hand as it rang through.

"General Capalli."

"General, Capt. Penso," he said and then a pause.

"Yes Captain, what is it?"

"Sir, they're not in the Tavern."

"What?"

"General, Mitchell said they were not inside. He questioned the help, and a waitress said Hancock was with Sheppard. She identified him by the photo. She said they had lunch and left a half hour ago."

"In what, Captain?"

"General, we don't know."

Earlier in the tavern:

Sheppard shut her cell phone off and slipped it into her side blazer pocket. She excused herself, went to the ladies room, and was back to the table in less time than it took to accomplish a normal pit stop. She looked at Hancock.

"Time to go," she said.

"Where?" he asked.

"I'll tell you in the car. There's been a change of plans, don't ask any questions, just do as I say."

He eyed Sheppard with a hint of suspicion. He figured the phone conversation was a new set of instructions. Hancock had listened carefully as she spoke, but he couldn't decipher any information from what she had said. He examined the bill, threw a bunch of pounds on the table, and said, "alright, you lead."

Hancock was careful not to show his face as they left the Tavern. He walked most of the way with his head tilted down as his hand rubbed his forehead. When they reached the door, Hancock exited first and hurried over to the Tahoe.

"No, Hancock, we're not going in the Tahoe," she said, "we're taking another vehicle."

Hancock looked confused but didn't say a word.

"The blue Taurus, over there, in the corner of the lot," she said. "I'll explain later."

As Sheppard approached the car, she reached inside her blazer pocket and pulled out the set of keys she retrieved from underneath the sink in the rest room. She pushed the fob and the doors unlocked. Hancock climbed into the passenger's side, and Sheppard jumped into the driver's side. She started the engine, put it in reverse, backed up, and headed out the lot toward A232. Hancock hadn't said a word as Sheppard drove onto the entrance ramp and pushed the gas pedal toward the floor. As Sheppard reached full speed, Hancock slipped his hand into the right side pocket of his sports coat and checked his weapon. It was there, and he rubbed the metal garrote with his thumb as the loop laid in the curve of his fingers, and out of the corner of his eyes, he examined the curve of Sheppard's neck just below her rounded chin.

CHAPTER 57

As Sheppard drove down 232, she felt an odd sensation well up in her gut. Her head snapped to the right and caught the intensity of Hancock's stare. Something was different about Hancock, and studying the road up ahead, she tried to put into thought what she detected in Hancock's eyes. She rested both hands on the steering wheel, still alarmed by what she sensed, and voiced the questions in a detached and cautious tone.

"So, what did Hamilton do that was so important, Hancock, and what is in the sealed correspondence in Washington's desk that prompted two innocent people to die?"

Hancock removed his hand from his pocket and gathered himself. He looked out his window and studied the old Tudor homes that passed by. *Tell her? What would it matter?* They were on the last leg of their journey and soon anything she had learned would be safe upon her death.

As he focused his eyes back into the Taurus, he felt a rush of his own significance rise up within him. Randolph Hancock, The Prince of Mercy, was about to experience what all his predecessors had hoped in their lifetime to accomplish, and he felt the presence of his revered brother masons pour into his soul.

The esoteric connection that would consume his being, as he touched the correspondence hidden inside the desk, would transcend him through the centuries of time, to when his great grandfather times six, John Hancock, waited at the Governor's Mansion in Massachusetts for the documents to arrive. And now, for centuries to come, as the Masonic elite viewed the handwritten letters in the secret vault at the 23rd Street lodge, Randolph Hancock would be remembered as the Masonic brother who recovered the correspondence from inside George Washington's desk, and the thought made him shiver.

"Well?" She asked again.

Why not!

"All right, Christina, here is the final piece of the puzzle. The founding Masonic consul, and their counterparts in Great Britain, agreed, that if their reign of the new world order was to continue with absolute control, one single, significant, financial institution must be created in order to assure the consul's success. They recognized, as the new government began to take shape, the measure they would introduce would be met by the opposition of individuals like Jefferson and Madison, but brother mason, George Washington, as President would have the final say.

So they brought in Alexander Hamilton to be the architect, under the guidance of John Hancock and John Langdon, and hoped, by the time Washington was sworn in as the first President in 89, the structure would already be in place. But the correspondence went missing in 86, and this fact, unknown to anyone but the Masonic high consul, delayed the plan until 1791."

Sheppard looked from the road to Hancock.

"What institution?"

"I'll get to that." Hancock said adjusting the control of the air flow from the car's air conditioning. "But first, answer this: what one constant must all nations have in order to exist?"

"A leader?"

"A means of exchange, Christina, whether its Nero's head stamped on a piece of metal, or George Washington's face on the dollar bill, a nation cannot exist without some form of exchange for their labor and their goods. Control that means and you become the invisible force which powers the economics of an entire nation. More powerful than the politicians that run it, or the military that protects it. The high consul recognized that to maintain complete control of this newly formed nation, they would have to establish a singular standard for a unified currency and, be the sole source of distribution. Control the currency, they understood, and you control every individual dependent upon it. So they looked to a man named Alexander Hamilton.

Hamilton, as first Secretary of the Treasury, developed the proposal for The First Bank of the United States which was chartered in 1791. And Hamilton, invisible brother mason, presented the blue print for how it would work. That day the charter was signed by President Washington, the twenty first of February, 1791, signaled that the Masonic plan was fully realized and now in place."

"It was the Bank of the United States, not The First Bank of the Masonic order." Sheppard said.

"Hardly, Christina, the United States government didn't have the money to fund a bank. They borrowed from Holland and France to fund the revolution. After its success, revolutionary soldiers were left with promissory notes, which speculators bought for pennies on the dollar. The newly formed nation was broke.

The term "Bank of the United States" was an intentional title. It sold the American public, and the congress and the senate, on the belief that their country, the United States of America, would have a centralized banking system of which the federal government controlled and owned. But in reality Hamilton proposed the bank be funded by selling ten million in stock, which they did. The federal government was to buy two million, but they didn't have the two million to buy the stock, so they were loaned the money by guess who, The First Bank of the United States. The federal government owned nothing.

So who owned the bank? In actuality the Masonic consul in this country and, get this, Great Britain. That's right, Christina, The First Bank of the

United States was, in fact, a private bank owned by Masonic investors of an international flavor. Its purpose was to loan money to the federal government, individual states, and the general public. And, they were the only institution which could print this new currency to be distributed throughout the United States: the U.S. Mint was part of Hamilton's proposal and, whoever owned the stock in essence owned the Philadelphia Mint and the profits that went along with it."

"Wait," she said, as she focused on the upcoming turn off.

Sheppard approached M25 and slowed to enter the roundabout. She eased around to the left, completed the half circle and turned onto the entrance ramp to 25. The Taurus was headed toward Dunton Green. As Sheppard pressed the gas halfway to the floor, she told Hancock to continue.

"By 1792 they had four more branches, Baltimore, Boston, Charleston and New York. That's within one year of the original charter. The power of The First Bank of the United States was staggering."

Hancock was getting intoxicated by his own exclusive membership in the high consul of the New York Lodge. It took great restraint to camouflage his emotions.

He reached into his right side pocket and grabbed hold of the garrote. It grounded him, and he felt the giddiness drain from his body. He imagined how he would approach Sheppard, from behind, and with the speed of a seasoned assassin, he would sling the wire over her head and clasp the garrote shut with his hands. And as it snapped closed, he would hear the gasping gurgle of her attempt to take her last dying breath.

"Hancock?"

CHAPTER 58

He entered the room as Brosconni looked up. The tycoon was still drenched, tired, and had a crazed look streaming out of his opaque eyes.

"You fuck," Brosconni said, "I kept my end of the bargain, now undo the cuffs and let me go."

The hooded man said nothing. He paced back and forth with his hands clenched behind his back, and his head rose toward the cathedral ceiling. He stopped, looked down to the desk, and then continued his aggressive stride from one end of the room to the other.

"I said, un…."

"Shut up you deranged psychopath. You think this is about the money……you ignorant letch."

The man picked up his pace. The black hood moved in and out around his mouth with his breathing.

"Take these God damn cuffs off—now!" Brosconni shouted.

The hooded man stopped, reached down and pulled his pant leg up enough to slide out his knife. It flipped in his hand from the handle to the blade. In one fluid motion he turned toward Brosconni, fell to one knee, and whipped the knife from behind his shoulder. It cut through the air like a silent missile, and Brosconni felt the concussion as the blade cut into the elm wood just above his head and stopped with a thud. The man lifted up off his knee, walked over and pulled the blade from the wood and put it to Brosconni's throat.

"I could kill you in a millisecond, Brosconni, but that's too good for you."

The man slapped Brosconni's chin with the flat of the blade and then stepped away and sheathed his knife.

"There's not enough money in the world to settle our score, Brosconni. And I'm only a representative of all the countless others whose lives you've destroyed. And for what, more money, more things, more inanimate objects you can sit and stare at? Most men have a soul, Brosconni; you have a narcissistic black hole where human life is a disposable means by which you acquire your fortune. Life's meaning is what you can take and what you can own and you have no conscience about how you get it. You and I have a score to settle Brosconni, and justice, for a man like you, can only take one form."

"Go ahead kill me," he said with a grin on his face, "do it now so I don't have to listen to your pathetic bullshit anymore."

"Hancock," she said again.

Hancock came out of his Masonic trance. He had decided it was time to change the subject.

"What were your instructions?" He asked.

The blue Taurus, the hooded man at the farm house had rented with a stolen credit card, and parked at Journeyman's Tavern, continued south down 25 which turned into A21 at Chevening. Hancock had cleared his mind and now gazed out through the eyes of a man whose focus had sharpened to the constricted light of a laser. The long protracted act of Ray Sheppard look alike, famed historian, and psychological master, had vanished. He had two lights to douse, and the cold heart of the skilled tactician had taken center stage. Hancock looked to Sheppard and asked again.

"What were your instructions?"

She felt a chill inside the Taurus and turned to Hancock with a deep sense of concern. She understood now what was different. His whole demeanor had changed; it had gone from kindness to cold. She decided to investigate further and asked a question to observe his response.

"You haven't finished yet, Hancock, you still have not told me what's in the desk."

Hancock was in a zone. As he began to speak, the words rolled off his lips like a technical recording, and Sheppard noticed the change in his tone. As she drove, her mind clicked into recall mode. The image of the open back of the Hepplewhite desk was as clear as the evening in Villa Marcella. And locked into her mind's eye was the picture of the two documents with their wax seals still in place. But clearly disturbed now by the instinctual alarms going off inside her gut, she listened with apprehension as Hancock completed the Masonic secret he had known for almost twenty years.

After Hancock's indoctrination as Prince of Mercy he was instructed by The Sublime Prince of the Royal Secret to examine the first volume of his predecessor's writings dated 1787. He had two weeks to learn its contents at which point Hancock participated in the most sacred and secret rites of the Masonic Craft. With the high consul present, Hancock was led, again robed, into the Colonial room lit only by candles. He was subjected to a series of pagan rituals which depicted his death at the hands of each reigning member of the present high consul. Each mock murder, carried out with vivid detail, had its own unique form of death. It symbolized the breath and the depth of the arsenal which Hancock had at his disposal. The grotesque simulations had been carried out for centuries and commenced the consecration of the twenty sixth degree. And as the final rite of passage, while on his knees before his grand consul, Hancock had to swear an oath to fulfill his mission, even at the cost of death.

The podium was set up in the Piazza Sant' Lgnazio, just below Carabinieri headquarters. The satellite trucks and press had begun to assemble just before noon. The speculation was General Capalli would announce the art squad had recovered one of the most significant finds of the twenty first century—the Hepplewhite. The major international channels had set up their portable new rooms, and the commentators spruced up their makeup in the trucks. Even though the news conference didn't start for hours, the correspondents were broadcasting live, recapping the theft and summarizing each step of the investigation. The buzz in the piazza was electric and the speculation was running wild.

By late afternoon upstairs, at his desk, Capalli stared at the clock which hung on the wall, 4:25. His wife was due to come out of the coma sometime in the afternoon as the doctor had briefed him, and Alberto intended to race off to the hospital right after his resignation speech. With his elbow on the wooden arm rest, and his finger wrapped around his mouth, Capalli wondered if he would still, given his wife's condition, step down had it not been for Brosconni. In his heart he responded yes, but his mind said no. After all, he had committed his entire adult life to the Carabinieri Art Squad, and what if Brosconni was already dead? The clarity The General had exhibited this morning when he spoke at his wife's bedside had suddenly grown into a dense fog, and the conflict between his head and his heart was taking its toll.

As he studied the citations on what he had called his wall of honor, Caprina chimed in on the intercom.

"Yes," he said, "what is it Caprina."

"Sir, Capt. Penso's on the line; he says it urgent."

Capalli steered his eyes to the phone.

"Put him through, Caprina."

Capalli pushed away from the desk and swiveled back around to the window.

"Yes Capt." He said.

"General, we've compounded the white Tahoe and forensics is going through the vehicle for prints. The waitress at the Tavern, as I indicated, identified Hancock from the photo we showed her."

"Capt."

"Yes, General?"

"If that's true, and our suspicions about Hancock are confirmed, this American is in grave danger."

"We agree on that General. Inspector Mitchell has intensified the search, and put a helicopter in the air over Kent."

"How can you locate them if you have no idea what you're looking for, Capt.?"

"General, a blue Taurus was rented three days ago in Bromley using a stolen credit card. The man that picked up the vehicle had proper ID, obviously forged documents. We're scouring Kent trying to locate the vehicle."

As Capalli studied the masses assembling in the piazza, he felt the end of his career sliding away. He hated going out under the circumstances, things could fall apart quick, particularly if Hancock dropped Sheppard. The whole investigation could blow up in their face, and the press, even though Capalli had valid reasons for leaving, would say he abandoned the ship. Capalli closed his eyes at the thought and swiveled around to his desk.

"Stay on it Capt." Capalli said and then pushed the button and hung up. *Stay on it,* he said again to himself, *you're a good man Capt. Penso,* as his head dropped toward his chest and froze, *Stay on it.*

CHAPTER 59

Inside the Taurus neither one had spoken since Chevening. Hancock was busy check listing every contingency possible. Sheppard was back at Heathrow, at the car rental counter, with the image of Arket's face frozen in her head. By the time she had passed through Sevenoaks Weald, she had flipped through every photo she had of Arket at the airport. Right now, with both hands glued to the steering wheel, and Pembury approaching up ahead, Sheppard was stuck on the image of Arket as he crossed the airport road. And as he reached the curb on the other side of the street, Hancock's voice evaporated the replay going on inside her head.

"Pembury, two kilometers," he said.

"I see it, Hancock." She replied clearly agitated by the interruption.

Hancock was all business now, and her squinted eyes and twisted lips indicated she hadn't been paying attention.

"I wasn't sure you saw it." He responded back.

She hadn't seen it, but she wasn't about to admit it to Hancock.

The inside of the car went silent again and Sheppard retreated back to her thoughts. She recalled the phone call back at Journeyman's Tavern. She was glad it was almost over. Emotionally, Sheppard was drained. Every step of the way had been a struggle to maintain her focus. From Villa Marcella, to the county of Kent, to the stories of Randolph Hancock, she felt she'd made a mistake. She had wished on numerous occasions she had boarded a plane and flown back to New York. But something had pushed her through, and now, with such a short distance left, she was glad she stuck it out.

Sheppard spotted the sign for Lamberhurst.

"About four kilometers on the left," she said, we're looking for Lady Oak Lane."

Hancock nodded.

The tension in the car since Chevening had intensified. She thought Hancock seemed on edge, so as the Taurus sped down A21, she tried to crack the thick air with the still unanswered question.

"The desk, Hancock, how long are you going to go without answering my question?"

He didn't have to say a word to confirm what she thought. The features of his face had changed, something was different.

"Alright," he said, the emotion drained from his voice. His role as a passionate historian was over. The sworn oath he had taken as The Prince of Mercy was now in full command. He completed the saga of the desk because it didn't matter now; the end was near for Sheppard, Brosconni, and the chaos the Masonic secret could have caused. So he continued his narration and exposed the contents of the sealed correspondence inside the desk, but now his recitation had become mechanical and rote.

"Prince Henry, Duke of Cumberland, in 1786 was the Grand Master of the Premier Grand Lodge of England. His brother was King George the III, the king who lost the Colonies in the revolutionary war and who later lost his mind. King George believed the Premier Grand Lodge was directly involved in instigating the uprising in the colonies, but he could never prove it. By the time the Revolution ended in 83, Prince Henry had been the Grand Master for a year, and, along with his fellow masons of the high consul in the States, was planning the footprint for the new world order. Colonel William Smith, John Adams son in law, was, in fact, the liaison between the New York Grand Lodge and its counterpart in England."

Hancock paused. "Two kilometers," he said.

"I see it." Sheppard responded, "finish the story!"

Hancock let her aggravated snip pass. He continued.

"Prince Henry, with help from the high consul, sculpted the likeness of the Bank of England, to be used as the master plan for the First Bank of the

United States. But the crucial difference was the Masonic Lodge was to control its ownership through the stock. Fellow masons, Hancock and Langdon, were to oversee its birth."

"Up on the left," Hancock said, "Lady Oak Lane,"

Sheppard stung him with a look. She turned onto the road and headed toward the instructed farm house. Hancock again continued.

"The desk was to leave Great Britain in 1786 bound for Boston Harbor aboard the Lucretia, but it did not.

Sheppard slowed to turn right onto the long dirt access road. Hancock searched the landscape for anything suspicious as he talked. The Taurus bounced in the pot holes as Hancock finished, but he kept a sharp eye on his surroundings.

"Recognizing it could compromise the entire Masonic plan, a massive search ensued but the desk was never found. New correspondence was sent via a secure courier, but that took months of preparation and months more of travel. Eventually, the First Bank of the United States was established and the Masonic new world order was complete."

Hancock looked ahead.

"There it is, pull around to the front."

Sheppard slowed the car and eased around the circle toward the front door. The Taurus stopped at the brick walk. She shut off the car and turned to Hancock.

"So?" She asked.

"It was a detailed blue print of how the bank was to be structured, the amount of stock to be issued and, most important, the establishment of a U.S. Mint. It listed names such as Hancock, Langdon, Washington, and Hamilton, which, if exposed, might well have ignited a civil war. It exposed that the real governing force of the United States was the Masonic lodge not the Senate or the Congress. The new government was a political puppet to be used for the benefit of the Craft. Just as damaging was the decree by the Premier Grand Lodge of England that French Masons were to be excluded from ownership of the stock—a feud which fueled the hostilities between the two Masonic nations for decades. In the end, if those documents were exposed to the American people today, and they realized their lives were controlled by a wealthy few, it would throw an already disgruntled nation into chaos."

Sheppard sat silent staring past Hancock toward the front door. She pulled up the image of the two documents, tied with string, the red wax seals still intact, and tried to comprehend the power the sealed correspondence held. She shook her head and said, "let's go."

Hancock stalled. He had spotted the surveillance cameras at the end of the road and was now conducting a meticulous visual search of the property. He scanned the farm house, the empty grazing fields, and what he could make out of the barns behind the house.

"Let's go," Sheppard said again.

"Go ahead," he said, "See if Brosconni's inside; I want to look around."

Hancock exited the Taurus and headed for the barns. Sheppard watched as Hancock disappeared behind the farm house, and she climbed out of car, stepped with caution toward the front door, and when she reached it, she pounded on the wood.

Earlier at the farm house:

"Go ahead," Brosconni said, "shoot me!"

The man in the hood turned and stared at Brosconni, then turned back toward the desk.

"I'll tell you why you're here, Brosconni, and if you make one more sound, I'll cut your tongue out."

He started to pace across the room again and then moved to one of the windows and gazed out to the pastures. He kept his back to the room.

"You're here, Brosconni, because of what you stole from me," he said, still focused on the hedgerow dividing the meadows, "a long time ago."

He put one hand up to the window sash, turned the sash lock, and reached to the rail of the window with both hands.

"You smell like the sewer you live in, Brosconni." He said as he threw open the bottom sash and leaned on the sill and poked his head outside and drew in a full breath of fresh air. Then he knelt, laid his arms on the sill, and put his chin on his arms.

"You employed a young man once," he said, "and he worked the ungodly hours you demanded and received the pittance you paid. Not only was the schedule horrific, but the conditions should have been condemned, and would have been had you not paid off the inspectors. But you didn't care; all that

379

mattered was to turn as big of a profit as you could squeeze out of your overworked labor.

Your foreman had been warned by the dockworkers that the booms were frail and in need of repair. But he was under orders, he said, and anyone who didn't like it could quit. One day, as the man stood on deck directing the boom operator loading the containers, the boom snapped and let go its grip on twelve tons of metal. When it landed on the deck, the dockworker was nowhere to be found."

He turned and looked at Brosconni.

"There was nothing left to even indentify: the twelve tons crushed the man beyond recognition."

He turned back toward the sunny landscape.

"He didn't even receive his full day's pay. His wife argued. She had no money, a son to feed but was repeatedly turned away. She sued for a settlement, but your entourage of high paid lawyers blamed the man, and said he was negligent and incompetent, and she received nothing for her loss. If she had been reimbursed half the amount you paid one of those scum bag lawyers, she wouldn't have lost the house. But that's what you get, she said, when you work for the devil—a curse and a trip to hell.

After the failed lawsuit, she went to your office every day. She pleaded to have a word with you but was constantly turned away. One day she waited in the parking lot for you to go to your car. She had her six year old son with her. When she approached you, being the scum that you are, you threw the widowed woman to the ground. Her son tried to defend her, and you twisted and broke his nose. I never forgot that you son of a bitch," he said and he got up, walked over to Brosconni, grabbed his nose and twisted it like a door knob until it broke. Then he calmly walked back to the window.

Brosconni squirmed on the ground, unable to reach his nose with his cuffed hands. Even though it was bleeding and bent, he stared at the hooded man in defiance.

"She didn't last long after that." He said still staring at the pastures. "She worked two jobs and died two years later; she contracted pneumonia. She refused to treat the disease; she couldn't miss time from work, I was told, so by the age of eight, I went to live with an aunt."

He stood up and faced the handcuffed tycoon.

"Your inhumanity spreads like an incurable cancer, destroying everything in its wake."

He walked over to the Hepplewhite, stopped, and with his back to Brosconni raised his head upward.

"I realized a long time ago, Brosconni, justice comes in many forms. It's true," he said as he shook his head up and down. "I could split your mother's forehead with this Smith and Wesson forty five and you, Brosconni, wouldn't even blink. But Strike at those objects you prize and possess, and you lose all control of your bodily functions. There is only one way to deal with a man like you, and there is only one form of justice."

Without turning toward Brosconni he walked to the encased opening and disappeared. A few moments later he returned with a two gallon can and a long handled ax. He looked directly at Brosconni and spoke.

"You, Brosconni, are the lowest form of life on earth. All your money couldn't protect your precious desk, and you journeyed here, on your own free will, to witness its execution."

He raised the ax up toward the ceiling and as it came down toward the centuries old Hepplewhite, the man screamed.

"This is for my father who I never knew."

The ax blade hit a leg just below the body and the wood splintered and desk fell onto its side.

"No, you ignorant fuck, stop, I'll pay you double."

Again he raised the ax.

"Thiis for my mother who died trying to give me a life."

The blade struck a second leg which propelled itself across the room.

"You son of a bitch, I'll fucking kill you!"

"This is for my life which I never had."

The third leg flew against the far wall.

"And this is for all lives you've destroyed." He screamed with the look of insanity peering out the slits of the mask.

The fourth leg moved an inch as the blade stuck into the wooden floor.

The man flung the ax across the room and retrieved the legs of the Hepplewhite. He threw them into the fireplace, took the upper body of the desk and placed it against the back wall of the fire box, emptied the can of gasoline onto the mahogany veneer, struck a match, tossed it into the fireplace, and Washington's desk burst into flames.

"I'll kill you, you sick fuck." Brosconni screamed.

The hooded man pulled out the keys to the cuffs and threw them on the floor as he left the room. Brosconni's head fell down to his chest, and his eyes closed as his chin hit his overalls and the crackle of burning wood echoed into his ears from across the room.

CHAPTER 60

As she pounded on the wood, the dull sound echoed behind the door. Sheppard heard the screams of a man's voice and recognized the thick Italian accent as Brosconni's. She tried the handle, it turned, and she pushed the door open, peered inside, and scanned the empty living room. As Sheppard moved inside and took three steps toward the opening, Brosconni's obscenity laced tirade pierced her ears from the right. She approached the hall and realized Brosconni's words made almost no sense. It was a jumbled mixture of rage.

"Senior Brosconni?" She called out.

"Get the fuck in here," he screamed, "unlock these cuffs."

She stepped closer.

"Are you alone?" She asked from the living room as her voice echoed off the walls.

"You ignorant bitch, get in here."

She approached the encased opening and gazed into the room. Brosconni sat against the wall; his hands cuffed behind his back, and she hardly recognized the disheveled tycoon. She took one cautious step into the room and was nauseated by the stench. Sheppard turned covering her mouth and nose with her hand.

"Pick up the keys and take these fucking cuffs off!"

"Where are they?" She asked, the sound muffled by her hand cupped over her nose and mouth. Sheppard glanced around and spotted his foot. When she realized the swollen mess was missing a toe, she gagged.

Brosconni pointed with a jerk of his head. "Over there," he said.

She scanned the floor and noticed the smoldering ashes in the fireplace. Her stomach dropped from her belly to the floor. The silver draw handles, a melted puddle from the intense heat, stuck out from the ashes. *It's not possible,* she thought, *not Washington's desk.* Sheppard moved slowly toward the stone hearth until she reached the firebox. She was oblivious to Brosconni's rants as she stared into the ashes. Toward the back, almost against the stone, she spotted two small piles of melted red wax. Sheppard's other hand raced to her mouth, and she turned away doubled over.

The Hepplewhite was gone. The only evidence it ever existed was the commissioned receipt back at Villa Marcella encased in Mylar. With her hand still over her mouth, Sheppard turned back toward the pile of ashes and stared at what was once the magnificent work of an eighteenth century master, and her eyes grew moist. The challenge to unlock the craftsman's secrets, the letters and documents hidden inside, the sealed correspondence hand written by the Duke of Cumberland, gone forever. A tear rolled down her cheek, slid along her cheekbone, and dropped from her chin.

"Pick up the fucking keys and unlock these God damn cuffs—now!"

Sheppard's head jerked around. She looked down and spotted the keys, picked them up, and shuffled over to Brosconni. He stunk, not mild, but nose burning stink, and Christina turned her head as she tried to put the keys into the lock opening.

"Come on bitch!"

His breath smelled like month old garbage, and she held her breath. Finally, she unlocked the first cuff, and Brosconni slid the chain out from behind the wrought iron pole. He looked over to the encased opening.

"Who the fuck are you?" he asked.

Sheppard struggled with the second lock now in front of Brosconni.

"His name is Randolph Hancock," she said, he's with me."

Hancock's eyes turned to the fireplace.

"Yes," she said, "it's gone."

Although he didn't show it, Hancock smiled inside. After two hundred and twenty four years the threat was over; the documents were destroyed. As he watched Sheppard turn the key on the second cuff,

Hancock schemed in his head. He would take out Brosconni first.

Hancock had pulled the keys from the ignition of the Taurus, and there was no place for Sheppard to go. They both could ID him, and even though Washington's desk was destroyed, and the blue prints for the bank burned, Hancock had no choice. He had made the decision the first time he met Sheppard at the restaurant in Italy. Recover the documents, destroy the desk, and remove all evidence, leave nothing behind.

He slipped his hand in his right coat pocket and grabbed the garrote with his fingers. He stood cautious as Brosconni threw the cuffs aside and jumped to his feet.

"Give me your phone," he said to Sheppard.

Too much commotion, Hancock thought, *wait, the nearest help is at least forty five minutes away.*

Sheppard handed Brosconni the phone, and he dialed Capalli's number: it was the only person he could think to call.

"Nothing, the God damn phone's dead, no service. Let's go, everyone to the car." He said.

"I'll be out in a minute," Sheppard said, "I want to look at what's left of the Hepplewhite."

"Bullshit, to the car—now ."

Christina stared at Brosconni with defiance in her eyes.

"When I'm ready, Brosconni, I'll be out."

Perfect, thought Hancock, *wait till he got outside and take out the smelly tycoon first. That would eliminate a struggle from Sheppard. If she didn't see it, she wouldn't know what to expect.*

387

"I'll kill this mother f............," Brosconni's rage continued as he headed toward the encased opening. He turned around half way through.

"Don't touch anything!" He said to Sheppard.

Hancock was inches from Brosconni's back as they walked toward the living room. His right hand was in his right coat pocket rubbing the garrote with his thumb. Sheppard stayed behind and moved over to the fireplace and inched down on one knee.

She stared at the melted wax and the charred remnants of burnt paper. Its outline sat like a darkened rectangular ghost atop a pile of ashes. She examined what was left of Washington's desk and thought of all the years it remained safe, in an attic, only to be found and destroyed, and her head lowered toward the floor.

In the living room, Brosconni stepped across the floor with Hancock riding his back. Hancock removed the garrote from his pocket and held it behind his blazer as they approached the front door. When Brosconni reached for the door handle, Hancock brought the wire around to his abdomen, opened it up with each hand holding one end and prepared to sling it over Brosconni's head the moment he stepped outside. He had checked the barns and around the house for additional surveillance but had found none. There were tire markings inside one barn, but the barn was empty now. Brosconni opened the door as Hancock hugged his back. Hancock lifted the garrote to his chest. Brosconni, who had limped the entire way, lifted his wounded foot out the door.

One room away, Christina felt her eyes moisten as her head hung down to her shoulders. She remembered the evening at Villa Marcella as she sat in the chair and opened the back of Washington's desk. She pictured it with such clarity, her hand reached up toward the fireplace as if to touch the receipt from inside the desk. Then suddenly she fell from her knee to the floor and onto her side. She looked up toward the opening. The loud sound had frightened her, like a truck backfire, and she heard thuds of chaos in the living room. She raised herself to her knees and pushed with her hands and rose to her feet. The noise had stopped; there was only silence from inside the farm house. Sheppard inched toward the opening and peered her head around the corner, nothing. She slid out of the room in slow motion not knowing what to expect.

As Sheppard arrived at the living room, she fell to her knees in horror. She half covered her eyes and snuck a glance through her fingers. Brosconni and Hancock were sprawled out on the floor, inside the open door, on their backs, each had a hole in their chest with blood splattered around the room. Neither one moved. In Hancock's right hand she spotted a piece of wire entangled in his fingers. Sheppard looked out toward the open door afraid whoever shot them might take her out too. As she rose to her feet, she listened for any sounds outside, again nothing. She looked out the door and scanned the landscape, took another moment to be sure and then closed the door. Sheppard turned around, her back fell against the wood, and she stared at the bodies of two dead men.

CHAPTER 61

The man clipped the M16 with the high powered scope into the concealed gun rack in the back of the van. He checked the jamming devices, climbed into the front seat and turned on the ignition. The laptop which sat on the consul, in between the seats, showed all clear at the end of the road. He put the van in drive, stepped on the gas, and pulled away from his sniper's position and onto the dirt road.

The shot had occurred at two hundred yards, from out of the back of the van. The man had waited for Brosconni to come out of the house; he knew the hot blooded Italian wouldn't waste any time exiting after he discovered he couldn't make a phone call because of the denial of service attack. He hadn't expected the second man though. Hancock had lined up directly behind Brosconni, and although it was a surprise, in the end it really didn't matter.

The ex elite Special Forces commando had waited most of his life for the chance to take out Brosconni, and he wasn't going to waste the shot. And although the second man stood in a direct line, and the fifty five grain 5.56mm bullet passed through Brosconni's heart, exited out his back, and entered the second man's chest, it was just collateral damage. He'd experienced it before in special operations. It was an unavoidable part of war.

If Sheppard had been lined up behind Brosconni, however, he wouldn't have taken the shot. He would have waited until she was clear of the tycoon. Sheppard had no connection to the man, and had no part in his plot, but she was an invaluable asset to the operation. He needed to bring her in to verify the Hepplewhite's destruction. When he made the satellite call to Journeyman's Tavern, prior to contacting the other woman to tell her the money had been transferred and was in the Swiss account, he instructed Sheppard to retrieve the keys from under the restroom sink and proceed to the farm house in the rented Taurus. She believed she was on her way to pick up Brosconni and to retrieve Washington's desk. That's what the man wanted her to think, and it worked.

The man was a highly trained military machine, and surgically removing his intended target was so ingrained into his psyche, it had become an instinctual act. He had no reservations about taking a life. And although his heart was as cold as steel, his soul had a deep rooted passion. He loved the classics, its music, and the instruments like the legendary Stradivarius whose sweet tones captured the essence of a composer's work. And his adoration was not confined to just 17th and 18th century instruments; it encompassed all valuable relics with a significant past. Shooting a man like Brosconni was one thing, destroying a one of a kind masterpiece was quite another. It was not an act he could commit.

So the operation went exactly as planned. The inexpensive reproduction produced years before from a plate of Hepplewhite's book of designs never faced the tycoon. He only viewed the back. The pictures he had down loaded from Brosconni's Smartphone, with the photograph of the two pieces of correspondence in the back of the desk, was just the prop he needed. He had purchased two random letters from a dealer which dated from the late eighteenth century which incorporated red wax stamps, and he placed them in a drawer in the fake desk. And Sheppard's visual examination of the incinerated piece turned into the verbal proof he needed to verify the Hepplewhite had been destroyed, but just in case, if Penso or Mitchell decided to carbon date the correspondence, it would confirm it had indeed been the Hepplewhite.

As he started down the road, with the crate in the back, a smile cracked his stoic features. Stenciled on the front of the pine box it said: Property of Col. W.S. / G. W. In one of the drawers was a note, typed, which explained the origin of the piece. And he had no intentions of selling Washington's desk. No, he had other plans for the famous piece, and perhaps someday, far in the future, the Hepplewhite would surface again. He amused himself at the thought of that and the frenzy of speculation which would ensue.

And for that to happen, the needed infrastructure would soon be in place.

On the outskirts of London, a very exclusive warehouse has stood for the past hundred and fifty years. It has housed rare and valuable antiques under controlled conditions with a security force round the clock. The Hepplewhite, in its crate, will be stored on a vertical shelf with its own special number and its own special space. The man had instructed Clouster Van Templand, of Clariden Lue Bank, to set aside the sum of two hundred thousand dollars and to buy government bonds which must yield a minimum of six percent. The proceeds from the principle will be sent to pay the yearly storage charge until Templand, or his predecessor(s), is notified to stop. The cash was intended to never run out.

As he turned onto M21, he thought of Brosconni. He had caused nothing but pain and suffering to those unfortunate enough to be exposed to his wide reaching universe, but the 5.56 mm bullet had put an end to that. And before it did, Brosconni had witnessed what he believed was the complete destruction of the most valuable possession of his life—the Hepplewhite. Now, with Brosconni dead, Washington's desk saved from the clutches of pure evil, and a woman one million three hundred ten thousand dollars richer, his job, he had waited a lifetime to complete, was done.

He pushed the gas pedal toward the floor and reached down to the consul pocket and grabbed the pint bottle of Crown Royal. The man unscrewed the top, took two long slugs, and replaced the cap. He stuck a cigarette between his lips, lit the end with a plastic lighter, and stared at the road ahead as the smoke trailed out the end of his nose. The white Ford E-series windowless van left the district of Kent.

CHAPTER 62

She sat at the table and thought about what the man on the satellite phone had said, and it triggered a swell of emotions in her. The first time they'd met, at her cousins wedding, what started as an innocent conversation ended in a proposition she thought absurd. But that doubt and initial shock soon turned into an exciting prospect, and a way to escape her desperate pain and daily misery. And her decision, although at first suspect, had grown confident with each passing day. And now, after three years of waiting for the right set of circumstances, she couldn't believe it had worked and was done.

The man had targeted her because of her association with Brosconni. He knew her position on the estate gave her access to information about Brosconni, and, most important, his purchases of new, expensive antiques. She had learned of the escape tunnel by shear accident, having entered the room the day Benvennuto Saleno, the carpenter, had discovered the secret door in the paneling. She kept it to herself, for a time, not even telling those closest to her, until one day, after witnessing the constant abuse of those she loved by Brosconni, she disclosed the find to the man. After the disclosure, he coaxed her into exploring the tunnel to determine exactly where it led. With Brosconni away, and Antonio Capano in Amalfi at a doctor's appointment, she did just that.

The man had learned of Brosconni's ritual of consuming his latest obsession in the very room where the tunnel commenced. But he knew he had to wait for a piece Brosconni would become so obsessed by, he would forfeit all common sense to retrieve after it had been stolen. When the Hepplewhite arrived, the tension and extra security in the Villa was like nothing she'd ever seen. She called the man from a pay phone in town. And when he was told that Christiana Sheppard would arrive the next day, he planned the heist for the following night.

She was tired of the abuse, and she was sick of watching her husband loose a piece of his masculinity with each degrading remark. He had become the shell of the man she married, but he would not leave. He stayed for the love of his family and, as he said, where else would he make the kind of money that would allow them to take care of their son? So, she watched him die a little more each day, and decided, if he wouldn't leave, she'd figure a way out of their living hell. The escape tunnel and the man, she believed, had been sent by God.

The man had also assured her she would never be considered a suspect or questioned because of who she was. It turned out to be true. Her husband took the heat, and the questions, and the polygraph test, but she was left alone. And again, as if by the hand of an angel, after the theft her husband was fired. The new distance from Villa Marcella, and the investigation, turned out to be a gift from someone above. So it all went off better than expected, and all she had had to do was wait.

What the man had told her, she still couldn't believe was true. He said the money was for her and her family, compensation for all of the abuse. It was a numbered account, he said, untraceable, and he gave her the contact at the bank. Templand would help set up stringer accounts from which their funds would be allocated as if from a ghost. And the last thing he said choked her up.

"Take care of your family, he said, especially your son, and know you never have to worry about his care. Give him the best, you can afford it now. Goodbye, Giana," he said, and the phone went dead.

Giana looked across to her husband. His face looked tired, worried, and drained. He hadn't found a job since being fired from Villa Marcella. Brosconni had seen to that. She would tell him about the money soon enough, but first, she would contact the man at the bank and set up the proper invisible trail. She didn't want to disclose how their lives had changed until everything was meticulously in place.

As she studied his face, she thought back to the night he was fired as Brosconni's head of staff. She had never seen her husband in such a rage. As he yelled, spit flew from his lips. She had to stop him from going back into the Villa after Brosconni, and when he finally calmed down enough to tell her what Brosconni had said, his hands were squeezed into fists, and the veins in his neck looked like swollen pipes.

"You ignorant letch," Brosconni had said, "your fired! I want you, your wretch of a whore, and your brain dead kid out by sunset, or I'll have the three of you dragged out by your hair."

Giana reached to her husband's arm and put her hand on top of his.

"Antonio Capano," she said, "everything will be alright!"

The press conference was scheduled to start in five minutes. Capalli folded the paper which contained his briefing and slid it into the inside pocket of his General's jacket, walked over to the mirror and put on his General's cap, adjusted it, and shuffled over to the window behind his desk and looked down to the piazza. A large crowd of reporters were gathered around the podium, waiting for the General's remarks, talking in front of their camera men setting the stage for Capalli's statement. A knock broke his trance, and he turned toward the door.

"Come in," he said.

Capt. Tinelli opened the door and saluted.

"It's time General."

"Have you heard anything from Capt. Penso," he asked.

"Not yet sir."

He looked back out the window and took a deep breath.

"All right," he said, "let's go."

On the elevator ride down Capalli's mind was on his wife, Carlota. He wondered now what Carlota's condition would be when she awoke. And then he thought of Brosconni, and how far reaching the consequences flowed from anything he did. It never affected just one individual, it rippled through lives like a deadly Tsunami, and the carnage left in recession was proof of his satanic work. As the bell sounded, and the door opened, Capalli looked to Tinelli and stepped out.

As Capalli approached the podium flashes went off like the opening display on the fourth of July. He waited for the crowd to settle, reached into his jacket, and pulled out his speech and placed it on the podium. He raised his hand indicating it was time to start, and the herd of reporters calmed down. Then Capalli turned toward Capt. Tinelli as he heard his cell phone ring. Capt. Tinelli stepped back, pulled out his phone, and answered the call. Tinelli raised his hand in a stop motion toward The General and then waived him over. Capt. Tinelli handed the phone to Capalli.

Capalli took two steps away from the crowd and listened as Capt. Penso told him about Brosconni and Hancock. Sheppard had called the police when her service returned, and Mitchell and Penso had rushed to the scene. And now Penso told Capalli Brosconni was dead. The General closed the phone, handed it back to Tinelli, and Capalli looked up toward his office window. Then he brought his head down to the piazza and placed his finger around his lip. Brosconni's threat to destroy Capalli was over: it died along with the tycoon.

Capalli stepped up to the podium. He looked out over the crowd, gazed down to his prepared statement, picked up the paper and slid it back into his pocket and then paused. A moment later he spoke.

"I have a brief statement to make, and I will not be taking questions afterward as this is an ongoing investigation. Enrico Brosconni is dead."

The crowd rumbled at the news and started shouting questions. Capalli raised his hand and waited for silence.

"Senior Brosconni was found murdered in a country farmhouse southeast of London, England. There is a second victim we will not name until we confirm his identity. The Hepplewhite is believed to have been destroyed; Scotland Yard is awaiting the results of the carbon tests to confirm it. That's all I have on the investigation at this time."

Capalli took a deep breath and raised his hand again. When the crowd came to order, he looked at his watch and then spoke.

"I have resigned my commission as commanding General of the Carabinieri Art Squad effective immediately. I am leaving my post for personal reasons, and that's all I have to say. It has been a pleasure to work with many of you for the past ten years, and I wish you all well—good bye!"

Two days later at the airport:

400

Sheppard sat in a small lounge, at gate twenty five in Heathrow airport. She had been interrogated by Inspector Mitchell and Capt. Penso and cleared to leave. She told them nothing of Hancock's Masonic story. With the proof incinerated, and Hancock dead, she was afraid they'd lock her up in an asylum. Who would believe a cockeyed story like that even with the documents intact? So she explained that Hancock, a respected and world renowned author, accompanied her because of the historical ramifications of the famed Hepplewhite, which he wanted to chronicle in his new biography on the first President of the United States, George Washington.

Sheppard was shocked when she learned he was a suspect in the murders of John Miller and Carlo Bennetto. And, when they explained what the wire in his hand was for, she almost passed out. For the past six years whether she lived or died had been meaningless to Christina Sheppard, but something had happened during the last two weeks, and the thought of being that close to death at the hands of Hancock spooked her back into reality. Not her pessimistic, dark sided reality, but back to life's reality, back into the light. And on the ride back to London, in the rented white Tahoe, she had a chance to think—a lot!

So now, as she sat at the table in the small lounge, and drank her hot black coffee, one image was stuck in her head, and she looked down to her iphone on the table. They remained locked on the touch pad as the loud speaker announced the boarding of her flight. She picked up the phone, dialed a number, and waited for an answer at the other end. After two rings a man's voice cut in.

"Jermaine," she said, "Its Christina............."

Made in the USA
Charleston, SC
10 January 2012